Christmas at the Cat Café

MELISSA DALEY

Christmas at the Cat Café

MACMILLAN

First published 2016 by Macmillan
an imprint of Pan Macmillan
20 New Wharf Road, London N1 9RR
Associated companies throughout the world
www.panmacmillan.com

ISBN 978-1-5098-3012-1

Cat illustrations by Ray and Corinne Burrows (Beehive Illustration)

Printed and bound by CPI Group (UK) Ltd, Croydon, CR0 4YY

For my sister, Emma

'What greater gift than the love of a cat?'
Charles Dickens

Christmas at the Cat Café

1

The honey-coloured buildings that bordered the market square glowed in the dazzling autumn sunshine. I sat in the dappled shade of an elm tree, watching as tourists and shoppers meandered back and forth along the cobbled streets, soaking up the town's atmosphere of prosperous gentility.

A cool breeze ruffled my fur and I inhaled deeply, savouring the scent of fallen leaves mingled with the aroma of meats and cheeses from the delicatessen behind me. The clock in a nearby church tower had just struck five and I knew that the bustling square would soon give way to a slower pace, as the shops closed for the day and the visitors made their way home. I yawned and jumped down from the wooden bench, taking my time to stretch languorously before setting off on my own homeward journey.

Keeping to the pavement, I trotted past the

numerous tea shops, antiques dealers and gift stores that lined the square, then cut in front of the stone steps of the imposing town hall. The gaggles of grey-haired ladies in sturdy shoes barely noticed me weaving between them, preoccupied as they were with making the most of their last opportunity to buy, before climbing back into their waiting coaches. When I first arrived in the Cotswold town of Stourton-on-the-Hill as a homeless cat, the indifference of strangers would have upset me, but now I strode along, my tail held high, buoyed by the knowledge I, too, had a home to return to.

Careful to avoid the many alleyways that led off the square, which I knew to be the fiercely guarded territory of the town's alley-cats, I turned onto a smart thoroughfare lined with estate agents' offices and clothing boutiques. I deftly picked my way beneath gates and over fences, until I found myself in a narrow, cobbled parade of shops beside a church.

The parade serviced some of the town's more mundane requirements, by means of a newsagent, bakery and hardware shop. But at the end of the parade, was a café. Like its immediate neighbours, the café was modest in size, but its golden stone walls exuded the same warmth as its grander counterparts on the square. Its front aspect was dominated by a curved bay window, framed by hanging baskets from which geraniums trailed, a little straggly, but still in flower after the long summer season. The only indicator that this café was different from any of the other eating establishments in Stourton was the chalkboard that stood outside its entrance, proclaiming the café 'Open for coffee, cake and cuddles'. This was Molly's, the Cotswolds' only cat café, and it was my name printed in pink cursive script across the awning above the window.

Nosing through the cat flap in the café's front door, I was immediately enveloped by the aura of tranquillity that only a room full of dozing cats can generate. The café had begun to empty after the teatime rush, but a few tables remained occupied, the customers chatting in hushed voices as they drank tea from china cups. The café's decor was as familiar to me as my own tabby markings, from its beamed ceiling and warm pink walls (the same shade as the trail of paw prints that snaked across the flagstone floor, the result of my encounter with a paint tray when the café was being decorated), to the candy-striped oilcloths on the tables and the handwritten Specials board on the mantelpiece above the wood-burning stove.

As I made my way across the flagstones I glanced around the room, making a mental note of my kittens' whereabouts. There were five of them – from my first and only litter – and their unexpected arrival just over a year earlier had, indirectly, brought about the café's transformation from rundown sandwich shop to thriving cat café. I saw Purdy first: she was draped proprietorially across the cat hammock that hung from the ceiling by the stairs, her white-tipped paws dangling over the edges of the hessian fabric. She had been the first-born of the litter and thus had assumed certain privileges over her siblings, which included laying claim to the highest napping spot in the room. As I picked out a path between the tables and chairs, I spotted her sister Maisie on the sisal cat tree that stood in the middle of the room. Maisie was the smallest and most timid of the kittens. She loved to observe her surroundings from the domed bed that protruded from the cat tree's trunk, her watchful green eyes monitoring the café's activity from her private refuge.

My destination was the sun-faded gingham cushion in the bay window. This had come to be known as 'Molly's cushion' by the café's staff and customers, because it had long been my favourite place to sit, allowing me to observe the goings-on both inside the café and on the street. I jumped up and turned in circles a few times, kneading its soft surface with my paws, enjoying the familiarity of its smell and feel. Around me, the last few customers pulled on their jackets, gathered their shopping bags and settled their bills. Abby and Bella, always an inseparable pair, had taken joint possession of one of the armchairs in front of the stone fireplace. They were curled up together, with their eyes closed, engaged in a reciprocal wash.

Debbie, our owner, stepped out from behind the wooden serving counter and moved methodically across the room, clearing tables. With the faintly weary air she habitually carried at the end of the working day, she went over to the table nearest the door, lifted her forearm to push the wispy blonde fringe out of her eyes, then began to stack the empty plates and cups onto the crook of her arm. Her blue eyes creased into a smile when Eddie – the only boy in my litter – jumped up onto the tablecloth and began to sniff hopefully at the half-empty milk jug. 'Eddie, you naughty boy! Where are your table manners?' Debbie chided him, giving him a gentle shove onto a chair. He gazed longingly after her as she – and the milk jug – disappeared back into the kitchen, before he finally jumped down and wandered disappointedly away.

A flurry of movement outside the window caught my attention. A song thrush was bouncing along the guttering on the buildings opposite, chirping persistently in a shrill warning call that announced the presence of a cat nearby. I craned closer to the window to scan the street and glimpsed a large black-and-white cat striding along the cobbles. Even at a distance, the cat's rangy frame and confident gait were instantly recognizable: it was Jasper, the father of my kittens.

Before he reached the café he turned a corner and vanished out of sight. I knew he would be heading to the alleyway that ran along the rear of the parade, where he always went to wait for the café's closing time.

The warmth of the low sun, intensified by the windowpane, began to take its soporific hold on me. I would meet Jasper outside later, for our customary evening walk, but first I felt myself succumbing to the irresistible urge to nap. I lay down on my cushion and tucked my paws neatly beneath my body, purring lethargically as a feeling of peaceful contentment spread through me. I was comfortable, I was well fed and I was surrounded by the people and cats I loved. Life was good, and as my head began to nod gently on the gingham cushion, I could see no reason why it would not stay like this forever.

2

I had just slipped into a doze when the brass bell above the café door tinkled. My ears flickered drowsily, but it took a shriek of surprise from behind the counter to jolt me back to full consciousness.

'Oh my God, Linda!'

Startled, I lifted my head to see Debbie dash across the now-empty café to greet a woman standing on the doormat. I knew immediately that the woman was not a regular Molly's customer. She was wearing a faux-fur gilet, tight white jeans and high-heeled leather boots, and her blonde hair fell in bouncy layers around a face that was half-obscured by a pair of giant sunglasses. As Debbie reached her, the woman pushed the glasses onto the top of her head and smiled. 'I was just passing and thought I'd pop in. It's about time I checked out the famous Cat Café,' she said, wrapping Debbie in a tight embrace.

'Well, this is it. What do you think?' Debbie replied, lifting her shoulders in a self-deprecating shrug.

Linda looked around, briskly surveying the café's interior. 'Very nice, Debs,' she nodded approvingly. 'I like it. Homely.'

Debbie glanced over Linda's shoulder at the door. 'Where's Ray? Are you both up from London for the day?' she asked.

'No, no, Ray's not here,' Linda replied, in a tone that made Debbie look twice at her. 'I'm allowed to visit my sister on my own, aren't I?' Linda added, a touch defensively.

'Of course you are,' Debbie gushed, 'I'm just surprised to see you, that's all. Why didn't you let me know you were coming?'

'It was a spur-of-the-moment thing,' Linda answered airily. 'I just thought it's about time I made the effort to come out here and see you – and Sophie, of course.'

'Come on, let me get you something to eat,' Debbie said, pulling out a chair and motioning Linda to sit down.

Linda shrugged off her gilet to reveal a clingy pink top and numerous necklaces draped around her neck. She picked up a menu card while Debbie stood beside her, patiently attentive. 'Feline Fancy; Frosty Paws Cake Pop; Cat's Whiskers Cookie – it all sounds delicious, Debs,' she murmured, while Debbie beamed with pride. Linda perused the menu with a look of tortured indecision, before announcing, 'I'll have a Feline Fancy and a pot of Earl Grey tea, please.'

As Debbie bustled around the wooden serving counter and into the kitchen, a beeping sound issued from the bag by Linda's feet. Frowning, she leant over, plucked a mobile phone from inside and began to tap rapidly on its screen. While she typed, I studied her from the window cushion, looking for signs of resemblance between the sisters. Everything about Linda's immaculately groomed presentation seemed at odds with Debbie's casual style, from the lacquered nails to her figure-hugging clothes and coiffured hair. I tried to imagine how Debbie might look if she put a similar amount of effort into her appearance, but my mind drew a blank. For as long as I had known her, Debbie had always prioritized comfort over glamour. On the few occasions she had attempted a more polished look, the episodes had ended with her slumped in front of the full-length mirror in her bedroom, staring at her reflection in despair. 'Oh, what's the point?' she had sighed, before tying her hair back in its customary ponytail and pulling on an old sweater.

Cheered by the last-minute arrival of a customer, my son Eddie padded over to Linda's chair to sit expectantly at her feet, hoping to charm her for titbits. Linda was unaware of his presence, however, and continued to scowl as she scrolled across the phone's screen with her thumb. Eddie, ever optimistic, raised a paw and patted gently at the leather tassel on her boot, making Linda jump in surprise.

'Oh, hello, Puss,' she murmured distractedly, leaning sideways to peer down at him.

Eddie gazed beseechingly at her, but Linda's heavily made-up face remained blank. I exhaled impatiently through my nose. This lady, I knew with absolute certainty, was not a cat person. No one who loved cats would have been able to meet Eddie's pleading eyes and not lower a hand to stroke him. Evidently, I concluded with a slight bristling of my fur, it was not just her appearance that distinguished Linda from her sister.

A few minutes later Debbie emerged from the kitchen, holding a tray. 'Here you go. One Feline Fancy and a pot of Earl Grey. Bon appetit!' she said, carefully placing the chintzy teacup and plate onto the table. Linda smiled with delight upon seeing the cupcake, which was decorated with pointy cat's ears and whiskers. Debbie took the chair opposite her. 'Have you got to rush off or can you stay for dinner? I'll be done in half an hour or so,' she said.

'Oh, I'm not in a hurry at all – dinner would be lovely. I've . . . got a lot to tell you,' Linda replied, before taking a bite of her Feline Fancy. 'Oh my God, Debs, this is *divine*,' she added quickly through a mouthful of cake, lifting a napkin to dab her lips.

A flicker of alarm crossed Debbie's face. 'Is everything all right?' she asked, a faint note of concern in her voice.

'Yes, of course,' Linda answered lightly, suddenly absorbed in examining the sachets of sweetener in a bowl on the table. Eddie, sensing that his chances of a fruitful scrounging mission were fading, sniffed disconsolately at the floor around Linda's feet, before padding over to the vacant armchair by the fireplace. Linda, meanwhile, seemed determined to look anywhere other than at Debbie's enquiring face.

'Well, look,' Debbie began brightly, 'I've got to clear up, but why don't you go up to the flat when you've finished your tea? Sophie will be back from college in a bit. We can all have dinner together.' She got to her feet and retied the strings of her Molly's apron behind her back.

'That would be lovely, Debs. Let's order a takeaway – my treat,' Linda replied.

Debbie brought the chalkboard in from the street and turned the door sign to 'Closed', before heading back into the kitchen, where I could hear her talking to the staff as they stacked crockery inside cupboards and wiped down the stainless-steel surfaces. In the café, Linda sipped her tea, pressing her fingertips against the china plate to pick up the remaining crumbs of cake.

The sun had now dropped behind the tiled rooftops on the parade, and the warm yellow light that had filled the café was replaced by the cool tones of the October evening. My ears flickered as a gust of wind rattled the awning outside and a draught seeped through the wooden window frame, sending a shiver up my back. Linda was engrossed in her phone once more, its blue glow illuminating her face. When she had drained her tea, she tossed the phone back into her bag and, as she straightened up, her eyes met mine for the first time. She appraised me coolly, as if I were merely another of the café's fixtures and fittings. For the second time since Linda's arrival, my fur bristled.

After a couple of moments my unblinking stare seemed to unnerve her. She stood up and carried her plate and teacup over to the counter. 'That was lovely Debs. I'll head upstairs now,' she called through to the kitchen.

Debbie appeared in the doorway, a pair of sopping wet yellow rubber gloves on her hands. 'Good idea. I won't be long. Oh, I almost forgot! Have you seen? That's Molly.' Debbie gestured with one dripping glove towards the window where I was still staring defiantly at Linda's back.

Linda turned and her eyes flicked briefly in my direction. 'Oh, yes, I thought I recognized the *famous* Molly,' she said, with an emphasis that struck me as somewhat sarcastic. There was a pause, during which Debbie smiled indulgently at me while Linda looked as if she was struggling to think of something else to say. 'She's been watching me since I got here,' she remarked eventually.

'Well, don't forget: it's her name above the door, so she does have the right to refuse entry,' Debbie joked.

Linda emitted a fake-sounding laugh and walked back to the table to fetch her belongings. Feeling suddenly protective towards the empty flat, I jumped down from the windowsill to follow her as she climbed the stairs, holding my breath as her sickly-sweet perfume filled my nostrils in the narrow stairwell.

Rounding the banisters into the hallway, Linda glanced briefly into the tiny kitchen on her right, before turning left into the living room. I slunk in silently a few paces behind her and crept across the room to an empty shoebox that sat on the floor next to the television. I climbed into the box to watch, as Linda made an inquisitive circuit of the living room, taking in the dining table cluttered with unopened post, a bowl of overripe fruit and a stack of lever-arch files; the well-worn sofa and armchair, whose threadbare fabric was concealed by an assortment of colourful cushions and fluffy throws; and the coffee table that was overflowing with old newspapers and an empty box of tissues.

Noticing two photographs among the jumble of ornaments that stood on the mantelpiece, Linda glided across the rug for a closer look. She glanced cursorily at the cardboard-mounted school portrait of Sophie, Debbie's teenage daughter, but her eyes lingered longer on the photo of Debbie beaming with pride, as she held me in her arms on Molly's launch day. Her curiosity satiated, Linda turned back to face the room, with a faintly bored expression. She casually swiped a magazine from the coffee table and dropped onto the sofa, kicking off her boots with a relieved groan.

Like all cats, I had an instinct for evaluating people's laps and, as I observed Linda, I tried to picture myself jumping into her lap for a cuddle. But, try as I might, I could not imagine feeling comfortable in it: it was not a lap that I would classify as *inviting*. Overall, there was something I found off-putting about Linda, and it was not just to do with her spiky boots and talon-like fingernails. I guessed that Linda was a few years younger than Debbie, probably in her mid-forties, but whereas Debbie's physique gave an impression of softness and curves, Linda seemed to be all angles and edges. Her face, which was a curious shade of orange, was longer and thinner than Debbie's, and her nose and chin were more pronounced.

Linda sat flicking through the magazine absent-mindedly for about fifteen minutes, until Debbie's heavy end-of-the-day tread could be heard on the stairs. 'One day my knees are going to pack up on me, I swear,' she complained, collapsing onto one of the dining chairs with an involuntary 'oof' noise and rubbing her kneecaps with both hands.

Linda sprang up from the sofa. 'Let me get you a cuppa, Debs. You stay here.' She rummaged about noisily in the kitchen, opening and closing cabinets in search of mugs and teabags.

At the dining table, Debbie began to sort half-heartedly through the unopened post. 'So, how've you been, Linda?' she called across the hall.

My ears flickered as I tried to make out Linda's reply over the clatter of teaspoons against the worktop, but the next thing I knew, Debbie had leapt up from her seat and dashed out of the room.

'Oh, Linda, what's wrong?' I heard Debbie ask over the sound of sniffing. 'Go and sit down,' she instructed her sister, 'I'll bring the tea through.'

Linda reappeared at the living-room door, her eyes rimmed with red. She pulled a tissue out of her pocket and sat down at the dining table, dabbing her eyes.

'Come on, now. What's happened?' Debbie asked tenderly, placing two steaming mugs on the table.

Linda's face flooded with colour. 'Ray and I have been arguing,' she answered.

'Oh, I'm sorry, Linda. What happened?' Debbie asked kindly, placing one hand on her sister's back.

Linda heaved a weary sigh, shielding her eyes with the damp tissue. 'Things haven't been great for a while, but it all came to a head last night,' she whispered. 'All Ray ever does is snipe at me. He says that I do nothing except shop, go to the hairdresser's and get my nails done, but it's not true!' She paused to blow her nose, and I saw Debbie's eyes fleetingly register her sister's pearly-pink nails and the diamond-encrusted rings on her fingers. She continued to stroke Linda's back in sympathetic silence. 'Besides,' Linda went on indignantly, 'he was the one who encouraged me to give up work, in the first place. He wanted a trophy wife, but now he resents me for it. I've had enough, Debs. I can't bear to be around him any more. I just can't . . .'

As Linda's words tumbled out, Debbie began to look troubled. 'So, Linda,' she began, tentatively, 'when you say you can't bear to be around him any more, do you mean . . . ?'

'I mean I've left him!' Linda's voice cracked melodramatically and she broke into fresh sobs.

A flash of sudden comprehension illuminated Debbie's face, and the hand that had been stroking Linda's back fell still. 'I see,' she said, but the calmness in her voice was betrayed by a look of growing panic. 'Well, have you spoken to him today? If you talk to him, you might find . . .'

But Linda's sobbing grew louder and more persistent, drowning out Debbie's efforts to reassure her. 'No, Deb, I can't talk to him – I can't go back! I just can't.' She slumped forward until her forehead practically touched the dining table, her shoulders shaking and her chest heaving.

Debbie resumed the slow rubbing motion on her sister's back. 'No, of course not, Linda. I understand,' she said soothingly.

Over the sound of Linda's sniffing, I heard cat biscuits being eaten from the dish in the kitchen, and a few moments later Eddie padded into the living room. With a cursory glance at the snivelling stranger bent double over the table, he spotted me in the cardboard box and walked towards me, his tail raised in salutation. I blinked affectionately and he climbed into the box beside me and began to wash, unfazed by the drama playing out on the other side of the room.

Several minutes passed while Linda wiped her eyes with the heels of her hands and blew her nose.

'So, have you thought about what you're going to do?' Debbie prompted, when Linda had finally stopped sniffing.

Still avoiding looking at her sister, Linda shook her head.

Debbie inhaled deeply, assuming an expression somewhere between resignation and dread. 'Would . . . you like to stay here, until you get yourself sorted out?' she asked.

At this, Linda turned to face Debbie. 'Oh, Debs, do you really mean that? Are you sure it won't be too much trouble?' she said, her red-rimmed eyes shining.

'Of course it won't, Linda,' answered Debbie, after a fractional hesitation. 'As long as you don't mind sleeping on a sofa-bed, that is. We haven't got much room, as you can see. And it won't be for long . . . will it?' A trace of a nervous smile danced across Debbie's lips, but Linda appeared not to have heard the question.

She leant over and seized her sister in a hug. 'Oh, Debs, thank you so much. I knew I could count on you,' she gushed, squeezing her sister tightly around the neck.

Intrigued by the noise of Linda's crying, the other kittens had now come upstairs to investigate. They prowled around the room, shooting curious looks at the newcomer and sniffing inquisitively at her boots and handbag on the rug.

As Linda and Debbie pulled apart, Linda gave her eyes a final dab. 'Well, I suppose I might as well bring my things in, before it gets dark,' she said, with an air of practicality, tucking her tissue back inside her jeans pocket.

'Your things . . . have you – you mean now?' I saw the corner of Debbie's mouth twitch.

'If that's okay?' Linda asked, with an ingratiating smile. 'I just threw a few things in the car this morning, to keep me going.'

'Er, okay,' Debbie answered, her eyes flitting anxiously around the cluttered room. 'I'd better clear up some of this mess, to make some space for you.'

'Deb, please, don't go to any trouble – it'll be fine. You'll hardly know I'm here,' Linda insisted. She jumped up from her chair, startling the kittens who scattered skittishly across the room, and grabbed a bunch of keys from her bag. 'I'll just nip down and get my stuff from the car. Back in two minutes,' she said, pulling on her boots.

'Hang on, you'll need the key for the café door,' Debbie called after her sister's retreating back.

Linda leant back through the doorway, smiling as Debbie tossed her a key. 'Thanks. I'll get a copy cut tomorrow,' she said airily.

Downstairs, the café door slammed shut. In the living room Debbie stood next to the dining table, looking slightly shell-shocked. Slowly the kittens began to emerge from their various hiding places, still jumpy after Linda's sudden departure. Debbie watched them with a preoccupied look for a few moments until, with a brisk shake of her head, she set about trying to tidy up. She had just picked up the stack of newspapers from the coffee table when the café door tinkled again.

'It's only me,' Linda shouted from the bottom of the stairwell.

Clutching the papers, Debbie listened as Linda mounted the stairs. Her tread was slow and laboured, accompanied by sporadic grunts of frustration, and every step was followed by a dull thud as something heavy hit the floor.

'Linda, are you all right?' Debbie called, hastily setting the newspapers back down. She winced at the sound of scraping against a wall in the hallway.

I watched from the corner of the room as a large plastic container came through the door, followed by Linda, pink-faced from exertion. In addition to the plastic container that she held in front of her body, she was also pulling a wheeled suitcase behind her. She edged past the dining table, almost knocking over a dining chair, and Debbie automatically stepped forward to take the container, placing it in the middle of the floor.

It took me a moment to register that the container was a pet carrier; and it was a further few seconds before I realized, with a sickening lurch in my stomach, that the animal inside was a dog.

3

Linda wheeled her suitcase across the room and stood it beneath the window, then puffed out her cheeks with relief.

'Um, Linda, what's this?' Debbie asked, looking dubiously at the pet carrier, which had begun to wobble on the rug.

'Oh, this is Beau. Didn't I mention him?' Linda's voice was offhand.

I narrowed my eyes suspiciously at her, before returning my gaze to the quaking plastic box. The kittens stood around the living room, fascinated and alarmed in equal measure. Purdy, who had always been the most confident of the siblings, strode brazenly towards the carrier, sniffing the air as she prowled in a circle around it. The box fell ominously still as its occupant sensed her silent movements. The other kittens looked on, happy to let their braver sister do the investigating for them.

'No, I'm pretty sure you didn't mention him. Beau is a dog, I take it?' Debbie replied, in the unnaturally even tone she used when trying not to lose her temper with Sophie.

'Yes, but he's only small, and very well trained,' Linda reassured her. She crouched down in front of the carrier, which started to rock violently as its occupant scuffled to the front and began to paw at the wire door. 'You're a good boy, aren't you, Beau? Do you want to come out?' she cooed in a babyish voice, her lips puckering into a pout.

A small black nose appeared through a gap in the door, and a pink tongue flicked underneath, reaching for Linda's face. I averted my eyes, repulsed by the demeaning display of canine submission, but the licking had the desired effect on Linda; she kissed the wet nose and began to unlock the carrier.

Before the door was even fully open, the dog had shot out into the room, where his demeanour changed instantly from submissive to aggressively territorial. He was a buff-coloured fluffy creature – not much larger than me – with short, stubby legs and a plume of a tail that curled back over his body. The fur around his cheeks had been neatly trimmed to emphasize the teddy-bear-like roundness of his snub-nosed face; and his dark eyes, which were half-hidden beneath feathery eyebrows, darted beadily around the room.

I scanned the area to locate all the kittens, praying they were near enough the door to be able to escape, should they need to. My eye was immediately drawn to Purdy, who was on the living-room rug behind Beau's carrier. The nonchalance she had displayed while Beau was incarcerated had vanished now that he was free. She had drawn herself up into a defiant arc, with her hackles raised and tail fluffed voluminously.

As if sensing her presence, Beau turned and fixed his dark eyes insolently on Purdy. She stared unblinkingly back at him and, for a moment, the room was silent and still. Then, with a vicious growl, he lunged across the floor towards her. Purdy responded instinctively, with an explosion of spitting and hissing, and for a moment it was impossible to distinguish dog from cat, as they merged into a writhing mass of limbs and fur. The other kittens leapt for safety, sending papers and empty mugs flying as they tried to get as far away from the melee as possible.

'Beau! Oh my God. Beau, baby – stop!' Linda shrieked, with absolutely no effect whatsoever.

Purdy scrambled on top of the pet carrier, from where, with her claws bared and ears flat against her head, she let out a rapid volley of bats against Beau's upturned muzzle. Confused by her sudden height advantage, Beau seemed rooted to the spot, powerless to defend himself against her repeated blows. The sound of claws snagging on skin was followed by Beau's high-pitched yelp and a gasp of shock from Linda. Then it was all over: realizing the battle was lost, Beau fled, scuttling into Linda's open arms.

She made soothing noises and kissed the tip of his nose as Beau whimpered pathetically. I turned to look at Debbie, wondering why she had gone to stand by the window, seemingly to stare at the ceiling. Following her eye-line upwards, I realized that Abby and Bella had both shot up the curtain and were now crouched on the curtain pole, rigid with fear, resolutely ignoring her attempts to coax them down. Throughout the drama Eddie had remained by my side, alert but sanguine, perhaps reassured by his proximity to me. Maisie, the smallest and shyest of my kittens, was nowhere to be seen; I hoped she had either escaped through the door or taken refuge behind the sofa.

Deciding to leave Abby and Bella where they were, Debbie turned back to face the room. 'Linda,' she said, rubbing her forehead, 'I think maybe we should keep Beau and the cats apart for now, at least until they all get used to each other. Don't you?'

Beau was lying on his back in Linda's arms, licking frantically at her face in a way that made my stomach turn. 'You might be right,' Linda replied, looking at

Beau with a distraught expression. 'The poor thing's traumatized, bless him.'

Downstairs, the café door slammed. 'Hi, Mum,' shouted Sophie. Beau immediately wriggled out of Linda's grip, dropped to the floor and started yapping demonically.

'Hi, love,' Debbie called back meekly, with a look that suggested she expected the situation was about to take a turn for the worse. We all listened as Sophie ascended the stairs, Beau's bark increasing in ferocity with every step she took. When Sophie appeared in the doorway, Maisie picked her moment to dart out from behind the sofa, shooting between Sophie's legs to make a break for the stairs. The combination of Maisie's escape and Sophie's arrival proved irresistible for Beau. He bolted after Maisie, practically knocking the unsuspecting Sophie off her feet.

'What the . . . ? Whose dog is that?' she asked, before looking up and noticing Linda, who was still crouched in the middle of the floor, ashen-faced. 'Oh, hi, Auntie Lin—'

'Stop him, Soph!' Debbie shouted, but it was too late. Beau had deftly swerved around the banisters in pursuit of Maisie. Linda jumped to her feet and barged past Sophie into the hallway. There were more yelps and scuffles in the stairwell, as Linda grabbed Beau and manhandled him back upstairs, finally depositing him in the kitchen and slamming the door shut. Seconds later, Linda reappeared at the living-room door. She smoothed her hair and arranged her face into a smile, before walking towards Sophie with her arms open.

'Hi, Soph, how are you? Good day at college?'

'I'm good, thanks,' Sophie replied, nonplussed, allowing her aunt to embrace her. She shot her mother a questioning look over Linda's shoulder.

'Auntie Linda's going to be staying here for . . . a few days,' Debbie explained. 'With her dog.'

'Oh, right.' Sophie smiled politely.

Linda released her from the hug, and I saw Sophie's eyes land on the large suitcase under the window.

No one spoke as Debbie, Linda and Sophie stood awkwardly around the empty carrier. Purdy had jumped onto the sofa and, with a look of complacent victory, had begun to wash, while Abby and Bella remained huddled together nervously on the curtain pole. I sat in the shoebox next to Eddie, taking in the bizarre tableau. The silence was broken only by the sound of Beau pawing at the kitchen door, his claws grating against the wood.

'I'm sure he'll settle down soon,' Linda murmured, at which Debbie tried to muster a smile.

'Well, I've got work to do, so I might just go up to my room,' Sophie said breezily, picking up her school bag.

'Good idea, love,' Debbie concurred. 'We'll order a takeaway later,' she added, in an artificially upbeat tone.

'Mmm, great,' Sophie replied, her phony enthusiasm not fooling anyone.

Debbie sank onto a dining chair, looking drained.

I would have liked nothing more than to restore my equanimity with a calming wash, followed by a long nap, but the dog's persistent scraping at the kitchen door, now accompanied by pitiful howling, ruled out the possibility of any rest.

Sensing tension in the atmosphere, Linda took it upon herself to tidy the mess caused by Beau and Purdy's stand-off, lifting the upturned mugs off the floor and straightening the disarrayed files on the dining table. She picked up the pet carrier and looked around for somewhere less obtrusive to put it, finally making space for it on the floor in the alcove next to the sofa.

The delivery of a Chinese takeaway later that evening went some way towards lifting spirits in the flat. Sophie shuffled down from her bedroom, wearing slippers and a onesie, her long blonde hair tied back in a loose ponytail, to reveal the almond-shaped blue eyes that so closely resembled her mother's.

'How's your homework going?' Debbie asked, as she placed a bunch of cutlery on the table.

'Okay,' Sophie shrugged.

'They work you hard at school these days, don't they?' Linda said, peeling the cardboard lids from the foil food trays at the table.

'It's not school, it's college,' Sophie corrected her. She had left school the previous summer to attend a local college, and was adamant that the distinction between the two should be recognized.

The three of them spooned out food onto their plates and began to eat, to the background accompaniment of Beau's pitiful whimpering in the kitchen. Linda cheerfully fired a succession of questions at Sophie and Debbie about their lives, the café and Stourton. There was a relentless, interrogative quality to her questions and, when she finally took Beau for a walk after dinner, it felt as though everyone in the flat – human and feline – breathed a collective sigh of relief.

Debbie flopped onto the sofa and patted her lap, inviting me to jump up. Sophie sat down beside us and tapped at her phone, while Debbie stroked me and sipped her wine. Neither of them spoke, and I sensed we were all enjoying the peace and quiet.

Twenty minutes later, however, when we heard the café door open, I felt Debbie's body tense underneath me. She inhaled sharply when Linda appeared in the living room with Beau tucked under her arm, although whether that had to do with Linda's return or the fact that, upon seeing Beau, I involuntarily impaled her knees with my claws, I could not be sure. Debbie unpicked my embedded claws from her jeans, one by one, while Linda placed Beau inside his carrier in the alcove, ordering him, 'Be a good boy and lie down.' Worn out by his walk and, presumably, grateful not to be locked in the kitchen, Beau did as he was told and, within a few minutes, was fast asleep and snoring.

When Jasper sauntered into the room a little while later I realized that, in the chaos of Linda and Beau's arrival, I had forgotten to meet him in the alleyway for our usual evening stroll. As I watched him slink silently between the table legs, it occurred to me that, having been outside all day, he would be unaware of the new arrivals. He did not break his stride when he noticed Linda sprawled sideways on the armchair, but a snuffly snort from the pet carrier in the alcove stopped Jasper in his tracks. He froze, glanced through the wire door at the sleeping dog, then lifted his eyes to shoot a look in my direction that seemed to say, 'You've got to be kidding me.' His tail twitched and his amber eyes narrowed in distaste at the unconscious Beau, before he swiftly retraced his steps into the hall. A couple of moments later I heard the cat flap downstairs swinging and I knew he had headed back out, no doubt planning to sleep in the alley.

Everyone agreed that an early night was in order. Debbie explained, between yawns, that she needed to be up early, and Linda was full of understanding and gratitude, acknowledging that it had been a long day.

Debbie opened out the sofa-bed and I sat in the hallway as they all waited their turn for the bathroom, before saying goodnight and disappearing into their respective rooms. One by one, the shafts of light beneath their doors disappeared, and the flat was silent, but for the ticking of the cooling radiators. I padded downstairs to join the kittens in the café.

4

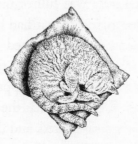

The next morning, I awoke on the window cushion with a start. The image of Beau's snarling face had appeared in my dream, accompanied by a panicky concern for my kittens' safety. Confused and alarmed, I scanned the café to check their whereabouts, and was relieved to see them all sound asleep in their various napping spots, their chests rising and falling with each breath. Jasper, however, was nowhere to be seen.

I slipped through the cat flap and padded down the side of the café, turning right into the narrow alleyway that ran along the back of the parade. This had been Jasper's territory when he had lived on the streets, and he still considered it his domain. A drystone wall bordered one side, facing onto the vista of mismatched fire escapes, dustbins and air vents that made up the rear view of the café and its neighbours.

As I moved noiselessly along the tarmac, there was

a flicker of movement beneath the iron steps of a fire escape, and a moment later Jasper's bulky black-and-white form emerged. He gave his square head a perfunctory shake, before stretching out, his fur rippling as the muscles flexed beneath his skin. When I had first stumbled into this alleyway as a half-starved stray, I had been intimidated by Jasper's imposing physical presence. The scars on his ears suggested he was an accomplished fighter, and my experience with another of the town's alley-cats made me instinctively wary around him. Over time, however, I had come to realize that his street-cat looks and taciturn manner belied a sweet-natured, chivalrous disposition.

I sat down next to the iron steps and Jasper came to sit beside me. 'Sleep well?' I asked.

'Not so great,' he answered, with a slight narrowing of his amber eyes. We contemplated the skyline in silence for a few moments: the rising sun had broken through the cloud, and the light mist that had swathed the nearby church spire was beginning to melt away. 'Who is she?' he asked finally, in a voice heavy with disdain.

'Her name's Linda – she's Debbie's sister.'

Jasper looked pensive. 'And is she . . . are *they* . . . staying long?' he asked.

I realized that, amidst the drama of the previous evening, Linda had not specified how long she planned to stay. 'Just a few days, I think,' I answered vaguely, with more hope than conviction.

'Hmm,' Jasper replied, returning his thoughtful gaze to the sky.

Having lived on the streets all his life, Jasper had an ambivalent attitude towards the cat café, at best. It had been a mark of his devotion to me, and his dedication as a father, that he had compromised his street-cat independence to spend time with us indoors, albeit on his own terms. He consistently avoided the café during opening hours, considering the idea of being 'on show' to customers demeaning; but, after closing time, he would slip through the cat flap, to enjoy some of the benefits of our lifestyle. I sometimes teased him about his double standards, pointing out that his proud asser-tion that he would 'always be an alley-cat' was not entirely credible when he spent his evenings sprawled semi-conscious on the café's flagstones in front of the dying embers of the stove. I suspected, however, that Jasper would draw the line at sharing his indoor terri-tory with a highly strung stranger and a lunatic lapdog.

The town was beginning to wake up around us; somewhere in the distance a dustbin lorry rumbled its stop–start progress around the streets, while the rooks and magpies in the adjacent churchyard cawed inces-santly, starting the day in dispute, as always. Behind me, I detected movement in the flat above the café: the swoop of a venetian blind being raised and the patter of water from the shower. I could picture the scene inside: Debbie hurrying from the steaming bathroom into the kitchen to fill our food bowls, before shouting up the stairs to the attic, to wake Sophie for college. My stomach began to growl with hunger.

'Are you coming in for breakfast?' I asked Jasper, knowing full well what his answer would be.

His nose wrinkled in distaste. 'Not today,' he replied dismissively, but when his eyes caught mine, I saw a trace of a smile. 'If he stays much longer that dog will need putting in his place,' he commented wryly.

'Don't worry, Purdy's already done it,' I said.

Jasper blinked his approval and puffed out his chest. 'Good for her,' he commented. Then he stood up, stretched and slunk away towards the row of conifers at the end of the passage.

Inside, the kittens had vanished from the café. I crept cautiously up the stairs, my ears alert for indications of Beau's whereabouts. The living-room door was still closed, but I could hear Debbie in the kitchen, talking happily to the kittens. 'There you go, Purdy; now, be nice, make room for Maisie. Bella and Abby, you can share the pink dish – there's plenty for both of you. Don't worry, Eddie, I haven't forgotten about you, aren't you a patient boy?'

Her loving chatter made my heart swell with gratitude; she knew my kittens almost as well as I knew them myself, and she always made sure they each received their fair share of food and attention.

I paused in the doorway to watch as they ate greedily from the dishes on the kitchen floor. With their heads lowered, the four tabby sisters looked so similar that they were almost indistinguishable, although Maisie's petite frame marked her out from the others. Eddie was at the far end of the line, noticeably taller and bulkier than his sisters, his black-and-white colouring a sleeker, glossier version of his father's.

Debbie stood at the worktop, waiting for the kettle to boil. 'Morning, Molls, I was wondering where you'd got to.' She smiled as I edged in alongside Purdy.

I had just taken my first mouthful when there was a scuffling sound across the hall, and Linda squeezed out of the living room, holding the door close to her body to prevent Beau from escaping. He yapped and scrabbled in protest as she pulled the door shut behind her.

'Cuppa?' Debbie asked.

'Oh, yes, please,' Linda answered, sidling into the kitchen to lean against the fridge. In her dressing gown, with mussed-up hair and eyes puffy with sleep, she was hardly recognizable as the immaculately presented woman I had met the day before.

At that moment Sophie raced noisily downstairs from her bedroom and steadied herself on the kitchen doorframe to pull on her trainers.

'You having breakfast, Soph?' Debbie asked.

Sophie glanced at her watch, considering whether she had time, and perhaps also whether she could face the contortions required to extract a bowl of cereal; the kitchen was compact at the best of times, let alone when it contained two adults and six cats. 'Er, actually, don't worry, Mum, I'll get something at the canteen,' she said. 'I've just got to get my art portfolio—'

Before Debbie or Linda could stop her, Sophie had crossed the hall and flung open the living-room door. Beau instantly darted out into the hallway, his feathery eyebrows twitching, his pink tongue hanging out. He looked as if he could hardly believe his luck at finding so many cats directly in his eye-line.

Experience had taught me that, when it came to dogs, attack was the best form of defence. As Beau hurtled across the hall, I braced myself for a fight: my hackles rose, my ears flattened and I growled in warning.

But before he reached me, Linda had lunged out of the kitchen and swooped down to lift Beau off the ground. Thwarted and humiliated, Beau tried to break free, but Linda kept a tight hold on him, cradling him in her arms as if he were an angry baby who needed soothing. Realizing that the dog would not settle with several cats in such tantalizingly close proximity, she dropped him back into the living room and closed the door on him.

'Sorry, I'd forgotten he was in there,' Sophie said sheepishly, before grabbing her things and thundering downstairs and out through the café.

Debbie sighed and stirred two mugs of tea. 'He's a feisty little thing, isn't he?' she observed, over the sound of Beau's determined scraping at the living-room door.

'It's the breed,' Linda concurred. 'He's a Lhasa Apso – they're very territorial. They were used to guard Buddhist monasteries in Tibet.'

Debbie raised an eyebrow. 'Oh, right,' she replied in a flat voice. 'Well, he's not in Tibet now, he's in the Cotswolds. In a cat café.' She handed Linda a steaming mug of tea. 'I mean . . . the clue's in the title, really.' She took a sip and fixed her sister with a look over the rim of her cup.

'I know, Debbie – sorry,' Linda replied. 'I think he's just a bit traumatized by the whole experience. I mean, all the arguing and shouting at home, it was so awful . . .' Her cheeks flushed with colour and I could see that tears were imminent. I watched as Debbie put her mug back on the worktop and touched her sister's arm.

'Sorry, Lind, I didn't mean to upset you.'

Linda's head dropped and she covered her eyes with the sleeve of her dressing gown, her shoulders starting to shake.

'Don't worry, Linda,' Debbie reassured her. 'I'm sure the cats will adjust to the situation. They'll get used to Beau soon enough.'

She leant in to hug Linda, and I caught Linda's eye over her shoulder. I held her gaze while the two women embraced, doing my best to convey that if anyone was going to have to adjust, it would not be me.

5

In spite of my determination to make as few conces-
sions as possible to their presence, it was impossible to
ignore Linda and Beau. With three adult humans, half
a dozen cats and one dog sharing the flat's limited
space, there simply was not enough room for us all.

The living room bore the brunt of the impact. The
opened sofa-bed took up so much of the floor area that
to get from one side of the room to the other, Linda
either had to edge sideways around the foot of the bed
or clamber across the mattress. The alcove next to the
sofa functioned as her makeshift wardrobe; she had
propped her huge suitcase open in there, alongside
Beau's upended carrier, and piles of clothes, jewellery
and cosmetics spilled out of it onto the floor.

But Linda's clutter was not confined to the room
she slept in. Boxes of floral-smelling herbal teas and
plastic tubs of vitamin pills appeared on the kitchen

worktop, and her extensive collection of creams, oils and lotions jostled for space on the bathroom window-sill. Even the hallway seemed narrower, what with Linda's jackets and gilets bulging from the coat pegs and her numerous pairs of boots and shoes snaking across the floor. When Linda took Beau for his daily walk, I tried to reclaim some territorial advantage by scent-marking the furniture with my cheeks. But in spite of my efforts, the combined aroma of Linda's cloying perfume and Beau's dog-shampoo continued to overpower any other scent in the flat.

To my great relief, the aggressive swagger that Beau had displayed when he first arrived did not last more than a few days. The scratch Purdy had inflicted on the dog's nose remained visibly raw and weeping, serving as a reminder of Beau's place at the bottom of the animal hierarchy, and the kittens soon learnt that a vicious hiss and the swipe of a paw, with claws bared, would send Beau scurrying to Linda for protection. His tufted eyebrows still twitched if a cat entered the room, but his growl lacked conviction, and he wore the resigned, resentful look of an animal that knew he was outnumbered. Like a piece of grit trapped between paw-pads, Beau was impossible to ignore, but in the short term at least he was an irritation that we could tolerate.

The highlight of his day was invariably his walk. He

would bounce up and down manically, his moist tongue hanging out, while Linda fetched his lead and the plastic pouch of poo-bags. She would tuck the excitable creature under her elbow and head downstairs to tell Debbie that she was 'taking Beau out to explore Stourton'. It didn't take me long to work out that when Linda said *explore*, what she actually meant was *shop*.

She returned from their first walk with a thick cardboard shopping bag slung over her shoulder. Intrigued, I followed her upstairs and watched from the living-room doorway as she tore open layers of rustling tissue paper to reveal an expensive-looking leather handbag. Her eyes wide with child-like excitement, she transferred the contents of her old handbag to the new one, before leaning over the side of the sofa to tuck the discarded bag beneath a pile of dirty laundry.

'What a gorgeous bag. Is it new?' Debbie asked that evening, catching sight of the bag sitting on the floor next to the sofa-bed.

Linda feigned surprise. 'What, this?' she said, nudging the bag casually underneath the bed with her foot. 'I've had it for years!'

As the week went on, her shopping habit became increasingly furtive. She and Beau would head out mid-morning, and hours would pass before she returned, laden with purchases from the many chichi boutiques that lined Stourton's cobbled streets. I would watch from the café windowsill as she clopped along the parade, with Beau bounding along next to her spiky-heeled boots. Only when she was sure Debbie was out of sight would Linda push open the café door – slowly, to minimize the tinkling of the bell – and dart between the tables to the staircase.

Once Linda had got her purchases into the flat, the majority of them seemed mysteriously to disappear. By the time Debbie trudged upstairs after work, there was no evidence either of the shopping bags or of their contents, and Linda never admitted how much time she had spent trawling the Stourton shops. The only purchases she ever admitted to were the gifts she had bought for her hosts. A silk scarf appeared in Debbie's bedroom one afternoon and, the following day, when Sophie returned from college, Linda was waiting to present her with a pair of pyjamas. 'They're cashmere – feel them!' she urged, her eyes twinkling as she handed the luxurious sleepwear to her stunned niece.

I was intrigued to know where Linda had put the rest of her shopping and so, one morning while she and Beau were out, I crept into the living room to investigate. There was no sign of her new purchases, just the usual messy pile of clothes on the floor next to the open suitcase. It was only when I scaled the suitcase that I discovered her secret: she was using Beau's pet carrier as storage. Concealed behind its wire door were boxed pairs of brand-new shoes and a stack of clothes, all neatly folded and wrapped in tissue paper.

Linda's shopping habits notwithstanding, by the end of their first week the overcrowded conditions in the flat were beginning to take their toll. Perhaps sensing that tempers were close to fraying, Linda insisted that she would make dinner for the three of them on Friday night, as 'my way of saying thank you'. And so, as the clock struck eight that evening, Debbie and Sophie waited at the dining table, while Linda bustled and clattered in the kitchen. Debbie looked worn out, but Sophie's slumped posture and bored expression conveyed something closer to ill will. She had foregone an evening with her boyfriend in order to be home for dinner and was making no secret of the fact that she resented the sacrifice.

Eventually Linda tottered through from the kitchen, balancing three plates in her hands. '*Voilà!* Superfood salad,' she announced, lowering the plates onto the table with a flourish.

Debbie smiled wanly at the pile of grains and pulses in front of her. 'Mmm, wow!' she murmured, with an unconvincing attempt at enthusiasm. Sophie scowled.

'Don't you like it, Soph?' Linda asked, as her niece began to push the contents of her plate around reluctantly.

I sensed Debbie's patience was wearing thin as she

watched her daughter's ill-disguised revulsion. 'Come on, Sophie,' she chivvied her. 'Eat up, please. Auntie Linda has gone to a lot of trouble to make this.' But Sophie merely glared sideways at her mother and picked at the mound of vegetation with her fork.

'You don't like quinoa?' Linda asked, looking concerned.

'No, I'm not a massive fan of *keen-wah*,' Sophie replied, her drawling enunciation carrying an unmistakeable hint of mimicry.

I watched as she picked up a single grain on the prongs of her fork and peered at it dubiously.

'There's no need for sarcasm, Soph. Just eat,' said Debbie, fixing her daughter with a stern stare. Sophie placed the tip of the fork into her mouth and began to chew the single grain, slowly. Debbie turned towards Linda. 'She's always been a fussy eater,' she said apologetically.

There was a sudden crash as Sophie's fork hit her plate. With a furious look at Debbie, she stood up and thrust her chair back, forcing the rug into messy folds behind her. On the sofa, the commotion made me jump, and I saw Beau's body spasm as he jerked awake in alarm under the table. 'I'm going to make a sandwich,' Sophie mumbled, picking up her plate of uneaten salad and carrying it into the kitchen.

'Sophie!' Debbie said tersely, sounding at once cross

and embarrassed. 'Linda has gone to the trouble of making that for you – the least you can do is try it,' she called after her daughter's retreating back. In the kitchen, Sophie was noisily scraping the contents of her plate into the rubbish bin.

'It's fine, really,' Linda said in a conciliatory tone. 'Quinoa is an acquired taste, I suppose.'

Debbie ignored her, and kept her eyes firmly fixed on Sophie who, after much tutting and slamming of cupboard doors, stomped upstairs with her substitute meal.

It troubled me to see Debbie and Sophie bickering. It reminded me of how things used to be, when Debbie had first taken me into the flat. Back then, their arguments had been a regular occurrence, usually culminating in Sophie storming out, leaving Debbie morose and tearful. For a while I had blamed myself for Sophie's unhappiness. Their relationship was already fragile, in the wake of Debbie's divorce and their move to Stourton, and I worried that Debbie's fondness for me had given Sophie another reason to feel hard done by. In time, however, Sophie's resentment towards me had mellowed, at first to tolerance, and eventually to something approaching affection. It had been a long time since she had deliberately flung her school bag at my head, or referred to me as 'that mangy fleabag'.

I sat in the cardboard box, listening to the ceiling

joists creak beneath Sophie's thudding footsteps. I was aware of stirrings of disquiet in the pit of my stomach and a feeling of foreboding that life in the flat might be about to get worse. Debbie had directed her annoyance at Sophie rather than Linda, but I suspected she might be harbouring frustrations of her own. As I watched Debbie chew her way stoically through her superfood salad, I wondered whether, in fact, she didn't much like quinoa, either.

Since Debbie had made the decision, a few months earlier, to close the café at weekends, Saturday mornings in the flat were usually a laid-back, leisurely affair. Debbie would stock up on pastries from the bakery, and she and Sophie would settle down on the sofa in their pyjamas, licking sugar and crumbs off their fingers while the kittens and I napped or washed nearby. The Saturday morning that followed the superfood-salad argument, however, did not begin in the customary relaxed manner. The effects of the previous evening's conflict seemed to hang over the flat and its residents like a cloud.

When I awoke at the foot of Debbie's bed, I discovered she had already risen. I padded downstairs and found her in the kitchen, shooting impatient looks at the closed living-room door, while roughly stacking dirty plates in the dishwasher. When, some time later,

Linda finally emerged in a state of puffy-eyed disarray, she found a frosty Debbie hanging damp laundry over the hallway radiator.

'Morning, Debs. Can I do anything to help?' Linda asked.

'The dishwasher will need unloading,' answered Debbie curtly. Linda rolled up her dressing-gown sleeves and headed diligently into the kitchen.

A little while later, Debbie was extracting the vacuum cleaner from the hallway cupboard when the bell over the café door tinkled.

'Deb, it's me,' shouted a man's voice from downstairs. It was John, Debbie's boyfriend.

'Hi, John, come up,' Debbie called over the banister.

Feeling relieved, I padded across the hallway to meet him. John's gentle manner was just what the flat needed on this rather tense Saturday morning.

John hummed to himself as he made his way up the narrow staircase and smiled jovially as he rounded the top of the stairs. 'Croissants,' he said, handing a large paper bag to Debbie, before kissing her lightly. John was tall but stockily built, with sandy hair and a kind, freckled face. I had always liked him, not least because I had been instrumental in bringing him and Debbie together.

'Come and meet my sister,' Debbie said, leading John into the living room, where Linda was sitting on the sofa reading the newspaper. 'John, Linda. Linda, John.'

'Nice to meet you, Linda,' John said, holding out his arm to shake Linda's hand, whereupon Beau, who had been asleep on the rug, jerked awake in alarm at the sound of an unfamiliar male voice. Upon seeing a strange man advancing, arm outstretched, towards his owner, Beau was unable to contain his guard-dog instincts. He leapt to his feet in panic.

'Beau, stop it!' Linda shouted over the animal's frenzied barking. 'I mean it, Beau!' she pleaded ineffectually, her cheeks flushing with embarrassment as Beau snarled and snapped around John's ankles.

John's eyes crinkled into a smile as he regarded his furry assailant with mild surprise. Dropping to his haunches, he put a hand out for Beau to sniff. 'At ease, fella. We're all friends, here,' he said placidly.

'I'm so sorry, John, he's not normally aggressive,' Linda apologized, as Beau's damp muzzle twitched across John's fingers.

'He's just being territorial,' Debbie cut in drily. 'He's a Lapsang Souchong, you know.'

Linda shot her sister a look over the top of John's head. 'Lhasa Apso, Debs,' she said crisply. 'He's a dog, not a cup of tea.'

Reassured that John posed no immediate threat, Beau retreated to his corner of the rug. He lay down and lowered his chin onto his forepaws, but maintained his beady surveillance of John, lest his services as Linda's bodyguard be required after all.

The buttery smell of freshly baked croissants had lured Sophie downstairs from her bedroom for the first time since her ill-tempered departure at dinner. She hovered in the doorway, watching hungrily as Debbie piled them onto a plate in the middle of the dining table.

'Morning, Soph, how are you?' John asked warmly.

'Good, thanks,' she mumbled.

While Debbie made coffee, John and Linda chatted at the dining table. Once John had established that Linda found Stourton charming and thought Molly's was fabulous, Linda swiftly turned the topic to John himself.

'So, Debbie tells me you've lived in Stourton all your life?' she enquired, popping a chunk of croissant into her mouth.

'Born and bred,' John nodded.

'And you're a plumber, I gather,' Linda probed.

'That's right. Did Debbie mention how her boiler nearly burnt the place down?'

Debbie had just placed their drinks on the table, and she rolled her eyes. 'Oh, all right, John – are you ever going to stop going on about that? Besides, if it hadn't been for the boiler, you and I might never have met.'

Whether it was the effect of the croissants or John's good-natured presence, the residual awkwardness from the previous evening seemed to dissipate. Debbie looked more relaxed than she had done for days, and even Sophie seemed in no hurry to leave. Once all that was left of the croissants was a scattering of crumbs on the table top, Debbie drained her coffee cup and glanced at her watch. 'Sorry to break up the party,' she said, with a sombre look at John, 'but we've got to get the cats to the vets.'

I had long accepted that visits to the vet were a non-negotiable aspect of life as a pet cat and, though I didn't exactly enjoy the experience, I never doubted that the long-term benefits outweighed the short-term discomfort. Jasper, however, had been born on the streets and had gone through life without ever experiencing the chill of the black examination table or the sting of the vaccination needle. His first-ever trip to the vet had taken place several months earlier, when he had begun to spend time indoors. Debbie had decided that Jasper deserved the same provision of care as the rest of us, and he had woken one morning to find himself being bundled into the cat carrier.

The fact that Jasper's first visit had resulted in him being neutered did nothing to endear the vet to him. When he had returned to the café after his ordeal, groggy from the anaesthetic, he had immediately taken refuge in the alleyway and proceeded to sulk for several days. Eventually, though, Jasper had realized that life would go on. In time, he had forgiven Debbie, although he retained his distrust of the vet, as well as his aversion to the cat carrier.

So it was that, on the occasion of our annual check-up, John had been roped in to help round us up, and we found ourselves sitting in a row of carriers on the back seat of Debbie's car. I shared my carrier with Eddie and Maisie; to our right, Purdy, Abby and Bella jostled for space; and to our left was a third carrier in which Jasper travelled alone, in bad-tempered isolation. I could make out his shadowy profile through the ventilation holes and, although he was silent, his resentment emanated through the plastic walls between us.

Over the sound of Purdy's frantic scratching, the occasional squeak of complaint from Abby and Bella as she trod on their tails, and Maisie's meek mewing behind me, I tried to concentrate on Debbie and John's conversation. They were talking about Linda.

'She is starting to do my head in a bit,' Debbie admitted guiltily.

'Has she ever left her husband before?' John asked from the passenger seat.

Debbie shook her head. 'Never. I thought she had

the lifestyle she'd always dreamed of: manicures, personal trainer, skiing trips with her friends.'

John raised his eyebrows. 'Very nice,' he remarked in a tone of diplomatic neutrality.

'Ray's the finance director for some marketing company in London. Linda used to work for him,' Debbie explained. 'He earns a fortune, though I always found him as dull as ditch-water.'

'Maybe money can't buy you happiness after all,' John said sagely, with the merest trace of a smile around his lips.

Debbie tilted her head in agreement. 'Apparently not.' She steered the car around a large roundabout, and there was a chorus of scrabbling on the back seat as we all slid sideways inside our carriers.

'Any kids?' John asked, once the car had joined the main road.

Debbie shook her head. 'Only Beau,' she joked, her eyes glinting as she glanced in the rear-view mirror. 'They never got round to it. Or at least that was the official version. Who knows what the real story is.' After a week in Linda's company, Debbie seemed relieved at being able to talk about her sister.

'She's lucky she's got you,' John said, turning briefly to face Debbie.

She shrugged. 'Linda's got loads of friends, but they're mostly the wives of Ray's colleagues. They're a gossipy bunch, from what I've heard. Linda would hate to think that her marital problems are the talk of north London.' Debbie drove on, concentrating on the road ahead. 'Sometimes I think I've been more of a mum to her than a sister,' she said, thoughtfully. 'And since Mum and Dad moved to Spain – well, who else has Linda got . . . ?' She trailed off, and John didn't press her any further.

The rest of the journey passed in silence, broken only by the sporadic yowls and mews from the carriers on the back seat.

When John pushed open the surgery door I was immediately assailed by the smell of disinfectant.

'Good morning,' the receptionist trilled in a sing-song voice, as we were lowered onto the grey linoleum floor.

'Debbie Walsh. Check-ups for seven cats.'

'Ah yes, Molly's Cat Café,' the receptionist smiled, scanning her computer screen. 'Quite a job just to get them all here, I bet.' She grinned, peering over her desk at the three carriers.

'I've got the scars to prove it,' Debbie replied, holding out her hand to reveal a livid red scratch left by Jasper in his struggle to evade capture.

The receptionist winced in sympathy. 'Take a seat, the vet won't be long.'

The young, enthusiastic vet seemed impervious to

Jasper's warning growls, which had risen in volume as soon as we entered the consulting room. 'Who's a handsome boy?' she cooed through the wire door, undeterred by the high-pitched rasp issuing from inside. 'Come on then, big boy, out you come,' she coaxed.

'Sorry, he's always a bit grumpy when he comes here,' Debbie apologized.

Unable to lure Jasper out, the vet had no choice but to upend his carrier. There was a scraping sound of claws against smooth plastic, as gravity took its course and Jasper slid out, backwards, on the sheaf of loose newspaper that lined the carrier floor.

On the examination table, Jasper's hostility was replaced by a look of stoic resolve. He gallantly submitted to the vet's ministrations, sitting motionless while she looked inside his ears and prised open his mouth to check his teeth, and did not even flinch when she briskly administered an injection between his shoulder blades. 'Good boy, Jasper! All done!' she exclaimed, giving him a congratulatory rub around the ears. He slunk back inside his carrier, to stare at her reproachfully through the wire door.

One by one, the kittens and I endured the same procedure. Maisie, whose timidity was never more apparent than at the vet's, trembled throughout; Abby and Bella clung together so insistently that the vet had to conduct their examinations in tandem; and Eddie was his usual placid self, gazing up trustingly at the vet and purring gratefully when she gave him a treat. Purdy, as usual, treated the whole experience as an adventure, leaping from the examination table to the vet's worktop, where she strode brazenly across the computer keyboard to sniff at the electronic scales.

Back at the café, Debbie unlocked our carriers and let out a long, relieved sigh. 'Thank goodness that's over for another year,' she said to John, watching Purdy follow Jasper out through the cat flap.

'I think we've earned lunch at the pub, don't you?' John replied, brushing Debbie's fringe tenderly out of her eyes.

'Now you're talking,' said Debbie. 'I'll just pop up and tell Linda.'

I followed Debbie upstairs to the hallway, registering the laundry hanging over the radiator and the vacuum cleaner standing amidst Linda's jumble of shoes. In the living room, the empty mugs and crumb-covered plates were still on the dining table, untouched since breakfast. When I saw Linda dozing on the sofa, with Beau snoring on the cushion beside her and the newspaper strewn messily across the floor, I felt my hackles instinctively rise with annoyance. Judging by Debbie's sharp intake of breath, I suspected that, had she been a cat, hers would have risen, too.

7

Debbie stood in front of the sofa with her hands on her hips while, behind her, John hovered awkwardly in the doorway. When it became apparent their presence was not enough to wake Linda, Debbie strode forward and began to scoop the sheets of newspaper noisily off the floor.

'Oh, sorry, I must have dropped off,' Linda mumbled, pushing herself upright with her elbows and shoving Beau off the cushion with her bare feet. Catching sight of John, Beau barked groggily, but quickly rearranged himself on the rug to continue his nap.

Any relief Debbie might have felt after spending time with John had been short-lived, and the fractiousness she had exhibited earlier returned. With pursed lips and a clenched jaw, she set about tidying the living room.

'Here, let me help you,' Linda said, jumping up from

the sofa and making for the table, where Debbie had begun to collect the dirty plates and cups.

'No, it's fine, thank you,' she replied testily, before striding out of the room towards the kitchen.

I watched from a distance as John and Linda exchanged an uncomfortable look.

'I think I'll take Beau for a walk,' Linda muttered, pulling on her shoes. 'Lovely to meet you,' she said, giving John a friendly peck on the cheek. She picked up the sleeping Beau and carried him, bleary-eyed and disorientated, downstairs.

John stepped across the hall and leant against the kitchen doorframe. 'Why don't you leave the tidying for now? It can wait till after lunch,' he suggested hopefully.

Debbie's face remained closed as she rinsed the plates under the tap. 'Actually, you know what, maybe we should just give lunch a miss today. I've got too much to do here,' she said over the splashing of water in the sink.

John's shoulders drooped with disappointment. 'Okay, well – if you're sure?'

'Really, I think I'm starting to get a headache anyway. I'd rather just get the flat tidy,' she insisted.

John gave a resigned shrug and leant into the kitchen to give Debbie a kiss, which she accepted without taking her eyes off the sink. I couldn't help but feel sorry for him as he grabbed his jacket and made his way downstairs alone.

As soon as the café door had closed behind him, Debbie heaved a sigh and gazed disconsolately around the kitchen. I pressed myself against her ankles in an effort to cheer her up, but she seemed too preoccupied to notice me. She pulled on her apron and set to work cleaning the flat: dusting, hoovering and mopping with ruthless efficiency. When she had finished and the dust-free surfaces gleamed, she sank onto the sofa.

Not wanting to waste the opportunity for some one-to-one affection, I jumped onto her lap for a cuddle and purred ecstatically while she stroked me.

All too soon we heard Linda's footsteps on the stairs, and I felt Debbie's muscles tense beneath me. Linda's simpering, orange-toned face appeared around the living-room door.

'Debs, I've got you something,' she announced gaily.

'Oh, really?' Debbie replied in a tone which suggested that, whatever Linda had bought her, she was not expecting to like it.

'It's a NutriBullet!' Linda proclaimed jubilantly, pulling a sizeable cardboard box out of a carrier bag and thrusting it at Debbie.

'A nutri-what?' Debbie asked, blank-faced.

'It's a fruit and vegetable juicer. They're brilliant!

You can chuck anything in there. Skins, pips, stalks – the lot. It was in the sale,' Linda added, as if this made the logic of its purchase unquestionable. 'Come on, I'll show you,' she said, grabbing her sister by the hand.

I had no choice but to jump down from Debbie's lap as she was dragged from the sofa. She stood in the kitchen doorway and watched listlessly as Linda unpacked the stainless-steel gadget and placed it on the cluttered worktop, where it occupied almost half of the available surface area.

Debbie eyed the device dubiously. 'But, Linda, I'm not sure we really need—' she protested.

'Trust me, Debs. You'll wonder how you ever lived without one,' Linda said authoritatively.

Debbie stared at the NutriBullet with sagging shoulders. 'Linda, please stop buying us gifts. It's not necessary,' she began in a small, tight voice.

'I know, Debs, but it's the least I can do, to say thank you for putting me up,' Linda riposted brightly.

'But, Linda,' Debbie persevered, 'there's no need for it, and it must be costing you a fortune—'

'Don't worry about that,' Linda cut her short. 'It's going on Ray's credit card.' A look of triumph flashed in her eyes.

Debbie took a short, exasperated intake of breath. 'Well, even if Ray's paying, it's not necessary. In fact it's making me uncomfortable.' There was a pause as Linda absorbed her words.

'Uncomfortable? Really? Sorry, Debs, I didn't mean . . .' A flicker of embarrassment crossed Linda's face. Her head dropped and she stared at the floor. 'I just wanted to say thank you, but I can take it back to the shop if you'd rather,' she whispered, a touch self-pityingly.

An uneasy hush descended on the kitchen.

Suddenly Linda's shoulders started to shake and she raised one hand to shield her face. 'I've made such a mess of everything,' she wailed. 'I'm sorry, Debs, I know I'm getting in your way, I'll pack up and—'

'Linda, there's no need for that,' Debbie groaned, putting an arm out to prevent her sister walking away. 'I'm not saying I want you to go, just that – well, maybe we need to find something for you to do.'

Linda dabbed her heavily made-up eyes with a tissue, and Debbie stood for a moment, chewing her bottom lip, watching her sister intently.

'Look,' Debbie said at last. 'If you really want to say thank you, why don't you help me out in the café? I could do with another pair of hands down there, and it would give you something to do during the day, other than shopping.'

Linda looked up, with watery eyes. 'Are you sure? I've never worked in a café before,' she said uncertainly.

'I'm sure you'll pick it up, Linda,' Debbie replied warmly.

A child-like smile began to spread across Linda's face. 'I'd love to help out, Debs. I always loved playing waitresses when we were little, do you remember?' she said, seizing Debbie tightly around the neck. Debbie returned the hug, but a wrinkle had formed between her eyebrows, and I wondered whether she was already having doubts about her spur-of-the-moment suggestion.

Linda's first day at work didn't get off to the most promising start. I watched from the window cushion as Debbie came downstairs on Monday morning and set about the usual tasks: she switched on the lights, placed the chalkboard on the pavement and stocked the till with cash. She was updating the Specials board when Linda appeared at the foot of the stairs, rubbing her hands together eagerly.

'Right then, Boss. Where do you want me?'

Debbie glanced doubtfully at Linda's spiky-heeled boots. 'Are you sure you want to wear those today? You'll be on your feet a lot,' she warned, but Linda was adamant.

'Don't worry, Debs, they're really very comfortable.'

By late morning, when the café started to fill up with customers, Linda's enthusiasm seemed to be waning. She struggled to use the till, and had mixed up two tables' orders. When the time finally came for her lunch break she limped upstairs, and the thought crossed my mind that she might not come back. An hour later, however, she reappeared for the afternoon shift, rested, refreshed and having swapped the spiky heels for a pair of flat, fleecy boots.

On Tuesday, Linda appeared downstairs wearing loose-fitting trousers, a sweater borrowed from Debbie and comfortable shoes. With her blonde hair tied back and a Molly's apron over her clothes, she bore more of a resemblance to Debbie, and sometimes I had to look twice to be certain which sister was which. She remained nervous whenever she had to use the till, but was relaxed and friendly with the customers, enthusing about the menu in a way that seemed genuine rather than pushy. 'Have you tried the Cake Pops? Oh, they're *delicious*!' she gushed, before trotting proudly to the kitchen with her order pad.

As the week went on, her confidence grew, and Debbie seemed both surprised and gratified by her sister's aptitude for the job. Working together gave them some common ground; for the first time since Linda had arrived, they had something to talk about other than Linda's marital problems and whose turn it was to wash up. On Friday afternoon, when Linda slipped out, saying that she had an appointment she couldn't miss, I was surprised to find that the café felt empty without her.

'Now, Debbie, don't be cross.'

I had been dozing in the window, but at the sound of Linda's voice I jolted awake. It was dark outside, the café had closed and Debbie was cashing up the day's takings behind the counter.

'What? Why would I be cross? What've you got there, Linda?' Debbie asked, a slight note of anxiety in her voice.

I looked sideways to see Linda standing on the doormat holding a large cardboard box. Smiling with excitement, she walked across the café and, with great care, placed the box on the counter.

'I know you said no more gifts,' she explained, 'but I thought this would be the exception. It's for the business really. I think it's just what the café needs.'

I sat up on my cushion, wondering what the café could possibly need that it didn't already have. I craned forward attentively as Debbie, with a look of trepidation, pulled the box towards her and flipped open its cardboard flaps. What I saw made my stomach contract: from inside the box, a pair of dark-brown, pointed ears appeared, quickly followed by the fine-boned face of a Siamese cat.

'This is Ming!' Linda exclaimed.

Debbie's mouth had fallen open. Speechless, she stared at the cat, who was looking around in wide-eyed alarm.

'Linda! What have you . . . ? You're not – you can't . . .' Debbie stammered.

'Now look, Debs. I know what you're going to say, but just hear me out,' Linda insisted. 'I've been working here for a week, and I think you're missing a trick. Molly and her kittens are lovely, of course, but they are – well, just *moggies*. I think it would really add to the café's appeal to have something a little more *exotic* in the mix. You know, to give the customers something a bit special to look at.'

'Linda, this is ridiculous,' Debbie replied with a mirthless laugh. 'We're talking about cats, not . . . clothes, or soft furnishings. *You can't just throw a new cat into the mix.* Our cats are a colony, for goodness' sake. This . . . Ming . . . will be an outsider.' She looked in desperation at the Siamese cat, whose disembodied, dismayed face was still peering out from between the box's cardboard flaps.

As Debbie talked, Ming turned to face her and let out a throaty, plaintive yowl. Debbie raised her eyebrows in surprise at the noise, which was far deeper and louder than anything I or the kittens could produce. Her expression softened and she instinctively reached to stroke Ming between the ears. I watched with narrowed eyes, feeling the hairs on my back bristle with envy.

When Linda next spoke, her voice was wheedling. 'Ming's owners put an ad in the paper. They're expecting a baby, so decided to rehome her. How anyone could give away such a beautiful creature is beyond me . . .' Linda trailed off, leaving the thought of such wanton cruelty hanging in the air. 'She's two years old, and has been spayed and vaccinated,' she added matter-of-factly, as if this would surely clinch the deal.

Debbie withdrew her hand from the box and began to rub her forehead in consternation. 'But, Linda, it's not that simple, is it?' she frowned. 'This is a cat café. What if Ming's temperament doesn't suit it here? She might hate living with other cats. And they might not like her.'

'Well, okay, that's a possibility,' Linda shrugged dismissively. 'But we won't know till we try, will we?' She looked shrewdly at her sister, sensing that Debbie's resolve was wavering. 'Why don't you give it some time and see how Ming settles in? If she seems unhappy, then you can rehome her. But at least give her a chance. What's the worst that can happen?'

I fixed my eyes on the back of Linda's head, allowing images of the worst things that could happen – both to Ming and to Linda – to run through my mind.

Debbie groaned and slumped against the serving counter. *Just say No!* I wanted to scream, wishing I could jump onto the counter and slam the cardboard flaps shut on Ming's beautiful, bemused face.

'Okay, fine,' Debbie said at last, looking at Linda across the tips of Ming's ears. 'We'll give her a few days and see how she gets on.'

Linda started to bounce up and down on the spot with excitement.

'But *only* as a trial,' Debbie added sternly. 'This is *not* a done deal. The cats' welfare comes first.' She leant over the side of the box and I heard the resonant rumble of Ming's purr as Debbie began to stroke her.

I had seen enough. I jumped down from the windowsill and crept, unnoticed by the sisters, past the counter and upstairs to the flat. Beau was lying in the hallway, and lifted his head drowsily as I passed. There was no aggression in the gesture, but I growled at him anyway. He instinctively averted his head, frightened I would take my anger out on his scab-covered nose. I strode past him into the living room, jumped onto the armchair and began to wash myself. But as I licked my flank furiously, Linda's words played on a permanent loop in my head. 'They are . . . just *moggies*,' she repeated over and over again, the disdain in her voice amplifying each time.

8

The following morning I crept downstairs early. The cardboard box had been moved to the floor between the serving counter and the fireplace. It looked empty and, as I moved silently across the floor, I indulged myself in the fantasy that Ming had escaped through the cat flap overnight and was at this very moment roaming the streets of Stourton, frightened and alone. But as I picked a path between the tables and chairs, I noticed Eddie sitting on the floor in front of the fireplace, gazing in rapt concentration at one of the armchairs.

'Have you . . . seen?' he asked.

I stepped closer and followed his eye-line. Curled up in a perfect crescent on the armchair, Ming lay sound asleep. Everything about her cream-and-chestnut-toned body oozed elegance, from her chiselled cheekbones to her dainty feet, which looked as if they had been dipped in liquid chocolate from ankle to toe.

'Who is she?' Eddie whispered.

'Her name's Ming. Linda brought her last night,' I replied curtly.

At that moment Ming's body twitched and her huge eyes opened dramatically, to reveal two orbs of the most intense blue I had ever seen. Beside me, Eddie gasped in surprise, or possibly admiration. Still prostrate on the cushion, Ming blinked, then unfurled her slender legs into a sideways stretch, throwing her head back against the cushion. As her mouth opened into a yawn, I saw the curve of her pink tongue behind pristine white teeth. Fully awake now, she looked around, and her azure eyes focused on me and Eddie on the flagstones before her.

She tilted her head quizzically to one side but said nothing, and I felt Eddie shifting uncomfortably next to me.

'I'm Molly, and this is Eddie,' I said, aware that my words didn't quite convey the authoritative tone I had hoped for. If anything, they seemed to confirm our status as supplicants eager for Ming's attention.

Her eyes narrowed slightly and flicked from Eddie's face to mine, but still she said nothing. I began to feel an impotent rage fizz in the pit of my stomach. *How dare she! Who does she think she is?* My cheeks burnt under my fur as I tried to preserve some semblance of dignity in the face of such insolence.

Within a couple of minutes, the patter of paws in the stairwell heralded the arrival of the other kittens. Maisie appeared first, raising her tail and heading across the room to greet me and Eddie. She jumped in alarm, on noticing Ming on the chair above us, instinctively diving behind me for protection. Purdy, Abby and Bella were not far behind, and soon they too were prowling around the hearth, throwing curious glances up at the feline stranger. Ming, meanwhile, lay resplendent on the armchair, looking down superciliously at us all.

I surveyed Ming with mounting dislike. *I've had enough of this*, I thought. Aloof, superior, rude . . . Ming seemed to possess every attribute that I had tried hard *not* to encourage in the kittens.

'Breakfast!' I instructed, herding them into a group and back upstairs to the flat, ignoring their protests that they had already eaten. Sensing my mood, they complied and made a show of taking a few mouthfuls from their bowls, before hurriedly dispersing. Feeling that I had not yet vented my annoyance sufficiently, I sought out Beau, who was fast asleep on the rug in the living room, and hissed at him so viciously that he woke with a startled yelp and scrambled under the sofa in panic.

I climbed into the shoebox in the corner of the living room and passed the day dozing fitfully, finding myself jerking awake in alarm at regular intervals before falling back into a light, restless sleep. It was dark when my rumbling stomach forced me out of the box. I padded into the kitchen and ate a few mouthfuls of cat biscuits. Sleeping and eating had done nothing to improve my mood, and I knew I needed some fresh air.

In the café, Ming was sitting on the highest platform of the cat tree, washing contentedly. I kept my eyes firmly on the door as I strode across the flagstones, determined not to pay her the compliment of looking at her as I passed. I headed out into the dark, quiet street and made my way purposefully along the alleyway. As I slipped through the conifers into the churchyard beyond there was movement in some nearby shrubbery, and Jasper emerged onto the grass in front of me.

'Evening,' he said, stepping forward to greet me.

'Hmmph,' I replied, turning my head away petulantly. I strode away from him towards the gravestones, aware that he was baffled by my uncharacteristic froideur.

'What's up?' he asked, trotting after me.

'Ming's up,' I replied sharply, taking a perverse delight in his confusion.

'What's Ming?' he said.

'*Ming*' – I practically spat her name – 'is the café's new cat. If you spent less time in the alley and more time indoors, you might have found that out for yourself.' I stalked off, feeling better for having vented my anger, but also guilty for taking it out on Jasper, who was no more to blame for Ming's arrival than I was.

I completed a solitary, troubled circuit of the churchyard before heading home, reaching the café at the same time as Debbie's friend Jo. Jo owned the hardware shop next door and was Debbie's closest friend in Stourton. She had a practical, no-nonsense air and unruly shoulder-length curls, which shook whenever she laughed, which was frequently.

'Oh, hi, Molly,' Jo said cheerfully, as I trotted up to her ankles. She bent down to stroke me, rubbing my back a little more roughly than was strictly necessary; but Jo owned a dog, and tended to misjudge the degree of physical force required when petting felines.

While she was stroking me, I sniffed at the brown paper bag in her arms, from which the combined aroma of garlic prawns, creamy chicken curry and spicy lamb emanated. Jo and Debbie's takeaways in the café had been a regular weekend occurrence for as long as I could remember, and I knew their menu selections by heart.

Jo stood up and waved at Debbie through the window. 'Come on then, Molly,' she said with a little whistle.

She opened the door and I darted in front of her feet and ran inside.

Jo deposited the bag of food on the serving counter. 'So, this must be the new cat?' she asked, pushing a brown curl out of her eye and making her way over to the cat tree, where Ming was curled up sound asleep on the platform.

'Her name's Ming,' Debbie replied, placing two wine glasses and a handful of cutlery on the counter next to the bag of food.

'She really is a beauty, isn't she?' Jo whispered admiringly. Debbie stepped up behind her, beaming proudly.

While they both gazed at Ming in awestruck silence, I jumped onto the counter, clumsily knocking the knives and forks to the floor, where they clattered noisily on the flagstones. *Oops*, I thought, smiling inwardly. Startled, Debbie and Jo both swung round and, sensing their eyes on me, I stepped precariously between the wine glasses to sniff the bag full of food.

'Oh, Molly, that's not for you,' Debbie said, leaping across the room to pull the bag sharply out from under my nose. I jumped down from the counter, satisfied that I had, for the moment at least, diverted their attention away from Ming.

Debbie set out their meal on one of the café tables, and I took up my usual position on the windowsill to watch them.

'No Sophie and Linda this evening?' Jo asked, heaping a spoonful of rice onto her plate.

Debbie shook her head. 'Sophie's gone to a party with her boyfriend, and Linda's gone . . . somewhere – I didn't actually ask where.' Jo chewed her mouthful, waiting for Debbie to elaborate. 'It's a bit of a relief to have an evening off, to be honest,' Debbie added guiltily, reaching for her glass of wine.

'How long's she been here, now?' Jo asked.

'Ten days,' Debbie answered instantly. 'Not that I'm counting, or anything.'

Jo grinned conspiratorially over the rim of her glass. 'Any idea how long she'll be staying?' she probed.

Debbie shrugged. 'It's complicated, apparently. She's adamant she won't go back to the house while Ray's there; and he's refusing to move out, since he pays the mortgage. I think solicitors are involved now, so of course the whole thing could drag on for ages . . .' She sipped her wine glumly.

'She'll be here for Christmas, at this rate,' Jo teased.

Debbie looked pained, and quickly took another gulp from her glass.

'Here's a radical thought. You could ask Linda what her plans are. Maybe give her a deadline to find somewhere else?' Jo's tone was supportive, but challenging. 'It's a fair question, isn't it? She can't expect you to keep putting her up indefinitely.'

Debbie winced. 'I know, Jo, but I feel bad for her.'

She sagged slightly in her chair, twirling the stem of her wine glass between her fingers.

'Of course you feel bad for her – her marriage has broken up. But that doesn't mean it's your responsibility to give her somewhere to live, does it? She could afford to stay in a hotel, by the sounds of it.'

'She probably could, but what kind of sister would I be if I asked her to do that?' Debbie's eyes were starting to shine. 'I'm just letting her stay until she sorts herself out, that's all. Besides, Linda is helping me out in the café.'

Debbie's cheeks were glowing, and Jo raised her hands in a placatory gesture.

'It's not just Linda you're putting up, though, is it, Debs?' she pointed out softly. 'It's Beau, and now Ming as well. Quite the menagerie she's brought to your door, when you think about it.'

My ears pricked up at the mention of Ming's name.

'She knows I'm cross about that,' Debbie said, rolling her eyes. 'I mean Beau is one thing – he's Linda's pet. But to dump a new cat on us,' she shook her head disbelievingly, 'and make out that she's doing it *for the business*. I mean, really, she just has no idea!' Debbie had drained her first glass of wine and seemed to be warming to her theme.

I was warming to her theme too, and found myself

feeling better than I had all day, as she began to open up about Ming.

'I mean, really – a bloody *Siamese*!' Debbie pulled an incredulous face. 'What was she thinking?' She laughed, and I preened with delight on the cushion. 'You'd be proud of me, though, Jo. I made it quite clear this is a trial period, just to see how Ming settles in.'

'Yeah, right,' Jo muttered sarcastically.

Debbie set her wine glass down on the table and fixed Jo with a stare. 'And what's that supposed to mean?' she asked flatly.

Jo grinned. 'Debbie, you and I both know that, when it comes to cats, you are the absolute definition of a pushover.' Debbie blinked at her in astonishment. 'You're more likely to give Sophie up for adoption than you are to hand Ming over to a rescue shelter,' Jo elaborated through a mouthful of naan bread. 'Debbie Walsh turn her back on a homeless cat? I don't think so. Not in a million years.' She gave a derisory snort.

Debbie took a moment to compose herself. 'First of all,' she began in a reasonable voice, 'I am *not* a pushover when it comes to cats. Or when it comes to anything else, for that matter. And secondly,' Debbie's voice was getting louder as she struggled to be heard over Jo's escalating laughter, 'this isn't just about me and what I want. I've got the welfare of the cats to consider and THEY COME FIRST!' Debbie was practically shouting, and her face was a picture of hurt indignation. She sat back in her chair and took a slug of wine.

Jo, sensing she had hurt her friend's feelings, backed down. 'Of course they do, Debs,' she said in a conciliatory voice. 'I know that. I was only teasing.'

My eyes flicked between the two of them, unsure whether I should feel reassured or alarmed by their exchange. Debbie's reaction had suggested that, like me, she saw Ming's arrival as an unwelcome imposition; but Jo was right about Debbie's proclivity towards taking in homeless cats. It was, after all, this very instinct that had led to her taking me in. And later, of course, she had done the same for my kittens. And for Jasper. I exhaled slowly through my nose. Perhaps Jo had a point: history showed that, when it came to cats in need of a home, Debbie found it difficult to say no. It had never occurred to me previously to consider this a shortcoming in her, but then I had never before found myself facing the prospect of living with an aloof Siamese.

Debbie and Jo continued to eat in silence for a few minutes, in unspoken agreement that they should let the subject of Ming drop.

Eventually Debbie put down her fork and said warmly, 'Speaking of pets, how's Bernard?' Bernard was Jo's dog, an ageing, arthritic black Labrador who spent his days snoozing by her feet in the shop.

Jo looked wistful and her eyes began to redden. 'Oh, he's hanging on in there,' she replied, trying to muster a smile. 'We've been back to the vet again this week. His hips are really playing up, and he's got a couple of worrying growths. They're going to do tests.'

Jo's eyes had turned glassy, and Debbie leant closer. 'Oh, Jo,' she said, giving her friend's arm an encouraging squeeze. 'He'll be okay.'

'I hope so,' Jo answered shakily.

Some time later, when Jo had gone home and Debbie had trudged upstairs to bed, the swoosh of the cat flap jerked me out of a doze. I looked drowsily across to see Jasper on the doormat, silhouetted in the semi-darkness. Still smarting from our encounter in the churchyard, I watched through half-open eyes as he moved stealthily across the room and jumped noiselessly up onto a table next to the cat tree. For several moments he stared at Ming's motionless, sleeping form on the platform. Then, perhaps sensing my gaze, he turned and glanced towards the window. I closed my eyes to feign sleep and, when I looked again, Jasper was grooming himself on the flagstones in front of the stove. I continued to watch him until he had completed his wash and I was quite certain he had gone to sleep.

9

When I awoke the following morning, Jasper had gone from the café, but Ming remained on the platform. She was sitting serenely with her eyes closed, her paws aligned and her tail neatly curled around the base of her body. Feeling fresh stirrings of envy in the pit of my stomach, I averted my eyes from her elegant profile, jumped down from the window and made my way outside.

The tip of my tail flicked indecisively as I stood on the doorstep considering my options. I knew I should seek out Jasper and make amends for snapping at him, but something about the way he had looked at Ming as she slept riled me, and I couldn't bring myself to apologize for my testiness just yet. Instead, I took a certain peevish satisfaction in setting off in the opposite direction from the alleyway, picking out a meandering route around the town's deserted back streets, which would give me time to ruminate in private on my grievances.

The raw sense of injustice I felt at Ming's arrival had brought fresh vigour to my simmering resentment towards Linda and Beau. I paced the streets for a good couple of hours dwelling on my woes before I felt ready to return to the café. When I finally made my way upstairs to the flat, I rounded the top step to see Debbie wrestling with the contents of the hallway cupboard. The ironing board had toppled out, along with the box of Christmas decorations, and Debbie appeared to be fighting with the hose of the vacuum cleaner. When she caught sight of me around the cupboard door, however, she smiled.

'Shall we go and see Margery, Molls?' she asked, finally yanking the cat carrier free. I let out an involuntary purr of delight, as the irritability that I had been carrying was suddenly lifted from my shoulders.

Before I had come to Stourton, my owner had been an elderly lady called Margery. In her devoted care, I had grown up with the unassailable confidence that comes from being an adored only pet. The cosy bungalow we shared had been my entire world, and it never occurred to me that there might be more to life than hunting in Margery's compact, tidy garden, or napping on the sofa while she watched television programmes about antiques.

As I grew older, however, there were occasions when Margery's behaviour began to unsettle me. They were infrequent at first: a sporadic forgetfulness, or a vagueness about the task in hand. But as time went on, her confused episodes became more frequent until, eventually, the decision was made by her son, David, that Margery could no longer live independently. Her bungalow – our home – was sold, Margery moved to a care home, and I was left distraught and alone.

Through a combination of perseverance and luck, I had been offered a second chance at happiness with Debbie. Nobody could ever replace Margery but, in time, I had accepted that, for me, she would exist only in my memories. And so, when Margery had appeared out of the blue in the café one afternoon, on an outing from her care home, it felt as though a part of me that had died had somehow come back to life.

After that blissful reunion, Margery had returned to the café every few weeks with her carer, invariably bringing a small bag of cat treats tucked inside her handbag, which she scattered onto the flagstones for the kittens, while I purred blissfully on her lap. When Margery's increasing frailty meant she was no longer able to come and see us, Debbie had persuaded the carer to let us visit her in the care home instead.

On the back seat of Debbie's car, I listened to the

thrum of the engine and watched the clouds scudding past the front windscreen. Excited as I was about seeing Margery, I could not keep my thoughts from returning to Ming. Was that simply an over-developed territorial instinct, or was I right to be suspicious of her? Debbie's insistence that the cats' welfare was her main priority gave me hope: if she knew I was unhappy, surely she would have no choice but to rehome Ming? And Debbie knew me well enough to recognize my horror at having to share my home with a pointy-faced, sneering Siamese – didn't she?

The sun had broken through the clouds by the time Debbie pulled up outside the care home, but there was a distinctly autumnal chill in the air as we made our way across the car park. In contrast to the freshness outside, the atmosphere inside the care home felt over-heated and stuffy, and the air was pervaded by the pungent smell of boiled vegetables. Debbie carried me through the vast lounge in which a television played loudly, but was largely ignored by the residents, who were seated in high-backed wing chairs, chatting to visitors or dozing with crossword puzzles on their laps.

We proceeded down a long, carpeted corridor lined on both sides with doors. Debbie rapped gently on one of them and, as she eased open the handle, the food smells in the hallway gave way to the scent of lavender. More than anything else, it was this fragrance that instantly transported me back to my life with Margery, when every item of clothing and piece of furniture was infused with her lavender eau de toilette. I inhaled deeply, and peered through the wire door of the carrier at the L-shaped room, which was like a pared-down version of the bungalow we had shared. All around me were familiar pictures, ornaments and knick-knacks; the bed was draped with the same blue-and-yellow crocheted blanket that I used to sleep on, and the dark-wood chest of drawers was covered with framed photographs of her family, just as I remembered it.

A recess next to the bathroom had space for two armchairs in front of a window that overlooked the care home's landscaped grounds. Margery sat hunched in one of the chairs, silhouetted by the bright light pouring through the windowpane beyond. As we moved closer, I made out the wispy waves of her silver hair, which appeared almost translucent in the sunlight.

'Hello, Margery – it's Debbie from the cat café. How are you?' Debbie said brightly.

Margery lifted her head slightly and her papery skin creased into a smile. 'Well now, who's this?' she asked, catching sight of the carrier. My heart swelled at the sound of her soft, tremulous voice.

'This is Molly. She used to be your cat,' Debbie answered.

'Molly, what a lovely name!' Margery said.

Debbie fiddled with the clasp on the carrier door and I walked over to sit by Margery's feet. She tilted the top half of her body sideways to look at me over the arm of her chair, her watery blue eyes gazing into mine. When she lowered a shaky hand towards me, I immediately rose up on my hind legs to rub her knuckles affectionately with my cheek.

'Molly, eh? What a pretty cat,' Margery cooed.

'She used to be your cat, Margery,' replied Debbie from the corner of the room, where she was filling a kettle at the sink. 'She lives with me at the café now, but I've brought her to visit you.'

'Oh, how lovely,' Margery clucked, tickling my ears as best she could with her stiff, crooked fingers. 'She looks like she's wanting a cuddle,' she smiled, leaning back in her chair and smoothing down her pleated wool skirt. I hopped up, making sure that I landed softly on her thin legs, with my claws fully retracted. I steadied myself in the centre of Margery's lap and gazed up at her face, allowing a deep purr to rumble in my chest as she stroked me.

Debbie carried over two cups of tea and sat down on the armchair opposite Margery's. 'I've brought you a Cat's Whiskers Cookie from the café. I know they're your favourite.' She pulled a paper bag out of her handbag and handed it to Margery.

'Oh, how lovely,' Margery repeated, carefully placing the bag on the arm of her chair.

They sipped tea and Margery took delicate bites of her cookie while Debbie chatted about the café, the kittens and the weather. As they talked, I allowed myself to drift into a doze on Margery's lap, savouring the fact that, for the first time since Linda had turned up at the café, I felt truly relaxed. There was something inherently comforting about Margery's small, tidy room overlooking the manicured lawns; whenever I was here, I felt as if all the responsibilities and irritations of adulthood had fallen away and that I was a kitten again, and life was simply a matter of feeling safe, warm and loved. I let out a contented noise that was part purr, part chirrup, and stretched out luxuriously on Margery's legs. I would have been happy to stay in that calm, sweet-smelling room, with the two people who meant most to me in the world, forever.

My purring stopped momentarily when Debbie drew her phone out of her bag and brought up a picture of Ming. 'We've got a new cat staying with us at the moment. A Siamese – look,' she said, handing the device above my head to Margery.

'A what?' Margery said, her brow furrowing. She plucked her glasses from the cord around her neck and pushed them onto her nose. 'Ooh, very fancy,' she remarked, and I felt my fur begin to bristle as she studied the screen. She handed the phone back to Debbie with pursed lips. 'But those fancy-looking cats are terribly fussy,' she added gravely.

'Well, you might be right, Margery. We'll have to wait and see.' Debbie chuckled, dropping the phone back into her bag. My purr resumed even more loudly than before, and I burrowed my face into the folds of Margery's skirt.

The comforting ambience of Margery's room stayed with me for the entire journey home, right up to the point where Debbie pushed open the café door and carried me inside. I was greeted by what, at first, appeared to be the usual Sunday afternoon scene: Maisie was scratching vigorously at the trunk of the cat tree, and I was aware of Abby and Bella racing up the wooden walkway that zigzagged up the wall by the door. As Debbie lowered the carrier to the floor, I saw Jasper washing on one of the armchairs in front of the stove, while Eddie chased a catnip mouse across the flagstones. My eyes followed him as he scampered towards the window, deftly batting the stuffed mouse back and forth between his front paws.

Only when Eddie reached the skirting board did I notice Ming watching him, motionless and sphinx-like, from the windowsill above. From *my* cushion. Eddie crouched victoriously over the mouse, and I saw him glance up at Ming. The look he gave her was one he had given me on many occasions. It was a look that said, *Want to play?* Ming stared back at him, her head tilted, her blue gaze curious.

I was seized by a sudden feeling of panic that, locked inside my carrier, I seemed to be invisible to all the other cats in the room. The warm feeling of well-being that I had carried since seeing Margery was giving way to an ice-cold rage. I had been gone for just a morning, and already Ming had taken my place, both literally and figuratively, while all I could do was watch from behind the bars of my carrier. And the worst of it was that neither Jasper nor any of the kittens appeared to think anything was wrong.

10

'Because it's *my* cushion, that's why.'

Jasper had followed me out onto the doorstep and was looking at me with a mixture of bafflement and concern. 'But, you weren't here. How was Ming supposed to know the cushion's yours?'

My tail thrashed angrily by my feet; my initial shocked dismay had been replaced by unadulterated fury, and Jasper's attempts to reason with me were making things worse. 'You could have told her!' I hissed, turning to face him, my eyes narrowed. 'But then I suppose you were all too busy playing happy families to think about me.'

I turned away to look down the parade, feeling my eyes prickle and my heart thump. I was cross not only with Jasper, but also with the kittens, for not telling Ming that the window cushion belonged to me; they should have known I would not take kindly to such an invasion of my personal territory. But it wasn't just the fact that she had been on my cushion that had upset me. It was something intangible that I had sensed as I observed them from the carrier: an atmosphere of relaxed familiarity, which had seemed to pervade the whole room and suggested, to me, that the kittens and Jasper felt quite comfortable in Ming's presence, and she in theirs.

Jasper sat beside me, looking contrite, but I was not in a forgiving mood.

'Oh, never mind,' I muttered, pushing past him and back through the cat flap. With as much dignity as I could muster, and keeping my eyes fixed on the flag-stones in front of me, I strode through the café and upstairs to the flat.

I awoke on Monday morning to a queasy feeling of dread. I had spent the night at the end of Debbie's bed, flitting between feelings of self-pity at the unfairness of having to share my home with a rival feline, and rage at everybody else's apparent inability to recognize my distress. In a few hours' time Debbie would open the café and I would have to bear witness to Ming's moment of glory, as she was unveiled to the public. Of course I could avoid the café altogether and spend the day outdoors but, after the previous day's trauma, I worried that to absent myself completely might have even worse consequences. Not only was there a high likelihood that Ming would lay claim to the window cushion again, but people might assume she had taken my place as the café's figurehead. So, after eating a breakfast for which I had very little appetite, I crept downstairs.

Ming was on her platform, surveying the room regally while Debbie prepared to open the café.

'We'll need to keep a close eye on Ming today,' Debbie told Linda, emptying a bag of coins into the till drawer. 'I don't know how she'll react to the customers.'

I padded past the cat tree with my eyes averted from the platform, as had become habitual for me since Ming had taken possession of it.

'If she looks like she's distressed, we'll need to take her upstairs,' Debbie continued, 'and that might mean putting Beau in his carrier. We don't want her being frightened by him, either.'

'Oh, I'm sure that won't be necessary,' replied Linda airily, avoiding Debbie's gaze as she pulled her Molly's apron over her head. I pictured Beau's bulging carrier in the living-room alcove and knew there was no way he could use it, unless Linda removed all her shopping first. Linda walked up to the cat tree and smiled approvingly at Ming. 'Besides, I have a feeling the customers are going to *love* her.'

One by one the kittens appeared at the bottom of

the stairs. Purdy headed straight for the cat flap while the others stalked across the floor, rubbing their whiskers against the chair legs or batting catnip toys across the flagstones, before taking up their usual positions around the room. Even the normally timid Maisie seemed unfazed and jumped happily into the domed bed directly underneath Ming's platform.

Just as Linda had predicted, the first customers gravitated immediately to the cat tree for a closer look at Ming. A grinning Linda shepherded them to a nearby table, explaining that Ming was the 'new addition to the Molly's family'. The customers, an elderly couple whom I recognized as regular visitors, normally requested a table near the window so that they could sit near me. On this occasion, however, they could barely take their eyes off Ming, even to look at their menus. 'What a gorgeous cat!' one exclaimed. 'Exquisite,' the other agreed.

I observed Ming from the windowsill, looking – hoping – to see signs of distress or, at the very least, mild displeasure at the increasing number of people filling the room. A party of day-trippers arrived just before lunchtime, chatting loudly and laden with shopping. As Linda bustled around them, scraping chairs and tables together across the stone floor, I fixed my eyes on Ming; surely this would disturb her equilibrium? But she continued to sit calmly on her platform with her eyes closed and one forepaw extended. She delicately licked the inside of her long, slender leg, unruffled by the commotion going on around her.

The day wore on, and I began to feel as if I were invisible on my cushion in the window. The buzz of conversation and the click of cutlery on plates were punctuated by coos of delight across the room whenever Ming moved. Linda stood earnestly beside the table of each new customer, revelling in telling them all about Ming. I noticed how, over the course of the day, she began to embellish details of the story, until Ming eventually became the victim of an abusive home, whom Linda had personally rescued, at great risk both to herself and to Ming. The customers lapped it up, oohing and aahing at the different beats of Linda's story.

When, at the height of the lunchtime rush, Ming yawned, stretched and jumped lightly down from her platform, an unnatural hush fell across the café. The customers all paused mid-conversation, to watch her sashay across the room. 'So elegant!' one lady gasped, as she sauntered past their table. Seething, I turned my back on them to stare furiously out of the window.

The week continued as it had started. There was something masochistic about my determination to remain in the café, largely ignored, while Ming was lavished with

praise and attention. I took some sort of perverse satisfaction from it, as if each compliment paid to Ming
confirmed my conviction that she was deliberately
trying to upstage me. The kittens, however, continued
to go about their daily routine as though nothing had
changed, playing with their toys, napping or, in Eddie's
case, scrounging for titbits at people's feet. Purdy
seemed to be spending more time outdoors than usual,
but she had always been more adventurous than her
siblings, so this could hardly be considered cause for
alarm. It was almost as if the kittens hadn't noticed the
change in the café's atmosphere, or the way we had
been relegated to the status of supporting artists to
Ming's show-stopping diva.

My resentment about the way my kittens had
accepted a rival female into the colony continued to
rankle, but feline pride made me want to hide my hurt
feelings from them. Though I kept my anger to myself,
I was aware that my behaviour towards the kittens
began to change. It was a subtle shift, almost imperceptible at first, but there was less casual intimacy of the
sort that would have come naturally to me in the past.
If I saw one of the kittens trying to wash a hard-to-
reach spot between the shoulder blades, I no longer
padded over to lick it for them; and if we caught each
other's eyes across the café, I no longer instinctively
blinked affectionately. I had no conscious desire to

punish them, and in my more self-pitying moments I told myself peevishly that, if they had noticed the change in my manner, they probably didn't care anyway.

As the week wore on, my frustration at the kittens' blasé attitude to our new living arrangements was wearing me down, and my efforts to maintain any semblance of composure were beginning to exhaust me. So when, on Friday morning, Eddie jumped onto the window cushion next to me, something gave way inside me.

Before Ming's arrival, I would never have begrudged sharing my cushion with Eddie; when the kittens were tiny they had all done so, burrowing deep into my fur for warmth and comfort. Over time they had outgrown the practice, with the exception of Eddie, who seemed reluctant to abandon the physical closeness of our bond. But, on this occasion, Eddie's proximity felt like an intimacy too far. When he sprang nimbly onto the cushion beside me, my heart did not swell with tenderness; instead, I felt a flash of rage at the invasion of my personal space. I hissed at him – a vicious, heartfelt hiss, which somehow gave vent to all the pent-up anger I had been feeling since Ming first set foot in the café.

Eddie's body retracted in shock and he cowered, flattening his ears against his bowed head. I instantly regretted my response. 'I'm sorry, I didn't . . .' I stuttered, horrified by his reaction. But before I had a chance to explain, Eddie had jumped down from the windowsill with a look of abject mortification. Shame and remorse flooded through me as I watched him slink across the floor with his tail between his legs; the shame made worse by the realization that the other kittens were watching and had no doubt witnessed what I had done.

I turned to face the window, feeling utterly wretched. Behind me I heard Linda talking to a customer, recounting what had now become an epic tale of Ming's rescue. When she had finally finished speaking and was jotting down the order on her notepad, the customer remarked, 'Molly 'n' Ming – now that's got a ring to it,' and Linda cackled in agreement, 'You're *so* right; it does!'

I had heard enough. The café, which for so long had been my safe place, my haven from danger, suddenly felt claustrophobic. The room was airless, the heat from the stove made my fur itch, and Linda's voice was as grating to my ears as her long fingernails on the Specials board. My head began to swim as I felt a wave of nausea rise from my stomach to the back of my throat. I tore across the café and out through the cat flap and did not stop running until I reached the alleyway.

It was a relief to leave behind the café's stifling atmosphere, its fawning customers and, of course, Ming. The November wind felt biting, but I took a few deep lungfuls of icy air, waiting for my nausea to subside. I found Jasper in the churchyard, prowling among the headstones. He looked surprised to see me; my withdrawn manner had also kept him at a distance, and we had not met for our usual evening stroll for several days.

'Everything all right?' he asked solicitously, sidling up to me.

'Yes, fine,' I snapped; but I felt my facade of indifference start to crumble beneath his concerned scrutiny. 'No, not really,' I admitted, dropping my gaze to the ground.

Jasper sat down beside me on the carpet of dry leaves and we remained in silence for a few moments, listening to the magpies cawing in the branches of the horse chestnut above us.

'Is it ... Ming?' he began, tentatively. I let out a snort at the mention of her name, aware that the tip of my tail had begun to twitch angrily by my feet. The remorse I had been feeling about Eddie seemed to evaporate, and anger swept in to take its place.

'*Ooh, Ming, what a gorgeous name! Oh, isn't she beautiful! So elegant!*' I mimicked, while Jasper listened patiently. 'More like stuck-up, stand-offish and rude, if you ask me.' My tail was now thrashing so hard that the dry leaves on the ground rustled noisily. Jasper's body remained still and his face composed, as he contemplated the moss-covered gravestones ahead of us.

'I know it's a shock,' he began in a careful, measured tone, 'but it can't be easy for her—'

I felt my stomach clench and turned sharply to face him. 'Can't be easy for her?' I interrupted, incredulously. 'What, exactly, can't be easy for her? Having a café full of people drooling over her? Having her every whim catered for by Debbie and Linda? Having the *whole of Stourton* think she's the most beautiful creature ever to grace this town? Oh, it must be *really difficult* for her,' I spat.

I paused for breath as Jasper sat in restrained silence, waiting for me to finish.

'Do you know,' I continued, feeling my cheeks burn, 'she has been here a week and she has not said one word since she arrived. Not *one word*.' I paused for emphasis, hoping to see some acknowledgment of Ming's indisputable rudeness, but Jasper's face remained impassive. 'At least she hasn't said one word to me,' I added, suddenly seized by a cold pang of suspicion. I narrowed my eyes as the thought entered my mind that, perhaps, it was only me that Ming hadn't deigned to speak to. Did she chat happily to Jasper and the kittens when I was not around? Was this how they had spent Sunday morning, while I had been visiting Margery? A shiver went through me, as though someone had poured ice down my back.

Jasper's face was still infuriatingly blank. 'I think

maybe she just needs time to settle in,' he said calmly, deftly evading the question that hung, unspoken, in the air between us.

I looked away in disgust. His reply seemed to confirm my worst fears: Ming's haughty demeanour was reserved for me alone. For all I knew, she and Jasper might already be firm friends . . . or more. Did that explain why the kittens were so relaxed around her, because they were following their father's lead? My heart began to race as the implications hit me. Ming was playing a game, of that I was sure. She was trying to isolate me from Jasper and the kittens. She was planning to take my place – not just in the café, but in my own family.

The kittens were sweet-natured and trusting; was it any surprise they had been taken in by Ming? But I was disappointed by Jasper's gullibility, his inability to see the situation for what it was. It was typical of him to be chivalrous, to give other cats the benefit of the doubt. Such generosity was one of the qualities I loved about him, but right now I found it maddening. It was one thing for him to be chivalrous towards me, quite another to be chivalrous towards a beautiful Siamese impostor.

Mustering what remained of my dignity, I stood up to leave. 'Besides, she's not perfect, you know,' I hissed, throwing a cursory glance over my shoulder. 'Have you noticed how she squints?'

As soon as the words left my mouth, I knew how they must sound: petulant and spiteful. But I didn't care. Jasper could think what he liked about Ming, but I knew the truth.

11

Although, like all the cats at Molly's, Ming was free to come and go as she pleased, she seemed content to spend almost all of her time in the café. She only ever went outside under cover of darkness, slipping out through the cat flap to answer the call of nature, and her brief forays into the flat were similarly fleeting: she crept upstairs at mealtimes to lurk in the hallway until the rest of us had finished eating, before swiftly polishing off whatever food was left in the bowls. Then she would slink back downstairs to take her usual place on the cat-tree platform.

Her pointed face and deep-blue eyes seemed only to convey two expressions: serene contemplation or mild curiosity; and, although she never sought out physical contact, she would purr gratefully if Debbie tickled her enormous chocolate-brown ears. I watched her obsessively, torn apart by some confused emotion that seemed to combine fascination, envy and contempt all at the same time. I was convinced there was something untrustworthy about Ming's implacable self-containment, and the fact that I was the only one who could see it simply made matters worse.

Since the hissing incident with Eddie, the kittens and Jasper had been wary around me. I desperately wanted to talk to my kittens, but feared that if I tried to explain how I felt about Ming, they would dismiss my concerns in the same way Jasper had, telling me I'd misunderstood her and that she was just *settling in*. So instead I allowed the rift between us to deepen, and became increasingly preoccupied with nursing my secret grievances.

Whilst Ming's arrival had brought agony for me, it seemed to have marked a turning point for Linda. Gone was the furtive shopaholic, prone to melodramatic outbursts of tears; in her place was a newly confident woman whose smugness and constant air of triumph were almost more than I could bear. Since Ming's debut in the café, Linda's face had worn a permanent self-satisfied grin, and in the evenings she crowed endlessly about the roaring success Ming had proved to be, how she had been right all along, and how Ming was just what the cat café needed.

I sensed that Debbie and Sophie were both starting to tire of Linda's self-congratulatory monologues.

Every now and then I saw them exchange weary glances behind Linda's back, as she piped up with yet another reason why Ming joining the café had been a 'commercial masterstroke'. I studied Debbie's face closely on these occasions, praying she would cut Linda off and announce that Molly's had been doing just fine before Ming arrived, and would continue to do so if she left. Instead, Debbie listened with patient forbearance and a polite half-smile.

When John came over for dinner one evening midweek, I felt a glimmer of optimism. Linda had gone out for the night, and I knew that if there was anyone Debbie would confide in, it was John. I climbed into the empty shoebox and watched, feeling almost giddy with hopeful anticipation.

'So, how's the new addition to the café been getting on?' John began as they sat down at the table.

'Who, Linda or Ming?' Debbie asked drily.

'Well, both, I suppose,' John replied, smiling.

Debbie sighed and slumped slightly in her chair. 'Well, much as I hate to admit it, Linda seems to have been right. Ming has settled in amazingly well, and the customers can't get enough of her. The cats seem to have accepted her, too, although Molly's been a little grumpy.'

In the shoebox, I bristled all over. *A little grumpy!*

Had Debbie really not noticed the extent of my anguish?

'So, does that mean she's staying?' John asked.

'Who, Linda or Ming?' Debbie shot back, mischievously.

John raised his shoulders in a questioning shrug.

'I'll keep an open mind,' Debbie went on, 'but, where Ming's concerned, it's looking hopeful.'

'And Linda?' John prompted.

At this, Debbie sagged still further in her chair. 'I'm torn, John, really I am. She drives me up the wall sometimes, but I just can't turn my back on her, not until she's got herself sorted out. And I've got to admit, she's been an asset in the café.'

John raised his eyebrows. 'Well, in that case, cheers to Ming,' he said, raising his glass of beer with a good-natured chuckle. In the shoebox I felt my heart sink in disappointment.

At the end of Ming's second week, the novelty of her appearance in the café was at last beginning to wear off. Linda no longer felt compelled to regale every customer with her life story, and Ming's silent, watchful presence was something I had, reluctantly, become accustomed to. My relations with the kittens, however, remained strained. I had not yet apologized to Eddie for hissing at him – not through pride or a reluctance to admit I had been wrong – but because I hated the thought of having to do so under Ming's supercilious gaze.

There was little comfort to be found upstairs either. The flat was, as Debbie put it, 'starting to look like a student bedsit'. Every room seemed to be perpetually in danger of overflowing with the collective detritus of people and animals. There was nowhere to put anything, and every surface was covered in dust and animal hairs.

Beau was starting to look unkempt, too; his fluffy fur, once neatly trimmed, had grown straggly to the point where it was impossible to make out the dark eyes beneath his eyebrows, or the mouth amidst his greasy beard. The scent of dog shampoo that used to follow him around had been replaced by a stale, musty odour. Other than his daily walk, he rarely left the flat, and consequently emanated an air of perpetual boredom, spending his time flopping around on the living-room rug, emitting disgruntled snorts.

The atmosphere in the flat seemed to simmer with low-level, unspoken discord. Sophie and Debbie had not argued again since the superfood-salad debacle, but Sophie had begun to spend more and more time with her boyfriend, Matt; and when she was at home, her interactions with Debbie and Linda were brusque. Debbie wore an expression of long-suffering forbearance around her. On Saturday, however, when Sophie sullenly announced she was going to Matt's house for lunch and wasn't sure when she'd be back, Debbie tutted with annoyance and protested that Sophie treated the place like a hotel.

'A pretty crap hotel,' Sophie muttered under her breath, grabbing her jacket from the coat rack. Debbie's face flushed and her eyes looked glassy, but she let the jibe pass. I followed Sophie downstairs and watched as she let herself out through the café. Eddie was padding desultorily between the tables. Ming was asleep and I wondered whether I should seize the opportunity to make my belated apology. As I made my way towards him, I tried to catch his eye but, sensing my approach, he picked up his pace and ran out through the cat flap. He was avoiding me, of that I was certain. Clearly, he was not yet ready to hear what I had to say.

Much as I felt sorry for Debbie, I could understand why Sophie wanted to spend as little time in the flat as possible. It was no longer a place I particularly wanted to be in, either. So when, after lunch on Sunday, Debbie dug the cat carrier out of the hall cupboard and asked, 'Shall we go and see Margery, Molls?' I was relieved, and craved more than ever the sanctity of Margery's lavender-scented room and the feeling that I was, for once, the centre of attention.

Outside, the sky was ominously grey and the wind whipped through the trees, shaking loose their leaves in a continuous cascade. As Debbie stood on the front step, locking the café door, I saw Jo outside her hardware shop, manoeuvring her Labrador, Bernard, into her van. His arthritic hips left him unable to jump, and she had hooked an arm under his hindquarters to lever him into the back.

As Debbie stepped onto the pavement the rain started – fat, heavy drops that the wind blew into us sideways. Grabbing the handle of the carrier in both hands, Debbie broke into a run towards her car, unable to stop and speak to Jo in the gathering rainstorm.

The drive to Margery's care home seemed to take forever as we crawled along in heavy traffic, Debbie drumming her fingers impatiently on the steering wheel. When at last we arrived and had parked the car, the rain bounced noisily off the top of the carrier as Debbie ran up to the sliding doors. Even once we were inside Margery's room, I was unable to relax. In spite of Debbie's best efforts to soothe her, the howling wind and torrential rain outside left Margery agitated and fearful. She eyed us nervously, seemingly unsure who we were and why we were in her room.

Debbie sensed Margery's discomfort too, and that our presence might be adding to her anxiety, so after about twenty minutes she got to her feet and lifted me back into the cat carrier. On our way out, my carrier collided with something in the doorway, and my view through the wire door was suddenly filled with a close-up view of a pair of grey trousers.

'Oh!' Debbie exclaimed, backing into the room to allow the owner of the trousers to enter.

'Oh, hello. Debbie, isn't it?' a man asked in a nasal, whiny voice, which I immediately recognized as belonging to David, Margery's son.

Debbie had moved aside to allow David into the room and I had a clear view of him as he stepped across the beige carpet.

'Yes, that's right,' she replied, politely courteous. 'How are you, David – keeping well, I hope?'

I had not seen David since the day Margery had been moved into the care home, but I felt my hackles instinctively start to rise. He looked just as I remembered him: small and wiry, with a pinched-looking face and thinning hair. I knew from experience, however, that David's weedy appearance hid a surprising pugnacity.

'Fine, thanks,' he replied tersely, before walking over to Margery's armchair and giving her a perfunctory kiss on the cheek. 'I didn't know you were going to be here today,' he said, turning to face Debbie, his voice faintly accusatory.

'Oh, we're just leaving,' Debbie replied, her apologetic

tone suggesting that she too had felt the intended barb. 'Well, take care, David,' she said, but he had his back to her and was yanking the vacant armchair closer so that he could sit down.

The journey home was even slower than the drive there and, on this occasion, I had no feeling of well-being to lift my spirits. Instead, I felt irritable and cross. Seeing David had unsettled me, bringing back upsetting memories of his callous disregard for Margery's – and my own – feelings when he had decided to sell our home. Recalling those unhappy times made me yearn to be back in the comfort and security of the café, with Debbie, Jasper and the kittens. But another part of me dreaded our return, and feared that I would find the same cosy scene that had greeted me after my last absence. When we finally arrived, however, the café was quiet. Ming was snoozing on her platform and her ears didn't even flicker when Debbie hurriedly unlocked the door and ran inside to escape the pouring rain.

I went upstairs to the flat and climbed into the shoebox in the living room. I undertook a self-soothing wash, inwardly bemoaning the fact that the world seemed full of people and animals who, in one way or another, were determined to pick away at the fabric of my life. When I had finished washing I lay down in the box, listening to the rain lashing against the window-panes, and waiting for the relief that only sleep could bring me.

'Has anyone seen Eddie today?' Debbie called up from the café a little later that evening, and instantly I was wide awake. She ran up the stairs and peered into the living room. 'That's odd,' she said, looking worried. 'He doesn't normally stay out for this long.'

Linda glanced up from the sofa. 'Which one's Eddie, again?' she asked vaguely.

'Black-and-white. Friendly,' Debbie replied testily.

Linda nodded. 'Oh yes, now you mention it, I'm pretty sure I passed him on the square yesterday afternoon, near the market cross.'

My stomach gave a strange jolt, and I sat up in the shoebox to stare at Linda.

'The market cross?' Debbie repeated. 'You're pretty sure, or you *are* sure?'

Linda frowned in concentration. 'Black body, white paws, silver collar?' she asked, and Debbie nodded. 'Yep, then it was definitely him. Why, is he not meant to go there?' Linda's face was a picture of innocence, but Debbie groaned with exasperation.

'It's not about whether Eddie's *meant* to go there, Linda, but he doesn't normally stray so far from the café. And if you're right, and he was there yesterday and

109

hasn't been home since, and now it's blowing a gale and bucketing down with rain out there . . .'

Debbie trailed off, but she didn't need to finish the sentence. She was right: Eddie had never strayed so far from the café before, and he had certainly never stayed away for so long. My little boy had been missing for more than a day, and I had been so fixated on my own problems that I hadn't even noticed.

12

The cat flap snapped shut behind me. I paused momentarily on the doorstep, sniffing the cold, damp air, before dashing along the wet cobbles to the alleyway behind the café.

In the dark, confined space of the passageway the rain seemed to fall more heavily, the raindrops pounding in a harsh staccato on dustbin lids and metal steps. I nosed through the conifers at the end of the alley and scanned the sodden churchyard. The front aspect of the church and its spire stood out against the black sky, lit from beneath by spotlights embedded in the gravel path, but the dazzling brightness of the stone facade merely emphasized the pitch-blackness all around. I stalked around the outer boundary of the churchyard, my ears alert for movement in the surrounding shrubbery. A rustle in a distant rhododendron caught my attention and I picked up my pace through the long, wet grass.

Jasper looked askance at me as I squeezed beneath the canopy of tongue-shaped, dripping leaves to the dry patch of earth where he sat. As I edged into his shelter, I gave my head and body a brisk shake, inadvertently spraying him with rainwater.

'Have you seen Eddie?' I asked, without preamble, and in a huffier tone than I had intended. A full week had passed since our argument about Ming, and since then we had barely seen each other.

It was Jasper's turn to shake off the drops of water that had landed on his face and whiskers, and he took his time to do so, before answering, 'Eddie? Not today. Why?'

'He's missing,' I replied tersely. 'He hasn't been home since yesterday. Linda saw him on the square by the market cross yesterday morning.'

Jasper considered me intently. 'Linda saw him yesterday?' he repeated. I nodded. 'So it's only been a day?'

My eyes narrowed. Sometimes I despaired of Jasper. I had always considered his laissez-faire approach to parenting part of his charm, but right now I found it infuriating.

'*Only* been a day? He's never stayed out overnight before. And in this weather?' I was aware of my face growing hot under my fur. 'What if he's run away?' I asked, willing Jasper to recognize the urgency of the situation.

'But why would he run away? That doesn't sound like Eddie,' Jasper replied calmly.

I opened my mouth to reply, but an answer wouldn't come. I wanted to tell Jasper that Eddie might have run away if he thought I didn't love him any more. The image of Eddie recoiling from my hiss filled my mind; the hurt and shock on his face, and how he had sloped away with his tail between his legs. I dearly wanted to tell Jasper the truth: that my jealousy of Ming, and my conviction that she wanted to usurp my position in our family, had so consumed me that I had taken my anger out on my sweet and loving boy, and that I had compounded the problem by procrastinating over my apology. But I was too ashamed to admit what I had done and, instead, kept my eyes on the ground and said nothing.

'He's young, and he's male,' Jasper went on, unperturbed. 'It's natural for him to wander. Twenty-four hours away from home is nothing.'

'It's natural for you, maybe, but you're not Eddie!' I cut in desperately.

Jasper's implacability was maddening. He seemed unable to recognize that what was normal behaviour for an alley-cat like him was not normal for our kittens; least of all for Eddie, who had always been a home-loving boy, far more interested in eating and sleeping than he was in roaming. My shame and remorse were swiftly giving way to a renewed frustration.

'I'm going to look for him. Are you coming or not?' I hissed, facing him with a look of defiant resolve.

Jasper's amber eyes studied me closely. He seemed – at last – to recognize that there was more to my distress than motherly over-protectiveness. 'C'mon then,' he said, springing to his feet.

We strode in silence through the rainy streets, dodging the kerbside puddles as cars swooshed past, dazzling our eyes with their headlights. Clusters of people dashed along the pavements beneath umbrellas, making for pub and restaurant doorways and the promise of open fires and hot meals within. We headed straight for the southern side of the square and climbed the soaking wet steps of the market cross. The imposing town hall looked down on us, its Gothic spire and turrets forming an eerie silhouette against the night-time gloom. All around, the street lights' orange halos were reflected in the slick cobbles, as sheets of rain were blown sideways across the market square.

I looked around at the wide square, trying to imagine where Eddie might have gone. My eye kept returning to the narrow gaps between the shop fronts, which marked the entrance to the alleyways that linked the square to the surrounding streets. I had arrived in Stourton on a similarly inhospitable night nearly two years ago and had sought refuge in the first alley I came to, mistakenly assuming I would find shelter and safety there, not knowing that each alley was the territory of a street-cat. What if, like me, Eddie had wandered into an alley, been attacked and was lying injured somewhere, feverish with pain?

As if reading my mind, Jasper murmured, 'I'll check the alleys, you stick to the road.'

I blinked at him, feeling a sudden rush of gratitude that at last he was taking my fears seriously. Jasper padded down the stone steps and crept stealthily across the tarmac, disappearing into the opening between the bank and the chemist's. I kept my eyes fixed on the spot where the tip of his tail had vanished, my ears alert for sounds that might indicate the presence of a hostile street-cat. But the alleyway remained silent.

My fur was soaked through to my skin, as I ran down the steps and took the road opposite the market cross. I made my way slowly along the pavement, checking underneath parked cars for any sign of Eddie. Every now and then I heard the yowl of an alley-cat somewhere in the distance and froze, rotating my ears to listen, lest I should hear Eddie or Jasper's voice in reply.

At the end of the street I turned right, onto a wide,

busy thoroughfare lined with pubs and hotels. Traffic rushed past me in both directions, and a group of people dressed for a night out stumbled out of a hotel, laughing. I pressed up against a wall and let them pass, the women's high heels clicking against the pavement just inches from my paws. A little further along the street they turned into a pub, pulling open the heavy wooden door and releasing a gust of warmth and light, which momentarily transfixed me. Could Eddie have found his way inside such a place? His sociable nature and love of people meant I couldn't rule it out. But the town was full of pubs like this – how could I possibly search them all? I sniffed disconsolately at the wooden porch around the entrance, before padding away down the street.

For nearly an hour I continued to prowl the area, probing into dark doorways and behind dustbins until my paw-pads were soaked and freezing. The hopelessness of my task had begun to dawn on me: there was no way Jasper and I could search the whole of Stourton tonight; and, even if Eddie had passed this way, the incessant rain would have washed away any trace of his scent. Tired and dispirited, I turned to head home, making no effort to dodge the splashing puddles as cars raced past me. Jasper was waiting for me in the café doorway, and I knew immediately from his downcast posture that his search had also been fruitless.

'He's a sensible cat, he'll be okay,' he whispered as I stepped onto the doorstep. I dropped my gaze, too exhausted to point out that just because Eddie was sensible it did not necessarily mean he would be all right.

'You coming in?' I asked wearily.

Jasper's tail twitched; since our conversation about Ming, he had hardly come indoors at all. But his face softened as we stood facing each other, equally drenched, on the doorstep. 'After you,' he replied, glancing at the door.

The following morning Debbie checked the alleyway for Eddie, returning from the kitchen with a look of mingled disappointment and concern.

'I'm sure there's nothing to worry about, Debs. He'll come back when he's hungry,' Linda said breezily, pulling her apron over her head. 'Our cat Toby used to do this all the time when we were little, d'you remember?'

Debbie inclined her head. 'Maybe, Linda – let's hope so,' she replied.

I spent the day in the window, keeping watch for any sign of Eddie, while Jasper headed out to continue the search. The kittens were subdued, spending most of the day sleeping or pacing the floor, sniffing at Eddie's usual napping spots, throwing anxious glances in my direction. In my vulnerable state I resented Ming's mute haughtiness more than ever. I kept it to myself, but I could not quell the growing suspicion that Ming had had something to do with Eddie's disappearance. Had some covert conversation taken place between them after the hissing incident, in which he had confided his hurt feelings, and she had encouraged him to run away? Or was I paranoid to imagine such a thing?

As the grey light outside the window gave way to darkness, I caught sight of Ming's reflection in the glass: a ghost-like apparition hovering, motionless, behind me. A flash of blue made me think she was watching me; but, when I turned to look, her eyes were closed.

13

Debbie was cashing up at the till one evening, when Linda sidled over to the wooden counter. 'Debbie,' she wheedled. 'Can I pitch you an idea for the menu?'

'Mm-hmm,' answered Debbie absent-mindedly, sliding piles of coins across the worktop into clear plastic bags.

'Ming's Fortune Cookies,' Linda announced, bouncing on the balls of her feet eagerly. On the window cushion, my ears flickered. Debbie's face was blank with confusion. 'I've made a prototype,' Linda went on, pulling something red and crinkly from her apron pocket and placing it on the counter.

Debbie picked up the twist of cellophane and unwrapped it, to reveal a small cookie and a folded slip of paper.

'That's Ming's Motto,' Linda explained earnestly.

'*Time spent with cats is never wasted*,' Debbie read, a faint smile playing at the corners of her mouth.

Linda whipped a notepad out of her apron. 'I've got plenty more mottoes,' she said keenly. '*All cats are equal, but some are more equal than others. To err is human, to purr is feline.*' She looked at her sister expectantly. 'See, not just a pretty face, am I?' she beamed, tapping her forehead with the tip of her pen.

'That's a good idea, Linda – I like it. If you print off the mottoes, we can make a batch and see if they sell,' Debbie said.

'Trust me, Debs, they'll sell like hotcakes,' replied Linda, practically glowing. 'Remember, I know a thing or two about marketing – that was my career until I married Ray,' she said, carefully folding the motto and cookie back inside their wrapper.

'And you no longer needed a career,' I heard Debbie mutter under her breath when Linda had bustled past her into the kitchen.

The following morning Debbie was at the dining table, reading the local newspaper with a furrowed brow. 'Linda, have you seen this? Ming's in the paper!' she called across the hallway.

In the shoebox, I froze in mid-wash and glanced across the room to see Linda appear at the living-room door, grinning broadly.

'As a matter of fact, I have,' she preened, leaning against the doorframe with an expression of barely suppressed triumph.

'Exotic New Kitty Joins Cat Café,' Debbie read aloud, before firing a disapproving sideways look at Linda. 'Popular new addition to Stourton's cat café . . . Beautiful Ming is a real glamour-puss . . . a tragic Siamese rescued from a life of neglect' – here, Debbie paused to raise a sceptical eyebrow at Linda – '"Ming has brought a taste of Eastern promise to the Cotswolds," says Molly's spokesperson, Linda Fleming.' At this, Debbie set her coffee mug roughly down on the table and sat back in her chair. '"A taste of Eastern promise", Linda – are you kidding?' she scowled. 'And since when have you been Molly's spokesperson?' she added scornfully.

But Linda was unrepentant. 'Trust me, Debs, it'll be great for business,' she winked, and trotted downstairs to the café.

Debbie reread the article with a look of growing displeasure. Then she tossed the newspaper across the table and sat for a moment, staring at the now-empty doorway with an expression of deep resentment on her face.

Trepidation mingled with curiosity in my mind, as I padded across the room and jumped onto the table. The newspaper lay open on the feature about Ming. In the middle of the page was a full-length portrait of Ming sitting regally on her platform, directing a haughty stare down the lens of the camera. The kittens and I were nowhere to be seen. In the bottom left-hand corner there was a second photograph: a small, professional-looking headshot of Linda, which must have been taken several years earlier: she was heavily made-up with immaculately blow-dried hair and looked a good five years younger. Beneath her image ran the caption 'Linda Fleming: rescues cats'.

I exhaled crossly and glared at the photo, aware of fury rising in the pit of my stomach. Everything about the newspaper coverage enraged me, from the made-up account of Ming's 'tragic' back-story, to Linda's positioning of herself as a 'cat-rescuer' and, most importantly, the misleading impression it gave that Ming was the café's sole charge and main attraction. It was as if the kittens and I had been air-brushed out of existence altogether. The article was inaccurate on every front and yet, seeing Linda's distorted claims in print somehow gave them credibility. Deciding I had seen enough, I sat down on top of the newspaper and began to wash, making sure to position my hindquarters squarely on top of Ming's conceited face.

Linda preened about her coup with the press for a couple of days, apparently oblivious to Debbie's tight-lipped frostiness on the subject. Watching from my cushion as she thrust the newspaper cutting – which she had now laminated – under the noses of customers, I couldn't help but remember what Linda had been like before Debbie had suggested that she help out in the café. In those early days she had been an unsettling presence; constantly close to tears and prone to emotional outbursts, which, I had suspected, were designed to trigger a sense of sisterly obligation in Debbie.

I had not exactly warmed to Linda even then, but at least she had divided her time between the flat and the shops, so my life in the café had been mercifully free of her interference. Now that she was working downstairs, however, there was no escaping her. Linda's involvement in the café went beyond simply *helping out*; there was something insidious about her enthusiasm. I was in no doubt that her plan was to stake a territorial claim on the business, and that promoting her protégée Ming was simply a means to this end. The newspaper article merely confirmed what I already suspected: Linda wanted the 'moggies' gone from the café, to be replaced with beautiful, exotic cats like Ming.

Jasper and I had continued to search for Eddie every day since he had vanished. Jasper performed a daily circuit of the alleyways during daylight hours, returning to the café at dusk. Every evening I watched hopefully from my window cushion, waiting for him to turn the corner into the parade. Each time, the droop of Jasper's whiskers and his lowered tail told me that his search had been unsuccessful. I took over the search in the evenings, revisiting all the places that might offer shelter for a frightened or injured cat: behind the recycling bins in the square, in the overgrown shrubbery beside the public toilets, plus every car park and green space in the town. There was no trace of Eddie anywhere.

I was more fearful than ever for his safety. Winter was creeping closer, and the conditions outdoors were getting harsher by the day. With every night that passed, the chances of Eddie returning uninjured, and of his own accord, seemed to dwindle. Debbie had done everything she could to raise awareness of Eddie's plight, asking customers to keep their eyes peeled for him, contacting all the local vets, and printing off 'missing' posters, which she dutifully pinned to lampposts around town. But there had not been a single reported sighting of him. I dreaded Debbie eventually giving Eddie up for lost, telling me sorrowfully that she'd done everything she could, but it was time to accept that he had gone.

One evening I made for the market cross, the location of Eddie's last sighting before he disappeared. I was convinced there must be a clue to his whereabouts, if I just looked hard enough. Around me, the square was almost deserted and the night air was damp and misty, as if a cloud had enveloped the town in its chilly embrace. My eye was drawn to the narrow alleyway directly opposite the cross. I knew Jasper had already searched it, but perhaps, if I could muster up the courage to talk to the resident alley-cat, I could at least ascertain whether Eddie had passed through.

I crossed the road and took a few tentative steps along the dark, clammy passage. I tiptoed forward, my face set, and was quickly plunged into the dank gloom of the unlit alley. Sticking close to the wall, I sensed rather than heard it, but knew something was standing further along the passageway, and a prickling on the back of my neck convinced me I was being watched. I squinted into the blackness, my heart racing. 'Hello?' I said, thinking it was better to find out as soon as possible whatever danger I faced. Something moved up ahead, and a low, dark shape hove into view from behind a dustbin. 'I'm just looking for a cat . . .' I said, aware of how small my voice sounded, and how frightened. A security light at the back of the chemist's flicked on, and the alleyway was suddenly bathed in a cold white light.

The alley-cat – I could see him now – said nothing, but continued to glide silently towards me. He had matted ginger fur and a tattered ear, and his yellow eyes narrowed maliciously as he stalked towards me. A low, rumbling growl from the back of his throat left me in no doubt that he was preparing to fight. Cursing my naivety, I turned and tore back down the path. Without pausing for breath, I sprinted across the foggy square, forcing a car to brake as I streaked in front of it, and did not slow down until I had reached the parade. Standing on the cobbles to catch my breath, I felt inordinately comforted by the sight of John's sturdy form on the café doorstep.

'Hello, Molly,' he said amiably, catching sight of me slinking along the pavement. He unlocked the door and I ran inside onto the doormat, waiting with my tail erect for him to stroke me. Smiling, John crouched down to tickle me around the ears.

'It's cold out there tonight, isn't it?' he murmured, gently wiping the layer of chilly moisture from my fur. I turned and rubbed against his hands with my cheek, grateful for the reassurance of his touch. When he stood up, I made straight for my cushion on the windowsill and set about washing away the lingering smell of the alleyway.

John walked across the café to the stairwell. 'Debbie, it's me,' he called. 'The table's booked for eight o'clock.'

'I'll be right down,' Debbie replied in a strained voice from the top of the stairs.

Above us, the sound of footsteps indicated that she

had moved to the living room. Through the ceiling I made out the muffled sound of Debbie talking in a tone that sounded plaintive and pleading. She was cut off mid-sentence by an angry growl from Sophie. The beams in the café ceiling creaked beneath the teenager's heavy tread, stomping across the living room.

'Well, can you blame me, Mum?' Sophie hollered from the landing. 'At least Matt lives in a normal house with a normal family. There's room to hear myself think, and it's possible to have a conversation, once in a while, that isn't about cats!'

John glanced at his watch with a look of weary resignation, then walked over to the fireplace. Jasper was sprawled across one of the armchairs and, as John lowered himself into the opposite chair, lifted his head sleepily. Perhaps it was some masculine bond between them, or they identified with each other being at once part of the café but also slightly removed from it, for John and Jasper had always had a particular fondness for each other. John leant forward in his seat to rub Jasper affectionately between the ears. 'I don't know how you put up with it, mate,' John murmured, as Jasper purred and closed his eyes lazily.

Debbie eventually ran downstairs, flustered and apologetic, and she and John headed out for their date. The flat above me was quiet and I spent a soothing couple of hours washing away the memory of the yellow-eyed alley-cat. It was only when I had curled up in a ball to wait for sleep that John's comment to Jasper popped back into my head. *I don't know how you put up with it*, he had said, and there had been something about his tone that troubled me. I had always taken John's devotion to Debbie for granted, rarely giving a thought to the impact the café's dramas might have on him. It suddenly occurred to me that his reserves of patience might not be infinite and that he might, eventually, tire of waiting on the sidelines while Debbie dealt with the successive crises in her life.

For the first time in a long while, the thought crossed my mind that John might decide he'd had enough of us all.

14

The rift that had opened between me and the kittens since Linda and Ming's arrival seemed to deepen in the wake of Eddie's disappearance. I was convinced that my bad-tempered hiss had been the trigger for him running away, but couldn't bring myself to talk to the kittens about it. My own sense of guilt was bad enough; it would be more than I could bear to hear them say they blamed me, too.

However, when a full week had passed since Eddie's last sighting, and our searches had led nowhere, I finally plucked up the courage to say something. Purdy was about to push her way out through the cat flap one morning when I intercepted her on the doormat.

'Can I talk to you about Eddie?' I asked.

It had been a long time since I had spoken to any of the kittens in private, and I felt surprisingly nervous when she turned her alert, inquisitive face to look at me.

'I was just wondering if Eddie said anything to you, before he disappeared?' I began, aware that my pulse was starting to race. If Eddie had confided in his siblings that he was angry with me, I knew Purdy wouldn't flinch from telling me.

Her green eyes held my gaze steadily. 'No – nothing,' she said. Then, after a pause, she added, 'I think you're assuming the worst.'

'What do you mean?' I asked.

'Well, you think something awful must have happened to him – that he's got lost or been attacked, but . . .' she trailed off, suddenly unsure whether to continue.

'But?' I prompted.

'Well, maybe he left because he wanted to see more of the world than just the café. Maybe it was just . . . the right time for him to go.'

In spite of her tactful tone, I instinctively bristled at her words.

'But if he thought it was time to leave, surely he would have told us first?' I replied, in a voice that was sharper than I intended.

Purdy's eyes narrowed and I knew that she felt dismissed by my response. 'Maybe he would, maybe he wouldn't,' she answered. She sounded nettled, and her tail was starting to flicker impatiently. She gave me a look that seemed to say, 'Can I go now?'

Reluctantly, I blinked to let her know she was free to leave, and she slipped silently out through the cat flap.

I waited on the doormat for a few seconds, then pushed my way through after her. Aware of Purdy loitering on the cobbles outside the hardware shop, but not wanting her to think I was pursuing her, I set off in the other direction, pondering her words as I walked. With hindsight, I knew that my response would have hurt Purdy's feelings. She had probably thought she was being helpful by suggesting that Eddie had simply decided it was time to move on, to see what life was like in the world beyond the café.

But my maternal intuition told me Purdy was wrong: no one knew Eddie like I did: how sensitive and home-loving he was and how, in spite of his grown-up appearance, he was really just a little boy at heart. The idea that he would choose to leave the comfort of the cat café in order to take his chances on the streets was barely credible. The notion that he might do so without talking to me first was out of the question. Purdy might have thought she was being helpful but, in fact, she was being naive.

I looked around and realized that, without any conscious intention, I had walked my usual route to the market square. Rows of market stalls had appeared overnight, their striped canopies flapping in the chilly breeze. Even in low season, the Saturday market drew a crowd, and the square was thronged with shoppers beneath a pale, grey sky. I sat down beside the wooden bench under the elm tree and soaked up the familiar sounds of the market: the slamming of car doors, the barks of excited dogs and the sporadic whines of complaint from overwrought toddlers.

I allowed my eyes to drift over the mass of people and colourful tarpaulins, towards the buildings that surrounded the market. Spying a gap between the sweet shop and an antiques dealer's to my left, I felt a sudden flutter in my stomach. Until now I had mostly left it to Jasper to search the alleys, but if my memory served me well, this alley was different from the others in town . . .

The afternoon light was already beginning to fade as I slipped into the narrow opening that marked the alley's entrance. I jumped onto the drystone wall that ran along one side, and made my way carefully along its jagged surface. Up ahead, in a garden that backed onto the passageway, an old shed stood against the wall, surrounded on all sides by overgrown brambles. Keeping my eyes fixed on its roof, I approached cautiously, dropping to my haunches so that my gait became a stealthy prowl. As I crept closer, I glimpsed movement in the brambles, followed by a lightning-quick flash of gold-coloured eyes through the tangle of thorny branches. I froze, my heart pounding, one paw hovering in the air as I stared at the spot where the eyes had appeared.

'Excuse me?' I said.

The face of a small tortoiseshell cat emerged from the midst of the brambles and peered at me, unblinking.

'I know you,' I said. 'We've met before.'

The tortoiseshell crept warily across the shabby tarpaulin of the shed roof and eyed me apprehensively. 'You came here a long time ago,' she said at last. 'You were injured.'

'That's right,' I replied, feeling a rush of relief. 'I wondered if you could help me again,' I continued, with a hopeful glance at her hesitant face. 'I'm looking for my son, Eddie. He's gone missing and I wondered if, maybe, he's been here?'

The tortoiseshell's golden eyes narrowed intently.

'Well, a black-and-white tom has passed through a few times this week,' she replied.

I felt my heart begin to thump. 'Was he wearing a silver collar?' I asked, trying to stem my excitement.

She wrinkled her nose thoughtfully. 'Hmm, no collar that I can remember. He looked like an alley-cat.'

My heart sank in disappointment; this must have been Jasper, on his daily tour of the alleyways.

The tortoiseshell tilted her head to one side. 'So your boy's missing, is he?' she said. 'That's sad.' It was a simple expression of sympathy that made my eyes begin to tingle.

'That would have been his dad that you saw. They look very similar. Eddie's been gone for a week now, and it's not like him. He's never lived outdoors.' I could feel her gaze on me, but I continued to stare at the uneven stone wall beneath my paws.

'When did you say he went missing?' she asked gently.

'He was seen last Saturday by the market cross.'

I watched as the tortoiseshell closed her eyes in concentration. Her face was mostly ginger, but there was a patch of black over one eye that lent her a slightly piratical look. Beneath her coat, which was a messy patchwork of ginger, white and black, her body was slim and taut. I was acutely aware of my own plump physique, maintained by a generous diet of cat food supplemented by café titbits, and felt a sudden burst of gratitude not to be living outdoors, in a constant daily struggle against the elements, having to hunt or scavenge for every meal.

The tortoiseshell's eyes sprang open. 'Look, I don't know if it was your boy, but I heard something about a pet cat hanging around the streets,' she said urgently, as if worried that she might be overheard. 'Caused quite a stir, strolling around town like he owned the place, in and out of the alleys – a bit like you did that time, come to think of it,' she added, her golden eyes twinkling.

'When was that, can you remember?' I pressed.

'Couldn't say for sure, but a week ago sounds about right,' the tortoiseshell replied.

I fixed her with a stare. 'Do you have any idea where he went?' I asked, my heart pounding so loud I could hear it.

Suddenly, her head dropped. 'From what I heard, an alley-cat chased him to the town sign on the main road south. After that, I don't know what happened to him,' she said sorrowfully.

I thanked the tortoiseshell and leapt down from the wall. I pelted out of the alley and across the middle of the square, dodging the legs of shoppers and dashing between parked cars until I reached the entrance to the churchyard. Spotting Jasper prowling between the headstones on the far side, I sprinted across the grass, causing a cluster of crows to flap skywards in alarm.

'I know what happened to Eddie,' I panted. 'A cat chased him to the main road south, about a week ago. An alley-cat told me.'

Jasper's eyes widened. 'An alley-cat told you?' he repeated, doubtfully.

'Yes, the one next to the sweet shop. She'd seen you go up and down searching for him, but she was hiding from you.'

Jasper stared at me with a mixture of surprise and admiration.

'I knew it,' I said, feeling self-righteousness bubble up inside me. I had been right not to listen to Purdy; Eddie had not gone off in search of adventure, he had been forced to run away. But any vindication of my maternal instincts was dwarfed by my concern for Eddie's well-being. The tortoiseshell had confirmed my worst fears: that he had got into a confrontation with an alley-cat and been chased out of town. He would be out there somewhere, alone, hungry and too frightened to come home.

I stared at Jasper defiantly, willing him to recognize the seriousness of the situation. 'So, what are we going to do?' I asked.

'Well, there's only one thing we can do,' replied Jasper soberly. 'I'll have to go after him.'

Later that evening Jasper bade farewell to the kittens and slipped out onto the street under cover of darkness. I walked by his side through the town's back streets until we picked up the main road heading south. There, we padded past the shops, the public toilets and the car park, to the point where the pavement ended and a grassy verge took over. All around us, the fields beyond the hedgerows looked inky-black in the darkness. An owl screeched, unseen, in a tree nearby.

We stepped off the kerb and made our way across the damp verge to the hedgerow. I knew Jasper would be able to handle himself, yet I still dreaded the thought of him leaving, and the fact that we would have no means of communicating while he was away. Much as I had felt vexed and frustrated by him in recent weeks, Jasper was my anchor. Without him, I would have no one to confide in and seek reassurance from.

As if he had read my mind, Jasper murmured, 'It'll be okay – I'll find Eddie.' He nuzzled his face against mine and I looked up into his amber eyes, wanting to commit their comforting gaze to memory.

Jasper burrowed into a gap in the hedgerow, there was a brief rustling sound, then he was gone. I turned and retraced my steps slowly back to the café. There was nothing I could do now except wait.

15

After breakfast on Monday morning I descended the stairs to find Debbie casting puzzled looks around the café. I could almost see her doing a head-count, as she watched the kittens file across the floor behind me. A few minutes later, I was settling into my habitual position in the window when I heard her rattling a box of cat biscuits on the back doorstep. 'Jasper, breakfast!' she called hopefully into the empty alleyway.

Linda, who was tying her hair back at the mirror beside the counter, registered the look of concern on her sister's face. 'What's up, Debs?' she asked casually.

'I haven't seen Jasper for a couple of days. He's not been in for breakfast, and he's not in the alley, either,' Debbie replied, frowning.

Linda's eyes slid back to her reflection in the mirror. 'To lose one cat may be regarded as a misfortune. To lose two looks like carelessness,' she observed, smiling wryly until Debbie's steely look sent her scurrying to refill the napkin-holders.

'Oh, hello, it's Debbie Walsh from Molly's. I'm afraid we've lost another cat,' Debbie told the vet, blushing, on the telephone later that morning. 'Could you let me know if you hear anything?'

However, there was no poster campaign for Jasper, as there had been for Eddie, and Debbie avoided mentioning his disappearance to the café's customers. I suspected that Linda's comment might have touched a nerve, and Debbie was embarrassed by the fact that the Cotswolds' only cat café had now mislaid two of its charges.

Throughout the day Debbie threw worried looks in my direction while I sat at the window, staring anxiously down the parade. 'Don't worry, Molls – Jasper's just gone wandering again, that's all,' she reassured me. I rubbed my cheek against her hand, wishing I could explain to her what was really going on.

I veered between telling myself that Jasper would find Eddie and bring him home, and feeling certain that I would never see either of them again. Even sleep brought no respite: I was troubled by unsettling dreams, from which I would wake with a sudden jolt of panic and an overwhelming sense that I should be doing more – that I should have been the one to go after Eddie. The powerlessness of my position, stuck at the café waiting, was agonizing. Every time the phone rang, my stomach lurched, as I hoped – and at the same time dreaded – that it was a call about Eddie or Jasper.

Although the kittens understood why their father had gone, the loss of Jasper in addition to Eddie had a de-stabilizing effect on our fractured family. I became more withdrawn and taciturn than ever, spending hour after hour gazing listlessly through the window. We were now an all-female colony, and in the vacuum created by Eddie and Jasper's absence, the kittens became more quarrelsome, as if they were jostling for position in the new hierarchy.

Purdy had always assumed certain privileges, as the most confident and outgoing of the litter; but, without their father around, Abby and Bella now became more extrovert and began to challenge Purdy's dominance. I kept out of their squabbles, thinking the best thing I could do was allow them to work out their sibling rivalries for themselves, but barely a day went by when I didn't hear a sudden hiss and spit as a minor disagreement boiled over into conflict. Their disputes usually ended with Purdy, realizing she was outnumbered, striding huffily out through the cat flap and marching off down the cobbles. She would often hop onto Jo's white van outside the hardware shop and look around insouciantly, before settling down on the van's roof for a proprietorial wash.

One morning, Linda took delivery of a large cardboard box at the door while she and Debbie were preparing to open the café.

'What's in there, Lind?' Debbie asked, watching Linda run a knife along the seam of brown tape.

'Ming's Mugs,' answered Linda brightly, enjoying Debbie's look of blank incomprehension. She ripped open the cardboard box and pulled out a white enamel mug, emblazoned with a photo of Ming. The disembodied image of her face against the stark white background of the mug emphasized Ming's pointed chin and enormous brown ears, and her slightly crossed eyes were a piercing, artificial shade of blue. Underneath the photos, in a bright-pink font, ran the hashtag #mingsmug.

Behind the till, Debbie's mouth fell open in dismay. 'And what are you planning to do with those?' she asked coolly, walking around the side of the counter for a closer look.

'Sell them, of course! It's called merchandising, Debs,' explained Linda pompously. 'I ordered sixty.'

She hoisted the cardboard box off the floor and teetered with it towards the fireplace, ignoring Debbie's expression of incredulity.

'We can display them next to the Specials board, see?' Linda had deposited the box on an armchair and was already arranging the mugs in a row on the mantelpiece. 'All the customers love Ming, and I reckon people will pay three ninety-nine—'

'Linda, stop!' Debbie shrieked suddenly.

The kittens and I fell still to look at her – it was not often that we heard Debbie raise her voice. Linda's hand hovered over the pyramid of mugs that she had begun to assemble at the fireplace.

'What's the matter, Debs?' asked Linda innocently, keeping her back to the room. 'Don't you like them?'

Debbie stood squarely behind her sister, taking deep, calming breaths. When at last she spoke, I detected a tremor of suppressed anger. 'Linda, you don't seem to understand. This is a café, not a . . . Ming theme park!'

A brief silence, then, 'Well, you could get some made of Molly too, if you like,' answered Linda airily.

'That's not the point!' Debbie snapped.

Linda finally turned to face her sister. Her mouth was fixed in a defiant smile, but two spots of pink had appeared on her cheeks.

'This is a cat café,' said Debbie, with a dismissive gesture towards the box of mugs on the armchair, 'not a . . . crockery warehouse. I'm sorry, Linda, but these mugs are . . . tacky.' She picked up one of them and studied the offending item closely. 'Besides, haven't you noticed? It looks like it says "Ming's smug".' Debbie held the mug up and pointed at the hashtag with a look of exasperation. 'Who would want to buy the merchandise of a smug cat?'

Linda looked momentarily crestfallen, then she turned wordlessly back to face the mantelpiece. 'Well, if that's the way you feel. You're the boss, after all,' she muttered churlishly. She began to dismantle the pyramid with pursed lips, the mugs chinking against each other as she carelessly looped them over her thumbs.

Once she had repacked the box, she heaved it into her arms and made her way awkwardly towards the door.

'I guess I'll just have to give these to a charity then,' Linda said loftily. Balancing the box between one hand and a raised thigh, she wrestled to unlock the door with her free hand, struggling for a couple of minutes, until Debbie walked over and opened the door for her. 'Thank you,' Linda mumbled grudgingly. She shifted the weight of the box between both arms and then, with her nose in the air, she and her mugs flounced out of the café.

The atmosphere between the sisters remained tense in the aftermath of the mug debacle. On Friday, Linda rushed upstairs straight after the café closed, and there was a note of triumph in the way she announced that she was to spend the evening with friends.

Debbie smiled politely. 'Have fun!' she called to her sister's back as it disappeared down the stairs. But she breathed a loud sigh of relief as soon as the café door slammed shut.

A little later that evening Jo turned up with a takeaway, and Debbie and I trotted downstairs to meet her. My spirits immediately lifted at the sight of Jo's mop of curly hair and jovial face at the bottom of the stairs. Her down-to-earth personality was in sharp contrast to Linda's tendency towards drama and self-pity, and she could always be counted on to help Debbie see the funny side of any situation.

It didn't take long for Debbie to begin to offload her frustration with Linda. 'I mean, you should have seen these mugs, Jo,' Debbie complained, grimacing as she poured out two glasses of wine. 'I've never seen anything so hideous in my life. The photo made poor Ming look like a cross-eyed freak!'

Jo had crouched down to stroke Purdy on the flagstones. Jo was affectionate towards all of the kittens, but had long-ago singled out feisty Purdy as her favourite. Her brown curls were shaking with laughter. 'Not so much "Ming's Mug" as "Ming's Ugly Mug", by the sound of it.' She grinned as Purdy rubbed against her knees. 'I wish you'd kept one to show me – they sound hilarious.'

She stood up and took her glass from the counter-top, while Purdy contentedly climbed the wooden walkway up to the cat hammock.

'Maybe Linda just got carried away, after the Fortune Cookies went down so well,' Jo suggested diplomatically, taking a sip of wine.

Debbie shrugged. 'Maybe. I can't decide whether she's a marketing genius or a total fruitcake, to be honest. Either way, she's doing my head in.'

Jo watched shrewdly as Debbie lifted a stack of foil trays out of the bag and placed them on the counter. 'If she's really doing your head in, you could always move into John's place,' she said, a mischievous smile playing around her lips. On the window cushion, my ears pricked up.

'Funny you should mention that,' answered Debbie quietly. 'John said the same thing.'

Jo did a dramatic double-take over her wine glass. 'Really? When?' Her eyes glistened with excitement, but Debbie was already shaking her head.

'A couple of weeks ago, but I said no.'

'Why?' Jo squealed, dropping disappointedly onto a chair. 'Surely that's the obvious solution? It's the natural next step for you two; plus it would give you some space from Linda.'

Debbie's face clouded and she braced her arms against the wooden worktop for support. 'But it's not that simple, Jo. What about Sophie? I can't ask her to move house again – not after all the upheaval of the divorce. Besides, the flat is my home, and I don't want to give it up just because . . .' she struggled to find the right words, 'just because my sister's driving me crazy.'

Jo's shoulders drooped despondently.

'Besides, if John and I ever decide to live together, I want it to be because it's what we both want, not because it's a convenient solution to an overcrowding problem.'

'I hear what you're saying, Debs, and I get it,' Jo replied, pushing a stray curl out of her eyes. 'But something's got to give, hasn't it? This situation can't go on forever. Maybe it's time you asked Linda to move out.' She eyed her friend surreptitiously between sips of wine, while I sat on the window cushion awaiting Debbie's response with bated breath. It felt as if it was *my* fate hanging in the balance, as much as Linda's.

At the counter, Debbie let out a long groan. 'Oh, I just don't know, Jo,' she wailed. Although she hadn't said it, I knew what she was thinking: that she couldn't turn her back on her sister at a time like this. So the next words to come out of her mouth surprised me. 'Maybe you're right,' she said. 'I can't take much more of this. I'll talk to Linda tomorrow.'

'That's the spirit!' Jo replied, raising her glass in a toast of encouragement.

Debbie looked up and I saw the corners of her mouth lift into a smile. 'Or perhaps Linda could move in with you for a bit?' she teased.

Jo pretended to choke on her wine, before composing her face into a look of sufferance. 'Actually, that might not be such a crazy idea,' she murmured. 'The way business has been going recently, I might need to take on a lodger soon, just to pay the rent.'

16

Later that night, curled up at the foot of Debbie's bed, I mulled over Jo and Debbie's conversation. It had reassured and alarmed me in equal measure. It was heartening to hear that John was sufficiently committed to Debbie to ask her to move in with him. However, I could not help but dwell on what life in the flat would be like if Debbie and Sophie moved out. Linda would be left in charge and would inevitably end up taking over responsibility for the cat café, too. That was a terrifying prospect. The first thing to go would surely be my name above the door. It would be Ming's café, rather than Molly's, and pictures of Ming's boss-eyed face would be plastered over every menu, napkin and apron in the place. Upstairs, the flat would become Beau's domain, and the kittens and I would find ourselves outcasts, both upstairs and down.

I drew my tongue vigorously along the length of my

hind leg, determined to drive the nightmarish vision from my mind. I had to remind myself that Debbie had swiftly dismissed the possibility of moving out, and she had even promised to speak to Linda about her leaving. When Jo had finally left the café and they were both slightly the worse for wear, Jo's parting words to Debbie had been, 'So, don't forget: you're going to talk to Linda tomorrow.'

Debbie had nodded emphatically. 'Absholutely,' she had slurred, 'I'm going to give Linda her marching orders. Or, if not, I'm going to send her round to your place!'

I drifted off to sleep, comforted by the thought that, as long as Debbie kept her word, there were grounds for hoping that the long ordeal of living with Linda might soon come to an end.

During the night, however, Debbie thrashed around under her duvet, waking up almost hourly to gulp down water from the glass by her bed. When her alarm clock sounded in the morning, she emerged from underneath the covers with dark shadows beneath her blood-shot eyes. She yanked the cord of the venetian blind and winced painfully in a shaft of early-morning sunlight.

Debbie was waiting for the kettle to boil in the kitchen when Linda finally stumbled out of the living room, looking similarly sallow-skinned and scarecrow-haired. She had not returned from her night out until after Debbie had gone to bed, and I guessed she too had been drinking. I had heard her unsteady footsteps in the hallway, and her tipsy shushing of Beau as she opened the living-room door.

Linda skulked around the hallway while Debbie stood watching the gurgling kettle.

'Morning,' Debbie grunted, to which Linda mumbled something indistinct in reply. They seemed in unspoken agreement that no conversation would be attempted until after they had both had a cup of tea. I stalked between the living room and kitchen while they prepared their breakfast, waiting twitchily for Debbie to fulfil her promise to Jo.

After they had consumed tea and toast, and the colour had begun to return to their cheeks, Debbie asked how Linda's evening had been. Linda launched into a tirade of gossip about her friends, to which Debbie listened patiently, her face a mask of polite indifference. 'She kept insisting it wasn't Botox,' Linda smirked conspiratorially at the conclusion of her complicated narrative, 'but I've never found a face cream *that* effective.' She raised her eyebrows and gave a knowing look over the top of her mug of tea.

Debbie gave a fake sort of laugh, waited for a moment until she was sure Linda had finished, then sat forward earnestly in her chair.

'Look, Linda, I need to ask you something . . .' she began, when suddenly a bedroom door flew open above us.

Sophie thundered down from the attic, complaining that she had overslept and was meant to have met her friend Jade twenty minutes ago. Debbie was quickly sucked into dealing with the crisis, helping her daughter find her shoes and purse, while Sophie frantically called Jade on her mobile phone. By the time Sophie was fully equipped and running downstairs, Linda had disappeared into the bathroom.

The moment had passed, and Debbie had no choice but to set about tidying the living room while Linda showered.

When Linda finally emerged from the bathroom in a gust of fragrant steam, she blithely announced, 'You know, I think it's about time Beau took a bath, too – he's been smelling a little . . . doggy . . . recently.' Under Debbie's disappointed and faintly disapproving gaze, Linda crouched over Beau on the living-room floor. 'Isn't that right, baby? Who's a smelly boy? Yes, *you* are!' she cooed, as the dog rolled onto his back and showed his belly submissively. She scooped the greasy-haired animal into her arms and carried him through to the bathroom, locking the door behind her.

Once Beau had been shampooed and blow-dried, Linda placed him on the sofa, where he sat wide-eyed and motionless, looking like a shell-shocked teddy-bear. No sooner had Linda sat down at the dining table with a newspaper than Debbie started to speak: 'Linda, I've been meaning to talk to you—'

This time Linda's phone began to beep, vibrating urgently on the dining table next to her newspaper. 'Sorry, Debs, I'd better just get that,' she apologized. It was a text from Ray, and Linda spent the next few minutes composing a reply, which entailed much frowning, eye-rolling and furious tapping on the screen.

Debbie sat beside her in silence, flicking unenthusi-astically through the pages of an old magazine.

I could tell that, the longer the conversation was put off, the more anxious Debbie was becoming. I began to worry that if she didn't speak soon, she might lose her nerve completely. However, once Linda had dealt with Ray's text, Debbie pushed the magazine aside and took a deep breath. 'Linda, we need to talk—'

The landline started ringing. Debbie groaned at the interruption and looked up at the ceiling in despair.

'Hold on a second, I'll just get rid of whoever that is,' she said to Linda, holding up a hand in a 'Stay there' gesture. She dashed across the room to the telephone in the alcove. 'Hello? Yes, this is Debbie.' As she talked, she kept her eyes fixed on her sister, as if compelling her not to move. She listened intently to the voice on the other end of the line, then suddenly turned away to face the wall. Her voice, when she answered, had dropped in pitch and volume. 'Oh, I see. I'm so sorry.' I stared fixedly at the back of her head, trying to quell the rising panic in my gut. 'Thank you for letting me know,' she said shakily, before putting the phone down.

'Something wrong?' Linda asked, cuddling the fluffy-haired Beau, who had recovered sufficiently from his bath-time ordeal to slink over to the table and jump into her lap.

When Debbie turned around, her eyes were brimming over with tears and her lip was trembling.

I padded across the rug to sit at her feet. The blood was rushing in my ears and I knew with absolute certainty what the phone call had been about. The question was: did it concern Eddie or Jasper? Or both of them . . . ?

Debbie lowered her eyes to look at me, and I saw a tear slide down her cheek. 'Oh, Molly, I'm so sorry. Margery's died.'

I felt as though the ground beneath me was falling away. I peered up at Debbie and tilted my head in confusion. I had been so convinced I knew what Debbie was about to say that her words seemed nonsensical. I stood there, feeling suddenly empty, my mind blank with shock. Then, as Debbie crouched down to stroke me and I began to process what I had heard, the first thought that came into my mind was:

at least it wasn't Eddie. Almost immediately I was hit by a wave of guilt; how could I think such a thing, at a moment like this?

Debbie was stroking my head, doing her best to comfort me, but comfort was not what I needed. I felt confused and numb, and I was suddenly seized by the realization that I needed to be on my own, to absorb in private what had happened. I bolted out of the room, down the stairs and out through the cat flap. I paused to look around me, in a blind panic, wondering which way to turn. Almost immediately I realized that I needed to go to my safe place: the fire escape in the alleyway. I ran around the side of the café, tore along the passage and made straight for the iron stairway.

My mind whirred as I tried to remember when I had last seen Margery. Somehow it felt important to recall our final encounter, and her last words to me. Then it came to me: it was that stormy Sunday – the very day, in fact, when Debbie realized Eddie was missing. Margery had been distracted and agitated and we hadn't stayed long, and had bumped into David on our way out. My throat tightened when I realized that, the last time I had seen Margery, she hadn't even seemed to know who I was.

I closed my eyes and allowed a wave of regret to wash over me. If I had known that would be the last time I'd see her, I would have jumped onto her lap and purred, and stayed there until she recognized me – so that she knew I would always love her. But it was too late now. I had wasted my last chance to say goodbye.

I circled slowly on the damp pile of flattened cardboard beneath the fire escape, listening to the sounds of the alley. A solitary pigeon cooed softly from a rooftop behind me, and a squirrel scampered across the wall opposite. A strange feeling of hollowness spread through me; I felt empty and insubstantial. It was as if my very identity was defined not by who I was, but by who I had lost: Eddie, Jasper and now Margery. Feeling utterly alone, I curled up on the cardboard and closed my eyes, praying for the relief from my mental turmoil that only sleep could bring.

That night, I slept deeply and dreamlessly, not stirring until the cawing crows woke me with a start at dawn. The sun was just coming up and the sky was a glorious pink, shot through with gold, and there was a crisp, wintry feel in the air as I crawled out from underneath the iron steps. In the churchyard the frost-tipped grass crunched under my feet as I made my way to the square, where I padded over to the elm tree and jumped onto the bench underneath its bare branches.

I had lived in Stourton for almost two years now, and had spent as much of my life without Margery as I had spent with her. I tortured myself with an almost unbearable dilemma: if I were offered the chance to go back in time – to remain with Margery in her cosy bungalow – would I do so? There would be no cat café, no Debbie, no kittens, no Jasper, but I would have had two more years of love from my precious Margery.

But there was nothing I could do to get back the time I had lost; there was no bargain to be made, no retrospective deal that could be struck. I had thought I had lost Margery two years earlier, but fate had intervened and, miraculously, she had come back to me. But now she really was gone, and I had to accept that I would never see her again.

17

Plodding back along the cobbles towards the café, my mind was foggy and my limbs felt heavy to the point of exhaustion. I nosed through the cat flap and stood on the doormat, flicking my tail, gazing aimlessly around the café. The kittens were nowhere to be seen, but Ming had assumed her customary meditative pose on top of the cat tree, facing the window with her eyes closed, her chocolate-brown tail neatly encircling her paws. I stared at her for a few moments. I had so often felt suspicious of her apparent ability to disengage from her surroundings; but, on this occasion, I deeply envied her imperturbable composure.

Perhaps Ming sensed she was being watched, because her eyes sprang open and she turned her head slowly in my direction. Her look was intense, yet inscrutable, conveying neither hostility nor warmth, but in my grieving state, her blue-eyed stare was more than I could bear. With my tail held as high as I could muster, I walked shakily across the café and climbed the stairs to the flat.

Upstairs, I heard Debbie humming softly over the splash of water from the kitchen sink. 'There you are, Molls!' she said fondly, catching sight of me as I peered round the doorframe. 'Where've you been? I was starting to worry about you.' She crouched down and began to rub my ears. 'You poor thing, you must be missing Margery,' she sighed.

Feeling my throat constrict, I nestled my head into her curved palm, savouring the familiar scent of her skin.

'Would you like some breakfast?' she asked, as if eating would help to assuage my grief. She stood up and reached inside one of the cabinets for a pouch of cat food, squeezing its contents into the bowl on the floor.

I stared at the mound of chunks dolefully, unable to summon up the energy to eat.

'Not feeling hungry?' Debbie asked, as I stood listlessly by the bowl. 'That's all right, Molly. It's there if you want it, okay?' she said, dropping to her haunches and pressing my nose gently with her fingertip.

Her attentiveness comforted me and I began to purr, tentatively at first, but louder as she continued to stroke me. I pressed sideways against her leg, nuzzling her hands gratefully and curling my tail over the top of her thigh. I realized with a pang how little time Debbie and I had spent alone together since Linda and Beau's arrival. We had lost the precious moments we used to share on a daily basis: the evenings spent cuddling on the sofa, or the lazy Sunday mornings dozing in bed. It was only now, as Debbie crouched over me on the kitchen floor, that I became aware of how desperately I missed being held by her.

As if on cue, the living-room door swung open and out strode Linda, with the fragrantly fluffy Beau trotting jauntily at her heels. I leapt up onto the worktop, so as not to get trodden on. Stepping awkwardly around the clutter, I found a space to sit down, between the dusty NutriBullet and the kettle.

'Cuppa?' Linda asked brightly, reaching for the kettle beside me, without acknowledging my presence.

'No thanks, I've just had one,' answered Debbie.

On the floor, Beau eyed the bowl of cat food greedily, drops of slobber forming at the sides of his mouth. Linda, oblivious to his nefarious intentions, squeezed past Debbie to reach the sink, and it was Debbie who deftly lifted the bowl from underneath Beau's salivating mouth and placed it out of his reach on the windowsill.

'I'm going to pop over to Cotswold Organic after I've taken Beau for a walk. Shall I pick up something nice for dinner?' Linda asked, thrusting the spout of the kettle under the gushing tap.

'That would be lovely, thanks,' Debbie replied half-heartedly.

Linda rammed the kettle back onto its base and bustled back to the living room, a disappointed Beau trailing after her.

Judging by Linda's cheerful demeanour and Debbie's wan look, I deduced that the subject of Linda moving out had not, in the end, been broached. I was not especially surprised. I could picture the scene from the previous evening, after I had fled to the alley: in the wake of the news about Margery, Debbie would have been too upset to risk Linda's histrionics upon being told that she was no longer welcome. I felt a dull pang of disappointment; but, given how low I was already feeling, the realization that Linda and Beau were as firmly ensconced in the flat as ever made little material difference to my emotional state.

In the days that followed the news of Margery's death I was plagued by persistent lethargy. I lacked the energy for anything beyond the basic demands of grooming, eating and sleeping. The thought of continuing to search for Eddie and Jasper seemed futile; I had looked everywhere, to no avail. Instead, I passed the daylight hours sitting on the window cushion, looking vainly for any sign of them on the parade, and every evening after closing time I slunk behind the café to the alleyway.

The gap under the fire escape became my private sanctuary, a space in which to think about Jasper and Eddie, and to remember Margery. Sometimes I could hear the high-pitched shrieks of alley-cats squaring up for a fight in a distant street. I shuddered at the sound, which instantly called to mind thoughts of Eddie's ordeal on the day he disappeared. I tortured myself by playing out the scenario in my mind: Eddie's guileless foray into an unfamiliar part of town, and his sudden realization that the alley-cat stalking towards him was no friend. Imagining his fear was almost harder to bear than my own feelings of loss – how he must have wished I had been there to protect him . . .

Was it my fault for not warning the kittens that the world was dangerous, that the love and security with which we were surrounded at home could not protect us beyond the confines of the cat café? Had our pampered, privileged existence made me overlook my responsibilities as a mother? If Eddie had paid the price for my complacency, I would never come to terms with my guilt.

My low spirits were not helped by the gradual appearance of signs all around Stourton that Christmas was approaching. Along the parade, coloured lights had been wound around windows and porches and, inside the café, Christmas carols issued tinnily from the kitchen radio. Christmas was not something I wanted to be reminded of, and certainly not something I looked forward to. To think of spending Christmas not only without Eddie, but without Jasper too, filled my heart with dread. The prospect of Linda, Beau and Ming taking their place in our celebrations made me feel physically sick.

About a week after we had received the news of Margery's death, Debbie ripped open a letter that had flopped onto the doormat. 'That's odd,' she frowned. 'It's from a solicitor, asking me to get in touch.'

'Get in touch about what?' said Linda quickly, peering at the letter over Debbie's shoulder.

'Something about Margery's estate. That's all it says,' Debbie replied, turning the page over, as if hoping for clues on the back. 'I'll give them a call tomorrow,' she said with a puzzled look.

But the solicitor's letter had piqued Linda's curiosity, and at dinner that evening she began to probe. 'So, tell me again,' Linda asked in a 'just wondering' voice, 'how exactly did you know Margery?'

'She was Molly's owner,' Debbie replied.

Linda's brow furrowed. 'I thought Molly was a stray when you took her in.'

'She was a stray,' Debbie laughed, 'but before she

became a stray, she had been Margery's cat, until Margery moved to the care home and Molly ended up on the streets. It was a complete coincidence that Margery happened to visit the café, but of course Molly recognized her immediately.' Debbie smiled fondly at the memory.

'That's a great story,' Linda mused. '"Café reunites owner with long-lost cat." Brilliant PR for the café, too,' she added shrewdly.

'PR had nothing to do with it, Linda,' Debbie said primly. 'It was just nice for them to find each other again. And nice for me, too. Margery was such a lovely lady,' she mused, starting to well up.

A few days later, Debbie slipped out mid-morning to attend a meeting with the solicitor, leaving Linda in charge of the café.

She returned at lunchtime, looking pale and distracted, swiftly swapping her coat for her apron and ignoring Linda's querying glances. Debbie continued to avoid her sister for the rest of the day, evading Linda's repeated attempts to catch her eye or initiate conversation. Linda's curiosity about the meeting was almost palpable, and although I sympathized with Debbie's reluctance to involve her, I also knew that the longer she put off talking to Linda, the more unbearable her sister would become.

Linda finally cornered Debbie in her bedroom that evening as she was getting ready for her date-night with John. I was grooming myself on Debbie's bed when Linda knocked at the door and, without waiting for an invitation, slunk into the room.

'So, I was just wondering what the solicitor said today?' she asked, with an unconvincing nonchalance.

I was washing my hind leg and glanced over at Debbie, who was applying make-up at her dressing table. I could see her closed expression reflected in the pedestal mirror. 'Um, not much,' she murmured non-committally.

Linda's eyes bored into Debbie's back. 'Well, they must have said something, otherwise why would they ask you to come for a meeting?' she persisted.

Debbie muttered something inaudible and began to rummage in her make-up bag.

'Sorry, Debs – I didn't catch that,' pressed Linda.

Debbie's shoulder slumped and she swivelled round on her stool. 'It was about Margery's will,' she said reluctantly, while I set to work on a patch of tangled fur at the base of my tail. 'Molly is a beneficiary.' With my hind leg tucked behind my ear and my tongue protruding from my mouth, I looked up in surprise.

Linda hooted derisively. 'Molly! Ha, really? What did Margery leave her? A year's supply of cat treats?

A hand-knitted blanket?' She was smirking, but Debbie's face remained stony.

'Everything,' Debbie replied levelly, her eyes fixed on the bedspread. 'Margery left her entire estate to Molly. With me as her named legal guardian.'

There was a moment's silence, during which I looked from Debbie's face to Linda's, and back again. I was aware of the absurdity of the way my leg was propped behind my head, but seemed unable to engage my brain sufficiently to lower it.

'Say again – what?' blinked Linda.

Debbie's breathing was shallow and the colour had begun to drain from her face. 'Apparently, Molly is Margery's sole beneficiary, and I am her legal guardian,' she repeated, and this time there was a slight tremor in her voice.

Linda made a strange spluttering sound. 'Well, did they tell you how much Margery left?' she asked, her eyes starting to glisten.

Debbie shot her a look of distaste. 'I didn't ask, Linda!' she snapped.

Chastened, Linda bit her lip, but continued to stare hard at her sister, who seemed absorbed in examining the backs of her hands as they lay in her lap. Eventually, steadfastly avoiding Linda's gaze, Debbie said, 'The solicitor said something about a property in Oxford, and some savings and investments, but that's all I know at the moment.'

Linda's eyes looked as if they were in danger of popping out of her head. 'A property in Oxford? *And* some savings and investments?' she screeched. 'Bloody hell, Debs – sounds like quite the nest egg she had tucked away!'

Debbie chose to ignore this remark, but began to fiddle distractedly with her fringe.

Linda's eyes flicked towards me. 'Well, Molly, aren't you a lucky cat?' she said covetously.

At this, Debbie fired her sister a look of disgust. 'Linda, please! I wish I hadn't mentioned it. I knew you'd react like this,' she said, twisting back round to face the dressing table.

'Oh, don't be like that, Debs,' Linda wheedled. 'I'm just surprised, that's all.'

Debbie said nothing, and began to apply make-up in front of the mirror again, acting as if Linda was not there.

I lowered my hind leg and repositioned myself into a neat loaf-shape on the bed, trying to process what I had heard. Linda's reaction had unsettled me; the unmistakably envious edge to her voice when she addressed me had made me deeply uncomfortable.

'So, what happens next?' Linda asked at last, doing a poor imitation of indifference.

Debbie was applying mascara, but her shoulders drooped. 'Well, obviously, I can't accept it. Margery had a family. This is their inheritance, not Molly's. I'm going to call her son David tomorrow.'

Linda chewed her bottom lip, fixing the back of Debbie's head with a cold stare. 'Are you sure you're not being too hasty, Debs?' she said silkily.

'Quite sure,' Debbie shot back.

Linda remained perched on the corner of the bed for several minutes. I sensed that she was hoping to continue the conversation, but Debbie's back stayed resolutely turned towards her. Eventually, her impulse towards interference having been thwarted by Debbie's determined silence, Linda slipped wordlessly out of the room.

They didn't speak to each other again that evening. In fact, I had the distinct impression that Debbie was avoiding her sister. She spent longer than usual getting ready to go out and, as soon as she heard the tinkle of the bell over the café door, ran downstairs to meet John, rather than inviting him up to the flat. While Debbie was out, Linda prowled around the flat like a cat unable to settle. She made a half-hearted attempt to tidy her belongings in the alcove, fidgeted on the sofa with her phone and made herself a cup of herbal tea. Her twitchiness made me so uneasy that eventually I padded downstairs, deciding that I would rather share a room with a watchful Ming than with a fidgeting Linda.

I curled up on the café windowsill, troubled by a nagging suspicion that life was about to get even more complicated than it already was.

18

I was in a heavy sleep when Debbie and John returned to the café later that night, and the sound of the door being unlocked startled me. The substance of my dream vanished as soon as I opened my eyes, but I was left with a feeling of guilt and a vague sense that I had been responsible for some unidentified calamity. I shook my head briskly and allowed my eyes to settle on Debbie, who had lowered the window blinds and switched on a lamp behind the till, instantly imbuing the café with a soft yellow light. John returned from the kitchen with two tumblers and they clinked glasses, before sinking into the armchairs in front of the fireplace.

'So?' John began.

'So – what?' Debbie replied, a little tensely.

'So, are you going to tell me why you've been on edge all evening?' he enquired gently, in a voice that conveyed concern rather than criticism.

Debbie took a sip, staring morosely at the unlit stove. 'Well, it's this ridiculous legacy, of course,' she sighed.

'What's ridiculous about it?' asked John.

Debbie gave a mirthless laugh. 'Everything about it is ridiculous, John. Margery disinherited her son and left her entire estate to Molly. And now it's up to me to sort this whole sorry mess out.'

I couldn't help but smart at Debbie's blunt appraisal of the situation, and the realization that I had unwittingly become the cause of such distress for her.

I had to squint to make out Debbie's expression in the shadow cast by the lamp behind her.

'But I'm right, aren't I?' Debbie said, looking anxiously for confirmation in John's face. 'I mean, it's out of the question that I could accept the money on Molly's behalf. Isn't it?' Her tone was urgent, desperate even. Curled up on my cushion, I willed John to say he agreed with her, to advise her to decline the legacy, so that the matter could be settled as quickly as possible and we could put the whole affair behind us.

John gave a helpless shrug. 'I don't know what's right or wrong in this situation,' he replied evenly. 'I didn't know Margery, and I have no idea why she chose to leave her money to Molly. It might have been something she felt strongly about, before the dementia took hold . . .' He trailed off, sensing that his words were not helping. Debbie turned away, looking as tortured as ever. 'I think you need to do whatever feels right to you,' he said at last.

At this, Debbie's head swung back towards him, and annoyance flashed across her face. 'But don't you see, John, what *feels right to me* has got nothing to do with it. It's about doing the right thing by Margery, and by her family. This money has nothing to do with me, or Molly,' she said curtly, gripping her tumbler tightly.

John raised the fingers of one hand in a placatory gesture. 'Well then, there's your answer,' he replied mildly.

Looking relieved, Debbie slumped back into her chair and took a sip from her glass.

On my cushion, I realized I had been holding my breath during their exchange. I exhaled deeply, relieved that Debbie had reached a decision she was happy with.

'So did you really have no idea Margery was going to do this?' John asked, looking at his tumbler as he swirled its contents lazily.

At this, Debbie frowned. 'Of course not! How could I have known?' she shot back, looking at him sideways.

John shrugged placidly. 'I s'pose. It's just that . . . you've spent a lot of time with Margery over the last few months. I thought maybe she'd have mentioned it to you.' His tone was light, almost offhand, but in the shadowy café Debbie's face seemed to darken.

'No, I didn't know anything about it,' she said, enunciating the words carefully. 'I never talked to Margery about her money, or her will. We talked about Molly and the café. That's all.'

Sensing Debbie's defensiveness, John stretched out an arm across the space between the armchairs. 'Okay, okay, don't worry – I was just wondering, that's all,' he reassured her.

Debbie glanced at his hand, which was resting awkwardly on the arm of her chair, but made no move to reciprocate the gesture. Instead she said coldly, 'Wondering about what?'

'I just meant—' John began.

But before he could finish, Debbie interrupted him. 'You just meant that surely I *must* have known Margery was planning to leave her estate to Molly. I'd spent all that time with her, how could I *not* have known.' She glowered at him.

At this, John pulled his arm back towards himself protectively. 'No, that's not what I meant at all,' he said, staring at his drink glumly while Debbie knocked back the contents of her tumbler in silence. The mood in the café, which had felt cosy and intimate, began to feel tense and oppressive.

I stared at the two of them helplessly. I was baffled by what had just happened: how they had gone from being in agreement that Debbie would decline the legacy, to this state of conflict in which John looked hurt and Debbie furious. I wasn't even sure who had been to blame for the turnaround; whether Debbie had been justified in taking offence, or whether she had read suspicion into John's words where there had been none. But I had witnessed enough arguments between Debbie and Sophie to realize that a stalemate had been reached, and that both parties were now too aggrieved to initiate a reconciliation.

Debbie yawned, then leant over to place her glass on the low table between the armchairs. John glanced at his watch and mumbled something about having to be up early. He leant over and gave her a perfunctory kiss, but there was no warmth in their touch. I could do nothing but watch as he picked up his coat and, without saying another word, left the café.

The following evening I watched through the window as a man made his way along the dark street towards the café. He carried a briefcase in one hand and pulled his anorak close to his body with the other. His head was bowed against the cold, and as he passed under a lamp post, he was hit by a gust of wind whipping down the parade. In the street light's orange glow, a few strands of hair on his balding head appeared to dance around his ears. He pushed open the café door roughly and stood on the doormat, smoothing his errant hair back into place. I felt my stomach lurch uncomfortably in recognition.

'Hello, David,' Debbie said warmly, coming out of the kitchen. 'I'm just finishing off. Take a seat and I'll bring you a cup of tea.'

David grunted in response. Even by his usual terse standards, he looked particularly sour as he stood on the flagstones, rubbing his hands against the cold.

Spotting the flickering flames in the stove, he walked towards the fireplace. Behind him, a burst of giggling issued from the kitchen, as Debbie and the kitchen staff shared a joke. The happy sound was in stark contrast to the chill that emanated from David.

'Thanks, ladies, see you tomorrow,' Debbie said, locking the back door shut behind them.

David hung his jacket on the back of a chair and sat down. He was dressed in his habitual palette of beige and grey and, without his bulky anorak, his thin, wiry frame was more apparent.

I had remained motionless, lying low on my cushion so as not to draw his attention, but as he looked around the café, he noticed me. I held his gaze, determined not to avert my eyes, and eventually he looked away, the merest sneer of contempt playing around his lips.

'Here we go,' Debbie smiled, carrying a tray of refreshments to the table. David swung his briefcase onto his lap, popped the locks and pulled out a slim cardboard folder, ignoring Debbie as she carefully set the teacups and plate of cookies on the stripy table-cloth.

David placed the folder on his place mat and waited with pursed lips while Debbie, brushing her fringe out of her eyes, sat down on the chair opposite him. Then he watched, with barely concealed impatience, while she set about pouring the tea.

'Milk?' she enquired. David gave a single nod. 'Sugar?'

'Two, please,' he answered gruffly.

'Help yourself to a cookie,' she said, nudging the plate towards him.

David grunted, glaring angrily at the biscuits as if they, too, were wasting his time. Although Debbie was doing her best to hide it, I could tell that, underneath her friendly demeanour, she was being made nervous by David's frostiness.

'I was so sorry to hear about Margery,' Debbie began, as she stirred her tea. 'She was such a lovely lady.'

At this, David breathed in sharply. 'Yes, well, it was probably for the best. She'd had a good innings,' he said matter-of-factly.

Debbie's eyebrows began to creep up her face, but she said nothing.

'This shouldn't take long,' David said, placing the

tips of his fingers on the cardboard folder on his place mat.

Debbie, still stirring her tea, glanced across. 'Oh, right,' she replied uncertainly.

'This is for you,' David said brusquely, attempting to push the folder across the candy-striped cloth towards Debbie. But the little table was so cluttered with crockery that the folder kept getting caught, dislodging sachets of sweetener from their bowl and almost knocking over the tiny vase of flowers. He tutted and picked the folder up, holding it above the tea cups.

With a look of polite courteousness, Debbie took the folder. David watched with a clenched jaw as she fished her reading glasses out of her apron pocket, removed them from their case and pushed them onto her nose. She opened the folder and began to read.

'Um, sorry, David – what is this?' she said lightly.

She looked up to find that David had hunched forward in his chair and was proffering a pen towards her. He had removed the lid and, as he twisted the pen, its brass nib glinted in the firelight. Debbie's questioning gaze took in the pen and David's posture of thinly veiled belligerence.

'What is this, David?' Debbie repeated in a small voice.

'It's a letter of renunciation, from you, saying that you renounce any claim to my mother's estate.' David's voice was calm but uncompromising. 'I would be grateful if you could sign it now,' he added, as if Debbie might not have understood the implication of the pen thrust in her face.

Debbie opened her mouth, then closed it again. 'Er, but, I haven't even read it yet,' she protested feebly.

David sneered and sat back in his chair, making a show of giving her time to read. He twiddled the pen between his fingers, while Debbie, now visibly flustered, scanned the letter.

'So, it's a letter from me, but written by you?' she clarified, concentrating hard on the sheet of paper in front of her. David nodded. Debbie cleared her throat slightly. '*I, Deborah Walsh, hereby renounce any claim on the estate of Margery Hinckley,*' she read.

'That's right,' David answered flatly, a muscle twitching at the corner of his mouth.

'But I never made any claim on Margery's estate, David,' Debbie said, mild indignation beginning to creep into her voice. 'And besides, I'm not the beneficiary – Molly is.'

At this, David let out a single bark-like laugh that was so sharp it made me jump. 'Well, in that case, maybe I should ask Molly to sign the letter?' His face split into a mean smile, revealing his yellow, uneven teeth. He turned to look at me, tilting his head sideways in a parody of courteousness. 'Molly, could you come over here and sign this letter, please?' he asked sarcastically.

I glared at him, unblinking, feeling a wave of fury course through me.

'No? Thought not.' He grinned maliciously, and his eyes flickered back to Debbie, who had begun to blush. I felt the heat rising in my cheeks, too.

David waved his hand at the letter dismissively. 'It doesn't matter who wrote it – we just need something in writing, to get the ball rolling. The solicitors can take it from there and get a contract of renunciation drawn up.' His tone was business like once more, and he leant forward again with his pen.

Debbie looked down at the page in front of her. 'But, David, this isn't a letter from me. These aren't my words—' she began.

'Doesn't matter,' David cut in. 'You just. Need. To sign. That's all.'

I felt my hackles rise at his aggressive tone. My heart was pounding and I could feel the blood pumping around my body; I had not felt so under threat since I had encountered the yellow-eyed alley-cat during my search for Eddie.

Debbie removed her glasses and placed them on the table. 'It matters to me, David,' she said quietly. 'As I told you on the phone, I plan to write to the solicitor and explain why I must decline your mother's legacy to

Molly, but I intend to do it in my own words.' She glanced at the hovering pen nib. 'And I intend to sign it with my own pen,' she added as an afterthought. She flipped the cardboard folder shut and held it across the table. 'I'm sorry, David, but I won't be signing your letter,' she said firmly.

David's face had turned a vibrant puce colour. 'I always knew you were up to something,' he muttered darkly, clicking the lid back onto his pen and snatching the folder from Debbie's hand.

'I beg your pardon?' Debbie said, looking scandalized.

'Why else would you visit my mother so often? Make all that effort to go to the care home to visit a complete stranger. I knew there was something fishy about it.'

Debbie's mouth had fallen open. 'Margery wasn't a complete stranger, David,' she exclaimed. 'She was a customer here, and she had been Molly's owner. I was taking Molly to visit her!'

David snorted. 'Oh, come off it. Do you really expect me to believe that? What kind of person would go to all that trouble, so that an old woman with dementia could see a *cat*!' A vein on his temple had begun to bulge, and beads of sweat had broken out on his forehead.

Debbie's breathing was fast and shallow, but she

took time to compose herself before she answered. 'The kind of person who understood what Molly meant to Margery, David. A person like me.'

'Well, I would beg to differ,' he hissed, opening his briefcase and shoving the folder roughly inside. 'I think it's the behaviour of someone who hopes that, if she puts in the hours and visits often enough, she might be remembered by an old woman in her will. *That's* the kind of person I think you are.'

Debbie's face had flushed a shade of pink almost as lurid as David's, and her bottom lip started to tremble. She surveyed the table, watery-eyed, taking in the rapidly cooling cups of tea and untouched plate of biscuits. 'I think maybe you should leave,' she said in a dignified voice.

David pushed his chair back noisily across the flag-stones and began to pull on his jacket. 'You know – letter or no letter – don't go getting any ideas about this legacy,' he said darkly. 'There's not a court in the land that would give any credence to the deathbed scrib-blings of a senile old woman. And if necessary,' he practically spat, 'I'm prepared to go to court to prove it.'

With that, he grabbed his briefcase and marched out of the café, slamming the door so hard that the window frame behind me shook, and I thought the little brass bell above the door might break.

Still seated at the table, Debbie dropped her head

and her shoulders started to heave. I jumped down from my cushion and walked quickly over to her. She was sobbing silently, fat tears rolling down her cheeks and dropping onto her apron. When I brushed against her leg, she glanced at me with a look of stunned disbelief.

'Oh, Molly,' she cried. 'What have I done?'

19

'Well, that sounded like a roaring success,' Linda smirked over the banisters as Debbie trudged upstairs to the flat.

Too numb with shock to register her sister's sarcastic tone, Debbie staggered into the living room and collapsed onto the sofa. I padded across the rug to my shoebox and watched as Linda shoved the snoring Beau off the other sofa cushion and sat down.

'I can't believe it,' Debbie whispered hoarsely. 'I can't . . . I didn't . . . Linda, what just happened?' she wailed, with a stricken look.

'From what I heard, Debs,' said Linda earnestly, 'you stood up for yourself admirably. David was trying to bully and humiliate you, the self-righteous little pr—'

'But, Linda,' Debbie cut in, 'that's beside the point! His mother's just died, and I refused to sign his letter. And now he thinks I'm a gold-digger, who only visited

Margery because I wanted her money, and he's going to take me to court and . . .' As the gravity of the situation hit her afresh, Debbie's eyes filled with tears and she let out a moan.

Linda placed a supportive hand on her sister's arm. 'Don't worry, Debs, he'll calm down,' she soothed. 'I'm not surprised you didn't sign his letter, given the way he spoke to you. In fact, I would have thought far less of you if you had signed it.'

Debbie looked tearfully at Linda. 'Really?' she asked meekly.

'Absolutely!' Linda insisted. 'How dare he turn up here and demand that you sign something on the spot. Dead mother or no dead mother, he's got a bloody nerve, the smug little w—'

'But, Linda,' Debbie interjected, 'he was only asking me to do something I had said I would do. I told him I would renounce the legacy and then, when it came to it, I refused! Oh my God, he must think I'm crazy.' She pulled a tissue out of her apron pocket and blew her nose noisily. Then she began to rock back and forth, her eyes glassy and unfocused, muttering, 'What have I done?' under her breath.

Linda appraised her sister. 'Debbie,' she said briskly, 'you need to pull yourself together.' Debbie appeared not to hear her and continued to rock silently. 'What happened just now was very unpleasant,' Linda conceded, 'but it can all be sorted out. Nobody is going to take anybody to court.'

At the mention of court, Debbie's eyes darted fearfully to Linda and her rocking redoubled in intensity.

'Oh, for goodness' sake,' Linda tutted. She leant back against the sofa, looking thoughtful. 'You know, there is another way of looking at this,' she said.

'Oh, really, what's that?' replied Debbie wanly.

'Well, what just happened with David has given you time to think, at least. The way I see it, David just showed you who he really is, which is a thoroughly unpleasant bully.'

Debbie gave an acquiescent shrug. 'So?'

'Well,' Linda went on, 'I'm starting to wonder if there was a reason why Margery didn't want him to inherit . . .' She trailed off, directing a significant look at her sister.

Debbie's brow furrowed. 'What are you saying, Linda? That he bullied his mother? That he . . .'

Linda hunched forward, clasping her hands tightly together in her lap. 'I don't know that for sure, Debbie. How could I? All I'm saying is, maybe it would be wrong to dismiss Margery's wishes out of hand.' Her face was full of fervour, and two spots of pink had appeared in her cheeks. 'There might have been more going on in that family than you realize. Margery may have had good reason for not wanting to leave her estate to David.' Linda raised her eyebrows and gave a slow, emphatic nod.

A look of panic started to spread across Debbie's face. 'Oh, God,' she cried pitifully. 'Oh, Linda, why did you have to say that? Now I *really* don't know what to do!'

Linda sat back again and glanced down at Beau, who had been staring longingly at her lap since being dislodged from the sofa cushion. Taking her look as a tacit invitation, he bounded onto the sofa, making a nest for himself in the space between the sisters. Debbie had stopped rocking and was staring blankly into the middle distance as if in a trance, while Linda picked at her chipped nail varnish. Between them, Beau seemed blissfully unaware of the drama unfolding around him; he cocked one leg sideways and began licking his genitals noisily.

In the shoebox, my tail twitched with frustration. It should have been me sitting on the sofa beside Debbie, not Beau, and I should have been comforting her, rather than Linda. My calm, purring presence would have soothed her far more than Linda's glib reassurances and dark speculations. Admittedly, I could not tell Debbie how proud I had been of the dignified way she had handled David, or that I knew that what she felt about Margery had nothing to do with money. But

I was confident that, without saying a word, I could have done more to help her than Linda.

It was only Sophie's unexpected appearance at the top of the stairs, and her blasé announcement that she would be home for dinner, that seemed to lift Debbie out of her trance. She disappeared into the hallway to greet her daughter and was soon ensconced in the kitchen, preparing a meal for the three of them.

For several days after David's visit the atmosphere in the flat was stiff with tension. Debbie seemed preoccupied, as if she were present in body, but not in spirit. She didn't mention Margery, David or the legacy at all, and steadfastly ignored Linda when she attempted, with varying degrees of subtlety, to talk to her about it. Linda found numerous ways to ask the same question, always in the same casual voice – 'Have you heard anything more from David?', 'Has the solicitor been in touch?', 'Have you thought any more about what I said?' – and 'Nope,' Debbie answered flatly each time, before standing up to leave the room.

Linda's frustration at her sister's stonewalling grew more apparent over time; her silent eye-rolls gave way to tuts of annoyance, until on one occasion she called pompously, 'You can't bury your head in the sand forever!' at Debbie's retreating back. To no avail. With Debbie stubbornly refusing to talk about it, Linda had no choice but to let the issue of the inheritance drop, and Margery's legacy became a taboo subject around the flat.

It occurred to me one morning, as I watched them eating breakfast in silence, that there were now so many issues being avoided by the sisters that it was a miracle they found anything to say to each other at all. Like Margery's legacy, the question of when Linda would move out also remained out-of-bounds; Debbie had either forgotten the promise she'd made to Jo, or was simply too taken up with Margery's legacy to contemplate revisiting the subject. Sophie continued to spend no more than the bare minimum of her time in the flat, but this too was something that Debbie seemed reluctant to address openly.

Eddie had been missing for over a month, but his and Jasper's continuing absence was similarly never mentioned, although I heard Debbie call their names into the alleyway every morning, and I knew she missed them keenly. As if that weren't enough, my fear that John would decide he'd had enough of us seemed to have been proved right. Almost a week had passed since Debbie and John's last date-night, when things had turned sour over the issue of the legacy. As far as I was aware, they had not spoken since.

All of which meant that conversation in the flat consisted of little more than discussing the day-to-day concerns of the café, and deciding what to have for dinner. Linda tried to cheer Debbie up one evening by suggesting that they buy a Christmas tree for the café.

'Mmm, not just yet, Lind, it's still a bit early,' Debbie replied apathetically.

'Come on, Debs, it's only a few weeks away. Show a bit of festive spirit! It'll be good for business,' Linda urged, but Debbie was not to be persuaded. The fact that Christmas was looming ever closer was something that she, like me, seemed unwilling to acknowledge.

Her plans for a tree may have been thwarted, but that did not stop Linda doing her best to impose a festive mood on the café by stealth. She filled the table vases with sprigs of holly and, one morning, I discovered she had pinned a string of fairy lights around the window frame overnight.

'Don't worry Debs, they're very tasteful,' she reassured her sister, as I sniffed disapprovingly at the plastic stars looped around my cushion.

A couple of days later, Linda returned from the market brandishing a large bunch of green foliage.

'Look, Debs,' she said excitedly, 'some mistletoe to go above the cat tree. I'm going to hang a photo of Ming from it – we can call it *Ming-istletoe!*'

'Whatever you say, Linda,' Debbie replied wearily. She watched with folded arms as Linda clambered onto a chair and attempted to fasten the mistletoe to one of the ceiling beams. She had been fiddling around with string and drawing pins for a few moments, craning her neck awkwardly, when Debbie said with a mischievous smile, 'If we're going to have *Ming-istletoe*, Linda, surely we should also deck the halls with *boughs of Molly?*' There was a moment's silence, during which Debbie bit her lip to conceal a smile.

'Hmm, I suppose we could,' Linda replied vaguely. 'Why don't you take charge of that, Debs?'

'Maybe I will,' Debbie replied primly, heading back into the kitchen.

The following day, Linda came bustling through the door just after closing time. 'Guess what I just found in the pet shop?' She grinned, swinging a plastic carrier bag onto the counter.

Debbie wandered closer as Linda pulled the bag open and rooted around inside.

'A Santa hat – for a cat!' she exclaimed, pulling out a miniature Christmas hat from the bag. 'Isn't it just the cutest thing you've ever seen?' The red, pointed hat was fringed with white fur, with a fluffy bobble at the tip. 'Look, there are slits for the ears – isn't it just *hilarious?*' she preened, holding the hat up for Debbie's approval.

Debbie sighed. 'Yes, Linda, it's very cute, but do you really think any of the cats will wear it?'

Taking this as a challenge, Linda spun around in search of a cat to model her purchase. Purdy happened to be striding across the café on her way to the cat flap, and was shocked and distinctly unamused to find herself scooped under the belly by Linda and carried across the room. *This should be interesting*, I thought, when Purdy was plonked ignominiously on the counter. She had begun to growl before Linda had even removed the item from its cardboard packaging and, when she lowered the hat towards Purdy's head, her growl turned into high-pitched shriek of warning. 'Come on now, Purdy, be a good girl,' coaxed Linda. Purdy's ears were pressed flat against her head and the whites of her eyes were showing.

'Linda, I really don't think—' Debbie warned, but it was too late.

Linda, smiling rigidly, placed one hand around Purdy's shoulder blades to steady her, and began to lower the hat over Purdy's flattened ears with the other hand. There was a furious explosion of hissing and spitting, then Linda swore loudly, dropped the hat and yanked her hands away from Purdy. 'Ow!' she shouted, sucking her bleeding knuckles. Purdy leapt down from the counter and streaked across the café to the door. 'That cat's vicious,' Linda complained, glaring at the swinging cat flap through which Purdy had fled.

'No, Linda, she's not vicious,' Debbie explained patiently. 'She's just a cat. There's a reason why you don't tend to see cats wearing hats. They're not big fans of hats, as a rule.'

'Huh,' Linda grunted, picking up the rejected item from the counter. 'Well, maybe that's true of some cats. But I bet Ming would wear it,' she said ruefully. She glanced across the room at Ming, who was curled up sound asleep on her platform. 'Although Ming's ears are so big, I'm not sure they'd fit through the holes,' Linda said disappointedly, waggling her bloodied fingers through the slits in the felt.

The corners of Debbie's mouth began to curl upwards. 'Maybe, when it comes to pet costumes, Beau might be a little more . . . compliant?' she suggested.

Linda said nothing, but returned her clenched fist to her mouth, sucking her knuckles solemnly. Debbie stood opposite her at the counter, struggling to supress a smile. Linda looked at her reproachfully. "S'not funny,' she said, her words muffled by the fistful of knuckles in her mouth.

Debbie's shoulders started to shake and she bit hard on her lip. 'Sorry, Lind, it's just – you should have seen your face!'

Linda removed her hand from her mouth. 'Debbie, don't laugh. It really hurts!'

Debbie's upper body was now shuddering with laughter and a sudden snort escaped from the back of her throat. 'Santa hats for cats! You really don't know very much about cats at all, do you?' she squeaked, while Linda glared at her. Debbie placed one hand over her mouth and stared fiercely at the till, doing everything she could to bring her fit of giggles under control.

Still sucking her injured hand, and with a look of hurt disappointment, Linda turned away from the counter and stomped upstairs.

Wiping tears of laughter from her eyes, Debbie picked up the discarded hat and dropped it into the bin.

I blinked at her approvingly, and not just because she had thrown the wretched hat away. For the first time in a long while, Debbie had found something to laugh about. The fact that her laughter had been at Linda's expense made my pleasure all the sweeter.

20

'Deb, there's another letter here from the solicitor,' said Linda, picking up the morning's post from the door-mat. Placing the envelope bearing the solicitor's insignia uppermost on the pile, she handed the mail to Debbie.

Debbie regarded the letter warily, as if it were a grenade at risk of exploding in her hand. 'I'll deal with that later,' she muttered, tucking it on the shelf beneath the till.

Linda moved between the tables, ostensibly refilling the sugar bowls, but watching her sister keenly out of the corner of her eye.

Later on, upstairs in the flat, Debbie was in the kitchen when Linda slipped in after her. 'What did that letter from the solicitor say?' she asked, gathering cutlery from the drawer.

'I don't know, I haven't opened it yet,' Debbie

admitted, then added morosely, 'It's probably a court summons.'

'Of course it's not a court summons, Debs. Don't be ridiculous,' Linda tutted. 'You can't put off dealing with it forever, you know,' she chided.

From my vantage point in the hallway, Linda's legs blocked much of my view, but when Linda shoved the cutlery drawer shut with her hip, I glimpsed Debbie twitchily brushing away her fringe – a nervous habit that I had begun to notice in her with increasing frequency of late.

'Have you thought about what I said, Debs, that maybe Margery—' Linda continued, but Debbie stopped her before she could finish.

'Yes of course I've thought about it, Linda,' she snapped. 'I've thought about very little else for the last week or so.' Although her face had disappeared behind her sister's body, there was no mistaking Debbie's defensive tone.

Linda produced the unopened solicitor's letter from her back pocket. 'Well, come on then – there's no point prolonging the agony,' she said decisively, holding the letter out.

I heard Debbie sigh, followed by the sound of ripping paper as she tore the envelope open.

'Well?' Linda sounded impatient.

'It's not a court summons,' Debbie answered, sounding relieved. 'They're just asking me if I've made a decision about the legacy. Impressing upon me the *urgency of having the matter resolved quickly.*'

Linda tapped the cutlery against the side of her thigh. 'Hmm, I bet David's behind that,' she said shrewdly. 'He must be all over the solicitor like a rash.'

'Well, I guess he just wants to know what's going on,' said Debbie meekly. 'Which is fair enough, I suppose . . .'

Linda snorted dismissively. Turning on her heels, she strode past me, gripping the knives and forks tightly, like a weapon.

No sooner had Debbie brought their food through and sat down at the table than Linda turned to face her. 'Now, Debbie, there's something I'd like to put to you,' she said, with an ingratiating smile.

'Sounds ominous,' Debbie remarked.

'Well, it's a business proposition, actually,' Linda explained.

Debbie assumed an expression of polite curiosity while, in my shoebox, I wondered what new item of Ming-based merchandise Linda was about to suggest.

'I've been working in the café for a while now,' Linda began, somewhat pompously, 'and, as you know, I've been trying to bring the benefit of my marketing expertise to the role.' The merest flicker of a sardonic smile passed across Debbie's face as she inclined her head in acknowledgement. 'I've been thinking hard about Molly's – its strengths and weaknesses – and where it can go from here.' Again, Debbie gave a single nod. 'Now, don't get me wrong,' Linda went on, 'the café is *fantastic*. It's popular, the cats are great and, most importantly, it's making money.'

At this, Debbie raised an eyebrow in a way that communicated – to me, at least – a wish for Linda to get to the point.

'But the problem with your current business model, Debs, is that it's just not scalable,' Linda intoned gravely.

'Scalable?' Debbie frowned.

'That's right,' said Linda. 'It's all well and good having a little café, Debs, but you really need to be planning ahead. These are tough times for small businesses, and you've got a lot of competition here in Stourton.'

'What competition?' asked Debbie, perplexed. 'There aren't any other cat cafés in Stourton – or anywhere else in the Cotswolds, for that matter.'

'Not yet there aren't,' shot back Linda. 'But how long do you think that will remain the case, once people start to get wind of Molly's success? Do you really think you're going to have a captive market of crazy cat ladies forever?'

'I . . . I don't . . .' Debbie stammered, the wind taken out of her sails.

Linda shook her head sadly, with the air of someone being the reluctant bearer of bad news. 'It's a jungle out there, Debs, and if your business isn't growing, it's dying.'

Debbie's composed neutrality had been replaced by a look of confusion, mingled with alarm. 'But how can Molly's be scalable? There's only one Molly, and only one café. I don't—'

'Debs,' Linda interrupted sternly. 'Let me spell it out for you.' Suddenly she spun round in her chair and looked straight at me. 'What do you see over there in that shoebox?' she asked, fixing me with a cold stare.

Mirroring her sister, Debbie turned to face me. 'I see . . . Molly,' she answered dubiously.

'And what is Molly?' Linda smiled.

Debbie paused. She wore the expression of someone who suspected she was walking into a carefully laid trap. 'A cat?' she asked.

Linda grinned; Debbie had given exactly the answer she was expecting. 'She might be a cat to you, Debs,' Linda observed loftily, 'but to me, she's a brand.'

Debbie and I stared at Linda with matching looks of utter incomprehension.

Linda flung one arm out, pointing at me with a chipped pink talon. 'That cat, sitting over there in that shoebox, has brand potential.' She was almost glowing with the fervour of her conviction. 'Or, rather, her name does. Personally, I've always felt Ming would be a better brand-ambassador than Molly, but it's too late to change the name now.' At this, Linda gave a disappointed sigh as she contemplated the commercial glory that might have been, had the café been named after Ming rather than me.

Debbie looked dumbstruck, and my head was reeling. Very little that had come out of Linda's mouth since she had uttered the words 'business proposition' had made sense to me. I didn't understand about business models, captive markets or scalability. The only thing I was certain of, as I sat in the relentless glare of Linda's professional scrutiny, was that I had absolutely no desire to become a 'brand'. It was quite enough of a challenge just being a cat.

'Think about it, Debs. Do you really want to still be clearing tables, and cashing up tills and . . . changing litter trays, in your sixties?' Linda wheedled.

'The cats don't use litter trays,' Debbie objected meekly.

'You know what I mean,' Linda retorted with a dismissive flutter of her beringed fingers. 'Wouldn't it be nice to delegate some of the more . . . hands-on aspects of the job?' She cast a sly glance in my direction, and I bristled at the implication that I was one such hands-on aspect.

Debbie opened and closed her mouth a few times, but no words came out.

'Look, I know it's a lot to take in,' Linda said coolly. 'There's no rush to make a decision, but I think it wouldn't hurt for you to start thinking about the future a bit more. After all, you're no spring chicken, are you? You'll be fifty in a couple of years, and your knees are already suffering from being on your feet all day, aren't they?'

Debbie gave a reluctant nod.

'Do you think you can carry on waiting tables until you retire?' Linda pressed, with a tight-lipped smile.

Debbie shrugged submissively.

'Nobody wants to think about growing old, but you've really got to start planning ahead, Debs. You know I'm right.'

Linda sat back triumphantly in her chair. Opposite her, Debbie's head was bowed and she wore the hang-dog expression of a chastised child.

'With my help, Debs, we could build the brand together,' Linda bore on. 'Within five years there could be branches of Molly's all over the Cotswolds.'

Debbie fiddled with her hair, gazing at the floor by her feet. 'But, Linda,' she said finally, 'what if I don't want to be responsible for a chain of cafés? It's enough responsibility just keeping this one going.'

'That's *exactly* my point, Debs,' Linda riposted brightly. 'With me as your business partner, and a management team in place, you wouldn't need to bother yourself with all the day-to-day responsibilities any more – you could delegate all of that.'

Debbie looked blank, as if she had run out of objections in the face of Linda's relentless sales pitch. She sat in silence for a few moments, trying to gather her thoughts. Eventually she said, 'But how would I pay for this *brand expansion*? Molly's is doing well at the moment, but to think about taking on new premises . . . I haven't got the money for . . . Oh!' A look of horror spread across her face, as Linda broke into a broad grin.

'But you could afford it, couldn't you, Debs, if you used Margery's legacy to pay for it?'

Debbie held up her hands, palms outwards, fingers spread. 'No way, Linda – that's out of the question!' she exclaimed, her eyes round with horror.

'Is it, Debs? Says who?' Linda was hunched forward earnestly. 'Margery left that money to Molly, remember, to make sure she would always be looked after. And what better way to look after Molly's interests than to make sure that her future – and the café's, and yours – is secure?'

Debbie lowered her hands to her lap and her head drooped. She looked defeated.

'Just promise me you'll think about it, Debs,' Linda pleaded. 'It's what Margery would have wanted.'

21

The following day brought ominous grey clouds scudding low across the sky, and by lunchtime the rain had arrived, driving down on the parade in icy sheets. The thought of Eddie enduring the wintry conditions alone, outdoors and without shelter, consumed me. In spite of the weather, I slipped out and made straight for the alleyway, to curl up beneath the fire escape. Hearing the relentless pounding of raindrops on the iron steps above me, and feeling the winter chill seep into my bones, was a kind of penance, as if I was sharing, at least to some degree, Eddie's suffering.

As I made my way back from the alleyway that evening, I rounded the corner to see Jo on the cobbles in front of the café. She was battling to steady her umbrella against the lashing rain, clutching a bag from the Indian takeaway close to her body with her free hand. I broke into a run and slipped in behind her when she opened the door and a blast of cold air rushed into the café with us, causing the paper napkins to flutter in their holders and the window blinds to tap against the glass.

'Hiya, Debs, food's here,' Jo shouted, shaking out her umbrella on the doorstep. She walked across the flagstones, pausing by the cat tree to deliver an amused double-take at the photo of Ming suspended from the bunch of mistletoe.

'It's *Ming-istletoe*. Linda's idea,' Debbie explained, deadpan, as she emerged from the kitchen carrying a bottle of wine and two glasses.

'Of course,' Jo murmured, stifling a smile.

She deposited the bag of food on the counter and walked over to the fireplace. Purdy, who had been spread out on the flagstones, jumped up and wrapped herself around Jo's ankles, scent-marking her jeans enthusiastically with the sides of her mouth.

'Hello, Purdy,' Jo cooed, bending over to rub her briskly around the whiskers. I could hear Purdy's purr from the windowsill. 'So, how're things with you, Debs?' Jo asked, drying the backs of her rain-soaked legs in the warmth from the stove.

Debbie made a face that was half-grimace, half-smile, then pulled something out of her back pocket. 'Have a read of that,' she said despondently, handing the folded envelope to Jo. The letter had arrived in the post that morning; I had recognized the solicitor's insignia, and noticed how Debbie had swiftly plucked the envelope off the mat and stuffed it in her apron, looking around furtively to make sure Linda hadn't seen.

'Hmm, they're turning up the pressure, aren't they?' Jo said, casting her eyes over the letter's contents while Debbie gathered plates and cutlery.

'I can hardly blame them,' replied Debbie. 'They need to know what I plan to do, but . . .' Her posture slumped and she stared at the crockery in front of her.

'But, what?' Jo asked. 'I thought you'd already decided to decline the legacy.'

'I had, Jo!' said Debbie fervently. 'But that was before Linda started going on about how Margery might not have wanted David to inherit. She thinks David's trying to bully me and that I should respect Margery's wishes and . . . Oh, I just don't know any more,' she wailed.

Jo pulled a stool towards the counter and sat down, hungrily ripping open a paper bag of poppadoms.

'She's making me doubt myself, Jo,' Debbie continued, looking dejected. 'Am I being naive for thinking the money should go to David, regardless of Margery's will? I know how much Molly meant to Margery, and David certainly isn't the easiest of people—'

'That sounds like an understatement, Debs,' Jo interjected, taking a bite of crispy poppadum.

Debbie's head dropped. 'He was awful, Jo, I've never felt so belittled by anyone in my life,' she admitted. 'But that doesn't make it right to disinherit him, does it?' she asked, her eyes round with worry.

'There's no easy answer,' Jo agreed. 'But Linda is right about one thing. A bit of financial security for you and Sophie wouldn't go amiss, would it?'

Debbie winced. 'You think I don't know that?' she asked. 'That's what's so horrible about this whole situation. Linda knows I've got no pension, and no one to depend on financially. She knows that thinking about the future terrifies me, and she's using it to justify taking the money.'

Jo did her best to convey sympathy whilst simultaneously shovelling a handful of poppadum shards into her mouth.

'If it makes you feel any better, Debs,' she said, as they moved their meal over to a table and sat down, 'I know exactly what you mean about financial security, or lack thereof.'

Debbie pulled herself out of her torpor and looked at her friend with concern. 'Business still slow?' she asked kindly.

'Stourton's changed, Debs,' Jo complained. 'My humble hardware shop isn't in keeping with the place any more. We don't fit in with all the beauty salons and designer boutiques and . . . cat cafés all over the place.'

Debbie poured out two large glasses of wine. 'On behalf of the cat cafés, I apologize,' she said sincerely, handing a glass to Jo. 'But people will always need Hoover bags, surely?' she asked hopefully.

'That's true, Debs, but they can get them from the market, can't they? Just like they can get most of what I stock from the market.'

Debbie gave her friend a sympathetic look and there followed a sisterly silence while the two of them ate and drank.

'I've got to be honest, Debs,' Jo said gloomily. 'If someone left Bernard money in their will, I'd think very seriously before turning it down.' She managed a half-smile and took a gulp of wine.

'Well, it could happen,' Debbie replied, determinedly upbeat. 'I'm sure there must be a rich benefactor out there somewhere, with a soft spot for arthritic Labradors.'

'Arthritic Labradors who are slightly incontinent and a bit smelly,' Jo clarified.

Debbie chuckled. 'How is Bernard, anyway?' she enquired.

Just as Jo had always taken an interest in me and the kittens, Debbie also felt an affectionate fondness for Jo's dog.

'Oh, he's plodding on, bless him,' answered Jo. 'I took him to see my dad last weekend on the farm. They were like two peas in a pod, wheezing and limping around the yard together.' She was smiling, but her eyes looked damp.

There was a sudden rattle and tinkle, followed by a gust of night air as the café door opened. Debbie and Jo both looked up, surprised by the unexpected interruption.

'Oh, hi, sweetheart,' Debbie said, twisting in her chair to see Sophie standing on the doormat. 'You're home early.'

Sophie shrugged. 'My plans changed. What're you eating?' she asked, drawn towards their table by the spicy aroma of their food.

'Indian. There's plenty left. Why don't you join us?'

Sophie stood beside them, considering the offer. 'Okay,' she said, and disappeared into the kitchen to fetch a plate.

'So how are you?' Jo asked, when Sophie had pulled up a chair alongside them and set about heaping her plate with lukewarm curry. 'I've hardly seen you recently.'

'That's because she's hardly ever here!' Debbie chipped in, with a pointed look at her daughter.

'And why do you think that is, Mum?' Sophie riposted drily.

There was a pause, during which Jo glanced from mother to daughter. 'I guess it must be a bit . . . crowded . . . in the flat at the moment?' Jo said diplomatically.

'You could say that,' replied Sophie, a distinct edge of bitterness to her voice. She tore off a chunk of doughy naan bread and dipped it into the sauce on her plate.

Next to her, Debbie had assumed a miserable expression and seemed to have sunk lower in her chair. Jo carried on eating, eyeing the pair of them surreptitiously.

'So,' Jo said, in a 'changing the subject' voice. 'What do you think about Margery's legacy, Soph? What do you think your mum should do?' At this, Debbie's body visibly tensed.

'I dunno, really,' Sophie shrugged. 'I think it's a bit of a weird thing to do, leave all your money to a cat. But then I also think David sounds like a bit of a d—'

'Sophie!' Debbie warned.

Sophie rolled her eyes, continuing to muse on the dilemma as she chewed. 'I think,' she said at last, 'that even if you're not going to keep the money, you should string it out for as long as possible. Make David sweat over it. At the very least, that might teach him not to go around treating people like sh—'

'All right, thank you Sophie,' Debbie said sternly, sitting up straight to address her daughter.

'She's got a point though, Debs.' Jo laughed. 'It might not be such a bad idea to sit tight till New Year. Give yourself time to think about it, before you decide one way or the other.'

'And prolong the agony even further?' Debbie grimaced. 'No, thanks. I don't want to receive a court summons on Christmas Eve, if it's all the same to you.' She heaved a sigh and slumped back down in her chair with an air of self-pity.

'I suppose,' Jo replied, glancing at Sophie, who responded with an eye-roll. 'What's John got to say about it?' Jo asked, hopefully. But the mention of John merely made Debbie's shoulders sag still further.

'Not much,' she said in a long-suffering voice. 'I haven't heard from him for a couple of weeks. I expect he's had enough of me.'

A gloomy hush settled on the table. It seemed that the more Jo tried to raise Debbie's spirits, the more determined she was to see the worst in her situation. No one spoke for several minutes until, eventually, Sophie broke the silence.

'Oh, for God's sake, Mum,' she hissed irritably. 'Enough with the pity-party.'

'Pardon?' Debbie replied, looking stung.

'Well, are you surprised you haven't heard from John?' Sophie snapped. 'The last time you saw him, you practically bit his head off about the legacy.'

Debbie's brow furrowed indignantly, and she looked at Jo for backup. But Jo was staring hard at her wine glass, keen not to get involved.

In spite of Jo's presence, Sophie made no attempt to soften her accusatory tone. 'Honestly, Mum, you don't get it, do you? First, you were so wrapped up in the whole Linda saga, and now in the whole legacy saga, that you seem to have forgotten that other people have feelings and might have stuff going on in their lives, too. You're not the only one with problems, you know.'

Debbie stared at Sophie with a hurt look. 'But I didn't . . . I'm just trying to do the right thing by everyone, Soph. I didn't ask for any of this—'

'I know you didn't ask for any of it, Mum,' Sophie interrupted impatiently. 'We all know that. But instead of letting Linda and David ruin your life, why don't you just get off your backside and do something about it?' Anger flashed in her eyes, and Debbie's mouth had opened, but no words came out. Across the table, Jo was looking increasingly uncomfortable. 'Honestly, Mum,' Sophie continued authoritatively, 'you need to start taking a bit of responsibility for your life. If you think you should decline the legacy, then do it. And if Linda's interference is getting you down, why don't you just tell her to f—'

'Okay, thank you, Soph,' Jo cut in with a tense smile. 'I think you've made your point beautifully.'

Sophie sat back in her chair. Next to her, Debbie looked stunned. 'You're right, Soph,' she said. 'I guess I have been a little . . . self-absorbed recently.' Sophie did not meet her mother's gaze, but a grunt indicated assent. 'And you're absolutely right: I need to make up my own mind about what to do.'

Another grunt.

Debbie placed a hand on Sophie's arm, and her eyes rested on her daughter with an expression of shrewd concern. 'So . . . I guess I've also forgotten to ask what's been going on in your life, haven't I?' she asked.

Sophie was staring at the piece of naan bread in her hands, breaking it into smaller and smaller pieces, until it disintegrated into crumbs on the table.

Jo drained her glass and tilted the empty wine bottle, looking at it with fierce concentration. 'I think I'll just pop out for another bottle,' she murmured, standing up and grabbing her jacket from the counter. Within seconds she was gone from the café, leaving mother and daughter alone. Two spots of pink had appeared in Sophie's cheeks and she looked like she was fighting back tears.

'Well?' Debbie prompted gently.

'Well, since you ask, Matt and I have split up,' answered Sophie, her bottom lip trembling.

'Oh, sweetheart,' Debbie replied, draping her arm

around Sophie's shoulders. 'I'm so sorry. When did that happen?'

'Tonight,' Sophie whispered.

As Debbie leant in, Sophie's restraint suddenly dissolved and she took a deep, shuddering breath. Debbie pulled her daughter towards her, resting Sophie's head against her neck and stroking her hair. As Sophie sobbed, Debbie murmured soothingly into her ear. 'It'll be okay, sweetheart, I promise. Everything's going to be okay.'

22

When Linda emerged from the bathroom the following morning, Debbie was waiting in the hallway for her.

'John's coming round for dinner tonight, Linda, so could you make yourself scarce this evening?'

I peered around the kitchen doorway to watch them. Adjusting her makeshift towel turban, Linda looked taken aback. 'No problem,' she replied compliantly.

'Great, thanks,' said Debbie, heading briskly into the bathroom and locking the door behind her.

Later, when Sophie finally wandered down from her bedroom, puffy-eyed and pale-faced in her pyjamas, Debbie patted a dining chair and beckoned for her to sit down. She disappeared into the kitchen and emerged moments later with a plate of sticky pastries and a mug of hot chocolate, topped with whipped cream and marshmallows.

'There you go, Soph. Sugar and carbohydrate. The best-known cure for a broken heart,' she said, lowering them onto the table.

'Thanks, Mum,' Sophie said, breaking into a smile. 'Did I hear you say John's coming over tonight?' she asked, licking icing off her fingertips.

'Yep,' Debbie said decisively. 'I took the advice of my ever-so-mature seventeen-year-old daughter' – Sophie smiled bashfully – 'and texted him this morning to invite him round, to say sorry for how I've been behaving recently.'

Sophie looked quietly impressed. 'Good on you, Mum,' she said approvingly, taking a noisy slurp of hot chocolate through the swirls of whipped cream.

After breakfast, Sophie retreated to her bedroom, Linda took Beau out for a walk, and Debbie set about tidying the flat with a look of resolute industriousness. I watched from the sofa as she ruthlessly disposed of piles of newspapers, emptied wastepaper baskets and cleared the dining table of its accumulated clutter. Eyeing the mound of Linda's belongings, she marched over to the alcove and shoved as many of her sister's clothes as possible inside the suitcase. When it was full to bursting, she forced it shut and pushed it roughly against the wall next to the pet carrier. Then she dusted the surfaces, and pushed the Hoover around with a look of grim determination. Finally satisfied, she fell heavily onto the sofa next to me. 'That's better, isn't it, Molls?' she panted.

The evening started well. Following her sister's instructions, Linda had gone out and – an added bonus – had taken Beau with her. I padded around the pristine flat, enjoying the change in atmosphere occasioned by their absence. In the living room the lights were dimmed, candles flickered on the table and music played softly on the stereo. Debbie had done a thorough job with the air freshener, and any lingering trace of Beau's musky odour was masked by the artificial scent of freesias. Stalking from room to room, I felt a glimmer of territorial pride; for the first time in ages, the flat felt like our home again.

Debbie and Sophie were in the kitchen when John appeared at the top of the stairs, freshly shaved and smelling of aftershave. He handed a bunch of flowers to Debbie in the hallway, which she accepted with a modest blush.

'Hi, Sophie,' John said through the kitchen doorway, surprised to find Sophie microwaving a meal for herself. 'It's not like you to be home on a Saturday night.'

Debbie, who was filling a vase with water at the

sink, glared urgently at him, shaking her head in warning.

'I . . . er, sorry . . .' John stammered, nonplussed.

'It's all right,' Sophie said, sounding sanguine. 'I split up with Matt yesterday is what Mum's oh-so-tactfully trying to tell you,' she explained.

'Oh, I'm sorry to hear that,' John said sincerely, watching Sophie tip her microwaved dinner onto a plate. 'Tell you what, Sophie,' he said, 'I've done a few plumbing jobs for Matt's mum, so I know where he lives. If you want me to go round and break his legs, just give me the nod.' John tapped the side of his nose conspiratorially.

'Thanks, but I don't think any leg-breaking is called for,' Sophie answered drily.

'Or, at the very least, I could tamper with his central heating. Make sure he's freezing cold over Christmas,' John suggested.

'Thanks, I'll think about it,' Sophie replied with a coy smile, filling a glass of water at the tap and placing it next to her plate on a tray. 'Have fun,' she said to them both, heading out of the kitchen and up to her room.

I followed Debbie and John across the hall to the living room and jumped onto the sofa while they began to eat. I closed my eyes, soothed by the sound of their voices and the clink of cutlery. The ambience in the clean, candlelit room was so calm that in no time I had dozed off, and had just drifted into a dream when I was startled awake by the sound of Linda's voice.

'It's only me, Debs, I'm just dropping Beau off,' she called up the stairs.

The tranquil atmosphere was shattered when, seconds later, Beau came skittering into the living room, leapt onto the sofa cushion opposite me and began to scratch furiously. I glowered at him, but he was too busy scratching even to notice my look of disgust.

When Linda appeared at the living-room door, John stood up courteously, but Debbie remained seated, pointedly ignoring her sister, while continuing to eat her dinner.

'Don't mind me, I'm not staying. I just wanted to drop Beau off before I meet my friends,' Linda explained, with an anxious glance at Debbie. 'How are you, John?' she said warmly, accepting John's polite kiss on the cheek.

'Good, thanks,' John murmured in reply.

Linda hovered in the doorway, taking in the romantic intimacy of the scene. John stood next to her, smiling awkwardly, while Debbie continued to glower at the table. The silence was broken only by the sound of Beau's teeth knocking together, as he scratched at his cheek with his hind paw.

'Well, I'll be off then. Nice to see you again, John,'

Linda said cheerily, determined not to acknowledge the tension in the air. She zipped up her quilted jacket and fished in her pocket for her car keys. Turning to leave, she said casually to John, 'Maybe you can talk some sense into Debbie about this legacy business.'

There was a loud clatter as Debbie let her fork fall against her plate. 'I beg your pardon?' she said, her eyes seeming to darken as she turned to look at her sister for the first time. 'What does that mean, Linda – "talk some sense into me"?' she asked, with a steely coldness.

'I just meant I thought it might be helpful for you to talk it over with John, to see what he thinks,' Linda blustered defensively.

Debbie glared at Linda with unmistakable anger. 'No, Linda, what you meant was: maybe John could convince me to keep the money.' It was a statement rather than a question, but Linda shook her head vehemently. Debbie's eyes shifted to John. 'My sister finds the idea of turning money down difficult to comprehend. She always has.'

John, who was standing just inside the living-room door, equidistant between the sisters, looked at his shoes in embarrassment.

'Deborah! How dare you!' Linda gasped, a flush of outrage rising in her orange-tinged face.

'Oh, for God's sake, Linda. Please, just be honest,' Debbie's voice was strident now. 'You want me to accept the legacy, and you're hoping John will persuade me to do so.'

Linda looked hurt, but she instinctively drew herself up straighter. 'I do think you should accept the legacy, Debbie, but only because I think you should honour Margery's wishes,' she said piously.

'Pah!' Debbie snorted. 'That's rubbish, and you know it. The only reason you're so keen for me to take the money is because *you* want to build a business empire with it. You can't bear the fact that I've made a success of Molly's without your help. Now you want to muscle in on my business to launch your *brand*' – she lingered mockingly over the word – 'and you want to use Margery's money to pay for it.' Debbie's face was rigid with anger.

Linda's mouth had formed an 'O' of scandalized outrage. John looked as if he would rather be anywhere else than caught in the sisters' crossfire.

'I don't know why I'm surprised,' Debbie continued bitterly. 'All you've ever cared about is money.'

'Oh, well, that's just charming,' retorted Linda sharply, rallying now that her initial shock had subsided. 'I've been working in the café – unpaid, I might add – for weeks now. I never heard you complain when I was scraping dirty plates and loading dishwashers for you. I never asked for a penny in wages, did I? If I'd known this was how you felt, then quite frankly I wouldn't have bothered.'

'That's not fair, Linda! We agreed you would work downstairs in exchange for staying here,' Debbie countered.

'Yes, and I've been working my backside off, haven't I?' riposted Linda fiercely. 'Not just being your skivvy and waitress, but doing everything in my power to help market and promote the café. I've got you press coverage, I've devised marketing campaigns, merchandising . . .' At this, Debbie let out a derisory snort and I knew she was thinking about *Ming's Mugs*.

Linda's eyes narrowed. 'You're not going to deny, I hope, that since I launched the Ming marketing campaign, the café's taken more money?' she said reprovingly.

Debbie groaned. 'That's exactly my point, Linda,' she answered shrilly, banging her hand on the table with sufficient force to make Beau stop scratching and look at her. 'You just don't get it, do you? Ming is a cat, not a *marketing opportunity*. And, whether you like it or not, Molly is a cat too, not a *brand*.' Debbie's eyes were blazing with conviction. 'Everything's about money for you, isn't it?' she went on fervently. 'You turn up here, expecting me to take you and Beau in indefinitely, and I'm not allowed to challenge it because *some* of your ideas have brought in a few extra quid to the café.'

When the telephone rang, John looked visibly relieved. He darted across the room to pick up the receiver, placing a hand over his other ear.

Still standing in the doorway, listening to her sister give voice to her pent-up frustration, Linda's eyes had become glassy. 'Well, if I'd known that was how you feel, Debs, I would never have come here. My marriage had broken down, in case you'd forgotten, and I had no one else to turn to. It's all right for you, with your lovely café and cosy flat. Life's not all cupcakes and kittens for everyone, you know. Some of us have real problems to deal with.'

If Linda had hoped this would elicit sympathy from her sister, she was mistaken. '*Real problems?*' Debbie repeated sarcastically. 'Linda, the only problem you've ever had to deal with is how to spend your husband's money. My God, you're still doing it now! Do you think I haven't seen the stash of shopping in Beau's carrier?' At this, Linda blushed deeply, but Debbie wasn't done yet. 'If you want to know about real problems, you should have tried walking in *my* shoes for the last few years. My ex-husband left me bankrupt, with a teenager to bring up on my own, remember?'

Linda looked close to tears, but Debbie showed no sign of relenting; the resentment that had been simmering for weeks had erupted in an unstoppable tide of bitterness and recrimination. 'You've been the same,

Linda, ever since we were little. You've always had a knack for getting other people to bail you out. First it was Mum and Dad, then it was Ray. Now that well is running dry, you can't wait to think of ways to spend my money instead!'

While she was in full flow, John slipped wordlessly past Linda to the hallway, leaving the sisters alone. As the argument had gone on, I had braced myself for histrionics from Linda, of the kind I had witnessed when she first moved in, but in fact she assumed a look of stoic forbearance.

When she finally spoke, her voice was eerily calm and her face expressionless. 'So it's *your* money now, is it, Debs? I thought you said it belonged to Margery's family.' There was a pause, during which Debbie blushed a deep pink. 'Maybe we're not so different after all, Sis,' Linda said coldly.

'I didn't mean . . . I know it's not . . .' I could tell Debbie was horrified by her slip of the tongue.

The tension between them was palpable, although apparently not to Beau, who, his itch satiated, had fallen asleep and begun to snore on the sofa cushion.

'Fine,' said Linda suddenly. 'If that's the way you feel, then I won't impose on your generosity any longer.' She strode across the room and grabbed her suitcase from the alcove. 'Come on, Beau!' she shouted.

Waking with a groggy bark, Beau stared wildly

around him, as Linda scooped him up. Dragging the suitcase clumsily behind her, with the bewildered dog tucked under her arm, she walked, with as much dignity as she could, across the room.

In the doorway, she looked back over her shoulder. 'Of course, legally, the money isn't yours or Margery's. It's Molly's,' she sneered, shooting a spiteful glance at me. 'Maybe you could save yourself a lot of heartache by asking Molly what she'd like done with it.'

Before Debbie could answer, Linda was gone. Debbie could do nothing but stare at the empty doorway, listening as Linda's suitcase thudded heavily down the stairs behind her.

I felt my heart thumping in my chest. I was furious that Linda had spoiled Debbie's chance to make amends with John, and livid that she had used me as a weapon in their argument. But, underneath my anger, what stung most was the sickening realization that Linda was right. Whether I liked it or not, Margery had left her money to me. All the upheaval of recent weeks – from the encounter in the café with David, to the argument with John, and this evening's showdown with Linda – had come about because it had fallen to Debbie to decide what to do about it. There was no denying that Margery's legacy to me was the primary cause of Debbie's anguish. The way I saw it, if anyone was to blame for Debbie's suffering, it was me.

23

As soon as the café door slammed shut, Debbie burst into tears. She staggered to the sofa and dropped down next to me.

'Oh, Molly, what a complete and utter mess,' she cried.

Outside, the wind had picked up and the window-panes rattled ominously in their frames. I climbed onto her lap and began to knead at her legs with my front paws, gazing up into her face and purring. I was desperate to do whatever I could to comfort her, although in truth I knew I was powerless to help.

After a couple of minutes I heard Sophie's soft tread in the hallway. 'Mum?' she said, peering anxiously around the living-room door. Her long blonde hair was loose and she was wearing her pyjamas and slippers. With a look of tender concern, she shuffled onto the sofa next to us. 'What just happened?' she asked.

'Linda just happened,' replied Debbie wanly. 'When she started talking about Margery's legacy, something snapped inside me. I told her exactly what I thought, as you said I should, Soph. You should be proud of me.'

'I am proud of you, Mum.' Sophie laughed. 'But couldn't you have picked a better time to tell her? This was meant to be your romantic night with John, remember?'

Debbie had covered her face with both hands. 'I *know*,' she groaned through her fingers. 'I didn't plan for it to happen like this! Linda promised to stay out for the evening.'

Sophie looked around the room, taking in the plates of half-eaten dinner lying on the table. 'Where's John?' she asked, sounding troubled.

'He left,' Debbie answered listlessly.

'What do you mean he left? Did you have a fight with him, too?'

Debbie shook her head. 'I'm not sure what happened. One minute he was standing between me and Linda, looking like he wished the ground would swallow him up, and the next minute he'd vanished. He must have gone while we were arguing,' she said in a flat, expressionless voice.

Sophie leant back against the sofa arm, frowning. 'Have you tried to call him?' she asked with an air of no-nonsense practicality.

Looking faintly surprised, as though the thought hadn't occurred to her, Debbie craned forward, reaching over me to fish her phone out of her handbag. She tapped at the screen, then held it to her ear, biting her lip nervously. 'It's just going to voicemail,' she said, before leaving a brief message: 'Hi, John, it's me, could you give me a call when you get this?'

'I'm sure he'll be fine, Mum,' Sophie reassured her, as Debbie tossed the phone back into her bag.

'He might have thought he was getting in the way and wanted to give you some privacy.'

'Hmm, I'm not so sure, sweetheart,' Debbie smiled thinly. 'I think he's probably had enough of me and my sister. And who could blame him?' She tried to muster a watery smile.

Sophie was beginning to look pained, as though she had exhausted all the avenues of reassurance she could think of and was struggling to come up with something else to say. 'Shall I make a cup of tea?' she asked at last.

Debbie smiled appreciatively. 'Thanks, Soph, that would be lovely.'

When Sophie had placed the two mugs of tea on the coffee table, she grabbed the remote control and curled up alongside Debbie. Leaning back against the sofa arm, with her feet pressing against Debbie's thigh and her toes touching my fur, Sophie flicked through the television channels. I stretched out lengthways on Debbie's lap and rested my chin on her knees, purring steadily as she absent-mindedly stroked my back. I closed my eyes and indulged in the blissful fantasy that Linda was gone for good and I would never see her again. I lost track of time, as I hovered deliciously between consciousness and sleep for what might have been a few minutes or a few hours, until the sudden slam of the café door reverberated through the flat.

I jerked awake and instinctively sank my claws into Debbie's legs in alarm. 'Ow, Molly!' she exclaimed, sucking air between her teeth as she gently unhooked my embedded claws, one by one, from her knees. 'Hello?' she called in a pained voice, shifting forward on the sofa under me.

Disorientated, I looked around, noticing that the candles had burnt down considerably since I had last noticed them.

'Debbie, it's me. You might want to come down.' It was John. Something in the tone of his voice made my heart lurch.

Debbie and Sophie exchanged surprised looks above my head and we all scrambled to our feet and made for the stairs, Debbie in front, followed by Sophie, with me at the rear. I was still in the stairwell when I heard Debbie gasp, 'Who is it?' Feeling my pulse start to race, I ran down the remaining steps and onto the flagstones.

John was standing on the doormat, unwinding a scarf from his neck. In a split second I noticed the cat carrier on the floor by his feet. Debbie ran forward and crouched in front of the carrier, fumbling to unlock its door. I felt strangely detached, as if I was watching the scene unfold from a distance, or in a dream. When Debbie flung open the door, there was a faint rustle of newspaper and a glimpse of black fur inside. Then, slowly, nervously, Eddie crept out.

He looked around warily, glancing first at Debbie, then at Sophie. Then, at last, his eyes found mine. In an instant, I saw a succession of emotions flash across Eddie's face: relief, shame and happiness – all conveyed in the look he gave me across the flagstones.

I felt a wonderful soaring sensation in my stomach. As Eddie began to walk gingerly towards me, I devoured him with my eyes. What struck me most was his height – I had forgotten how large and grown-up he was. During his disappearance, whenever I had pictured him in my mind, it had been as a gangly kitten. Seeing him in front of me, I was reminded that, outwardly at least, there was nothing kittenish about the rangy tomcat coming towards me.

His bulk was another surprise. I had convinced myself that Eddie would be half-starved after so long

on the streets, and yet I saw no hollow cheeks, no protruding hip-bones or concave flanks. Wherever he had
spent the past few weeks, I realized with a rush of relief
that he had found food. One of his ears bore a fight
scar, and his fur looked a little dull and scantily
groomed. Other than that, he seemed unhurt; his gait
was strong and his eyes as bright as ever.

He stepped closer and his wary expression softened,
as if my proximity was bringing out his vulnerability.
When Eddie sat down in front of me, he lowered his
head and looked up submissively, just as he had when
he was a kitten expecting a telling-off. 'I'm sorry,' he
whispered.

Feeling my throat tighten and my eyes tingle, I leant
towards him, allowing our noses to touch, before nuzzling my face into the fur of his neck. I closed my eyes,
the better to allow my sense of smell to glean all it could
about where Eddie had been. He smelt of hedgerows and
damp earth, but also of furniture polish and log fires and
people.

'Molly, look.'

I opened my eyes, fleetingly annoyed by the interruption. Across the café, Debbie was beaming at me,
one arm extended, her finger pointing across the floor.
I followed her arm and saw that, sitting in front of the
open carrier, with a look of paternal satisfaction, was
Jasper. I stared at him in stunned disbelief and, when he

blinked slowly, his amber eyes twinkling, I thought for a moment that my heart might burst with happiness.

Eddie's deep purr filled the living room as I drew my tongue in long, sweeping movements over his fur, determined to lick away the tangles and make him smell like home again. We were in the shoebox and Purdy was watching us from the sofa arm, her face alert and curious, while Abby and Bella huddled together in the alcove, taking it in turns to peek out from behind Beau's pet carrier. Jasper was sitting proprietorially on the rug in front of the fireplace, where Maisie had sidled up beside him, washing diligently in a manner that I knew was designed to elicit his approval.

On the other side of the room, Debbie and John were at the table, picking at the cold leftovers of their dinner. The candles had burnt down almost to stumps, the long flames dancing vigorously in the draught from the window.

'Someone called while Linda was here,' John explained. 'Said she thought she had your cats. I didn't want to get your hopes up, until I knew for sure. Besides, you were a bit busy at the time, so I just slipped out.'

Debbie smiled ruefully. 'So, where were they?' she asked, popping a piece of cold potato into her mouth.

'A village a few miles south of here. The woman said

Eddie had been visiting her house for a while. She'd assumed he belonged to one of the neighbours, till she asked around and realized no one owned him. Jasper had been hanging around too, but she thought he and Eddie were the same cat, until she saw them both in the garden together. It took her a few days to round them up and get them to vet to be scanned. She thought the vet was joking when he told her both cats were registered to the same owner.' Debbie chuckled.

'But what a coincidence that they ended up together,' Debbie said incredulously. 'They disappeared a good few days apart.' She looked towards the shoe-box, baffled.

'I've given up trying to make sense of what these cats of yours get up to,' John shrugged. 'I've always suspected they're playing us for fools.'

Licking the top of Eddie's head, I glanced towards John, but he had already turned back to face Debbie.

When I had finished grooming him, Eddie quickly fell asleep, his warm body pressed up against me, his legs entwined with mine. Debbie and John had taken their drinks to the sofa, and the conversation had moved onto Linda.

'I know I probably got a bit carried away,' Debbie said regretfully, 'but, to be honest, I'm relieved that she's gone. This business with Margery's legacy, on top of everything else . . . it was just the last straw.' She trailed off, a familiar weary expression flickering across her face.

'I think it was probably long overdue,' John said tactfully. 'Whatever you said to her, it needed to be said.'

Debbie yawned and stretched her legs out across John's lap. 'When I realized you'd disappeared tonight, I thought I'd blown it,' she said with a sleepy smile.

'It would take more than a row with Linda to scare me off,' John reassured her, rubbing her feet.

'You looked as if you wished the ground would open up beneath you,' she teased him. 'But, after the last couple of weeks, when I hadn't heard from you . . .' she persisted, biting her lip anxiously.

'I didn't want you to think I was getting ideas about the legacy – that I wanted you to keep it and was only hanging around for the money. I guess maybe I went a bit too far the other way, backed off too much,' John said apologetically.

'Perhaps just a little,' Debbie replied. Her eyelids were heavy and I could see her chin begin to sink closer to her chest. 'What a day,' she mumbled drowsily. Then her eyes closed and her head lolled sideways onto the cushion.

John stayed on the sofa, watching her sleep for a few minutes, before carefully extricating himself out from under her legs. He lifted the fluffy throw off the arm of the sofa, where Debbie had diligently folded it earlier in the day, shook it and lowered it over her slumbering body. Then he kissed her softly on the head, blew out the candles and left.

24

I awoke the following morning to find the living room bathed in pale, wintry light. It was now the middle of December and, outside the window, the first fluffy snowflakes of the season were twirling in the air, landing softly against the glass. Clearing my head with a vigorous shake, I jumped off the sofa and padded past the shoebox, where Eddie was still fast asleep, his long limbs spilling over the cardboard sides. I leapt onto the windowsill and peered at the alleyway below, where the grey-brown hues of stone and tarmac were rapidly being erased by a blanket of white.

There was no sign of Jasper downstairs, so I nosed through the cat flap and, head bowed against the swirling flakes, hurried around to the passageway. As I walked, my paws left shallow dips in the deepening snow, and soon my paw-pads were soaked and freezing.

I found Jasper in the churchyard, sheltering beneath the low branches of the rhododendron.

'I didn't have a chance yesterday to say thank you, for finding Eddie,' I said, squeezing in alongside him, savouring his familiar scent and the warmth of his body.

'You're welcome,' he replied contentedly.

We sat side by side, watching the snow fall silently in front of us.

'Do you think Eddie's okay, after everything that's happened?' I asked, trying not to betray my maternal anxiety.

'I think Eddie is absolutely fine,' Jasper replied levelly. 'He had to grow up, fast. Learning to fend for himself came as a bit of a shock after such a pampered upbringing.'

I turned away, stung by the implied criticism; Jasper had always let it be known that he thought the kittens were over-indulged, and that they lacked the skills required to lead independent lives.

'But he seems to have worked things out for himself,' Jasper added hastily, sensing my hurt feelings. 'What he lacks in street-smarts, he more than makes up for in charm.' I turned and looked at him, waiting for him to elaborate. 'By the time I found him, he had the whole neighbourhood queuing up to look after him. He could take his pick of at least half a dozen houses. There was never any danger he would go hungry,' he said, in a tone of grudging admiration.

I felt a wave of relief mingled with pride. In retrospect, it seemed obvious that my friendly, loving boy would have no trouble finding people to take care of him.

'That's not to say he didn't want to come home, of course,' Jasper added, giving me an affectionate nuzzle behind the ear, as a delighted purr began to rumble in my chest.

Beyond the shrubbery, the sky had lightened to a milky white and the snowfall was beginning to ease. I edged forward and peered out from under the canopy of leaves. The honey-stoned church looked as though it had been glazed in white icing, and a single, determined robin fluttered from one snow-capped headstone to the next in search of insects.

'Are you coming in for breakfast?' I asked brightly, feeling my stomach start to growl.

Back inside the café, I stood on the doormat and shook the slushy ice crystals from my fur. Eddie had come downstairs and was pacing around the room, methodically scent-marking the table legs with his cheeks. Maisie followed a few steps behind.

'What happened to your ear?' she enquired, a note of sisterly concern in her voice.

Eddie puffed out his chest proudly. 'Got into a fight

with an alley-cat,' he said offhandedly. 'It was no big deal.'

Maisie's eyes widened in alarm and, when Eddie set off towards the armchairs, she trotted keenly after him. 'And what did you do for food in the wild?' she asked eagerly.

Eddie paused and his gaze drifted to a point in the middle distance. 'Hunting, mostly. It's not easy, but you do what you have to, to survive,' he said grandly.

On the doormat, I stifled an inward smile. Eddie's account of his time 'in the wild' differed somewhat from Jasper's version. I wondered whether Maisie would be quite so awestruck if she knew the truth: that Eddie had been doted on by a streetful of surrogate owners for most of his time away. Regardless of his bravado, however, I could not begrudge Eddie the opportunity to bask in his sister's adoring admiration. I knew his blasé demeanour belied the terror he must have felt at finding himself homeless and alone. Let him enjoy his moment of glory, I thought, as I shook myself dry on the warm flagstones.

In the afternoon Debbie appeared at the bottom of the stairs carrying a large cardboard box full of Christmas decorations. She placed it on an empty chair and shouted up the stairwell, 'C'mon, Soph, I need your help.' When Sophie shuffled downstairs a few minutes later, she found Debbie rummaging inside the box. 'Untangle these, will you, love?' Debbie asked, handing Sophie a twisted coil of fairy lights.

With a sigh, Sophie tied her hair back in a messy ponytail and set about unthreading the tangled wires.

Once the decorations had been sorted into messy piles on the table, they started adorning the café. Debbie sang along to Christmas carols on the radio, ignoring Sophie's cringes and eye-rolling, while the kittens did their best to hamper proceedings, jumping in and out of the cardboard box, or leaping up from the floor to swipe at the rustling fronds of tinsel dangling enticingly over the table edge. Ming observed the scene from her platform, with her customary air of curious detachment.

John arrived a little later, hauling a Christmas tree by the trunk. He carefully manoeuvred the tree into position next to the fireplace and snipped away at the netting that encased it. The tree's branches instantly sprang outwards, filling the café with the scent of fresh air and pine forests.

When Jo passed the café window with Bernard plodding along by her side, she tapped on the glass, waving cheerily.

'What do you think of the tree, Jo?' asked Debbie, opening the door to let her in.

'About time too, Debs!' Jo teased, brushing the

snowflakes off her jacket with the back of her hand. Her nose was pink with cold and her knitted bobble hat struggled to stay on over her unruly hair. Bernard waddled into the room after her and, as soon as he was inside, sank down gratefully on the doormat.

'Hello, Bernard, you lovely old boy,' murmured Debbie, bending down to rub his tummy. Bernard's tail flopped up and down on the coir mat, and within minutes he had fallen wheezily asleep.

Debbie passed around tumblers of warm mulled wine and, as the afternoon sky darkened outside, all four of them set about dressing the tree with ornaments and lights. The kittens gamely did their best to bat the baubles off the branches as quickly as they were hung until, worn out by their exertions, they retired to their usual places for a recuperative nap. When the tree was finally finished, Debbie stepped back and looked at it approvingly. 'Ready, everyone?' she asked, with a look of child-like excitement.

She nodded to Sophie to switch off the overhead lights, and a hush descended on the dark room. Even Bernard drowsily raised his head from the floor, sensing anticipation in the air. Debbie flicked a switch and, suddenly, the café was transformed. Everywhere I looked, lights twinkled and glowed. The tree was enrobed in tiny berry-like bulbs that blinked mesmerizingly. A string of white lights wove its way across the mantelpiece, and a wreath of flashing stars framed the serving counter. In the semi-darkness the kittens' and Ming's eyes flashed a luminous green, and I had to look twice to be sure which were cats' eyes and which fairy lights.

'Oh, Debs, it looks beautiful,' Jo exclaimed.

'It does, doesn't it,' Debbie smiled proudly. 'I'm sure Linda would approve,' she added, looking suddenly wistful.

She flicked the overhead lights back on, and the room was flooded with yellow light once more. Bernard emitted a low groan of protest and repositioned himself on the doormat.

'Have you heard from Linda since yesterday?' Jo asked tentatively, as Debbie straightened the row of red stockings hanging from the fireplace.

Debbie shook her head. 'I know what she's like – she'll need some time to cool off before she'll speak to me,' she replied. 'I'll give it a few days, then I'll call her. Besides, I need to let Linda know that I've decided what to do about the legacy.'

The others exchanged surprised looks behind Debbie's back.

'Sounds fair enough,' Jo replied carefully. 'So, if it's not rude to ask, Debs . . . what have you decided?'

Snow still covered the ground on Monday morning

and, with logs crackling in the stove and the festooned tree by the fireplace, there was a definite buzz of Christmas in the air. Debbie had put a sign in the café window – *The boys are back! Welcome home, Eddie and Jasper!* – which lent a frisson of excitement to the festive mood; and before long, Debbie and her waitresses were rushed off their feet. Café regulars and Christmas shoppers streamed through the door, and Eddie was showered with attention, while Debbie dutifully repeated, ad infinitum, the story of how he and Jasper had been found.

It was almost seven o'clock when the staff hung up their aprons and went home. Debbie collapsed onto one of the café chairs, puffing out her cheeks with relief. She had only been there a few seconds when the door tinkled open.

My stomach jolted unpleasantly on seeing David standing on the doormat. His sour demeanour seemed more jarring than ever, now that the café was bedecked for Christmas.

'Oh, hello, David,' Debbie said, turning to look at him over her shoulder. She smiled politely, but I sensed a guardedness in her manner.

David nodded curtly and wiped his wet shoes on the mat, eyeing Debbie suspiciously as she went over to the counter and retrieved a sheet of paper from behind the till. Clutching the piece of paper, she sat down at the nearest table, motioning for David to join her. I couldn't help noticing that, this time, there were no cups of tea or plate of cookies. David sat down opposite her and there followed an awkward silence, during which neither of them seemed to want to be the first to speak.

'So, thanks for coming, David,' Debbie began at last, fingering the sheet of paper nervously. 'You can probably guess why I asked you here: to sort out this business of your mum's legacy.' David inclined his head fractionally, but said nothing. Debbie swallowed, she looked as if she was steeling herself to continue. 'What happened last time we met – all the talk about going to court – I'm sure neither of us wants it to come to that,' she went on, glancing apprehensively across the table.

David blinked at her, but his pinched expression gave nothing away.

Debbie ploughed on bravely. 'Anyway, I've been thinking a lot about Margery, and why she might have wanted to make Molly a beneficiary.' At this, David's lips parted, but Debbie carried on talking before he could speak. 'But I've also been thinking about you, and the fact that you'd only just lost your mum when you found out about this legacy. It can't have been nice to discover that you'd been . . . overlooked, in favour of a cat . . .' She trailed off, glancing nervously at David's hard-set face . . .

'You could say that,' he concurred.

'I think, if it happened to me, I'd be furious,' Debbie prompted.

David frowned at the place mat on the table. 'It was a bit of a shock,' he admitted at last. 'She'd never mentioned anything about it. Not to me, at least,' he said, looking at Debbie warily.

'She never mentioned it to me, either,' Debbie insisted. 'I promise you, David, I had no idea what was in Margery's will. This legacy was as much a shock to me as it was to you.'

David continued to stare sulkily at the place mat.

'Look,' Debbie persisted, 'I said it right from the start: I feel it would be wrong for me to accept your mum's money on Molly's behalf. But I can't ignore the fact that Margery wanted to make sure Molly would be taken care of.'

David had fixed Debbie with an intent look and seemed to be hanging on her every word. On the window cushion, I was also on tenterhooks. Debbie had not confided her plans to anyone, insisting that she needed to speak to David first, so I was as much in the dark as he was. Her agitated demeanour suggested that there was more to be said, that her willingness to decline the legacy would have conditions attached, and that she didn't expect David to like them.

'Things have been . . . tricky in the café recently,' Debbie explained evenly. 'We've been tripping over ourselves – the flat's too small. Put simply, cats need space, and there just isn't enough room for us all here. I've got to consider the welfare of all the cats, not just Molly.'

I felt a flutter of panic in my chest as I listened. I had never heard Debbie talk about us in such starkly practical terms. I had always believed that, when it came to cats, if she could make room for us in her heart, she would find room for us in her home. Why else would she have taken on not just me and the kittens, but Jasper and Ming as well? And yet here she was, talking about us as though we were a mere logistical consideration, and implying that the number of cats currently living in the café exceeded the available space.

'Margery was devoted to Molly. She wanted Molly to live somewhere she would be looked after properly. The way things have been recently, that just hasn't been possible.'

A sickening feeling of dread spread through me. Was I to be the sacrificial victim, the one to be removed from the café environment, so that the other cats would have more space? Did Debbie think that was what Margery would have wanted? Panicking, my eyes flicked towards David. He looked as horrified as I felt, and I wondered if, like me, he thought Debbie was about to ask him to take me in.

Debbie paused, and I could see the sheet of paper quiver in her trembling hands. 'I've written a letter to the solicitor, setting out what I would like to happen. I wanted to show it to you before sending it,' she said steadily.

David took the letter and read it with rapt concentration. I tried to glean something – anything – about the letter's contents from his expression, but his face was infuriatingly blank.

'That's not quite what I was expecting,' he said at last, a wrinkle forming between his brows.

'I thought long and hard about it, David. Margery wanted Molly to be taken care of, and I think my solution will make that possible.'

David grunted, and pinched the bridge of his nose between his thumb and forefinger. For the first time in my life I found myself in the position of depending on David to be my ally. I wanted him to challenge Debbie, to tell her that it was out of the question for him to look after me – that neither of us would be happy with such an arrangement. But he looked deep in thought.

'On balance . . . I think it's fair,' he said finally.

'Good, then I'll get the letter in the post first thing

tomorrow,' replied Debbie, breaking into a relieved smile.

Debbie walked with David to the door. As he was about to leave, he turned to face her. 'My mother was very fond of you, and of Molly,' he said, his eyes darting self-consciously across the floor by Debbie's feet. 'I'm grateful that you took the time to visit her. It meant a lot to her.'

Debbie looked stunned for a moment, and then her composure crumbled. 'Oh, David, come here,' she said, flinging her arms around him in a bear hug.

David's discomfort was evident, but he tolerated the hug, and even lifted one hand to pat Debbie's back.

With a final curt nod, he was gone. Debbie locked the door behind him, puffed her fringe out of her eyes and heaved a huge sigh of relief. As she wearily climbed the stairs, I stared after her in dismay, wondering what on earth it was that David had just agreed to.

25

During our walk that evening, I recounted to Jasper the conversation I had overhead. The moon drifted in and out of sight behind the shifting clouds above us, as Jasper loped along the slush-covered pavement beside me, one ear cocked attentively.

'So, did Debbie say anything *specifically* about rehoming you?' he asked when I had finished.

'No, not specifically,' I admitted. 'But she said there hasn't been enough room for us all recently, and that it's not what Margery would have wanted for me. What else could she have meant?'

We slowed to a halt underneath the elm tree in the square and paused to contemplate the town's festive decorations. Lengths of coloured bulbs were strung between the lamp posts, and the handsome Christmas tree by the town hall glittered with lights. After a few moments' silent deliberation, Jasper glanced at me sideways and said, 'Well, if Debbie thinks there isn't enough room for all the cats, maybe she's planning to rehome Ming.'

'No, it wouldn't be that,' I replied disconsolately. 'If Debbie decided to rehome Ming, she wouldn't need to tell David first. Ming has nothing to do with Margery's legacy.'

'Hmm,' he mused, unconvinced.

A knot of frustration formed in my stomach, as the conviction grew that Jasper thought I was overreacting. Jasper's equability was one of the things I loved about him – it anchored me, when my natural inclination was to worry – but at times his implacability infuriated me. He had never been a pet, and had never experienced the intense attachment to an owner that I had felt for Margery, and that I now felt for Debbie. As an alley-cat, how could Jasper possibly understand how it felt to lose your home and owner, or how terrifying it was to think it might happen again?

I stood up and wandered off dispiritedly, unable to bear his measured attempts to reason away my anxiety. A burst of raucous laughter issued from inside a pub to my left and I instinctively swerved away from the noise, skidding on an invisible patch of ice. As I rounded the corner of the square, I broke into a run, fleeing not only Jasper's scepticism but also my own disappointment that, once again, I was alone in recognizing the threat our family faced. I ran back to the parade, paying scant regard to the cars that rushed past me.

Ming was fast asleep on the cat tree, but Abby and Bella raised their heads drowsily as I pushed through the cat flap into the dark café. Upstairs, Debbie and Sophie had gone to bed and the flat was silent and still. In the living room Eddie was fast asleep in the shoe-box, with his tail draped over the cardboard rim. I jumped onto the sofa and settled my gaze on the rhythmic rise and fall of his chest, taking comfort in the fact that, although I did not know what our future held, at least all my kittens were safe. As I succumbed to the irresistible pull towards sleep, I was aware of a feeling of relief as my worries scattered and my mind drifted into darkness.

I was eating breakfast with the kittens the following morning when I heard Debbie on the phone. 'Hi, Lind, it's me. How are you?'

I swallowed my mouthful and stepped away from the food bowl, allowing Eddie and Maisie to devour greedily the last few biscuits in the bowl.

In the living room Debbie was standing at the window, the telephone pressed to her ear. 'Look, Linda, I think we need to talk. If you're free this evening, why don't you come for dinner?' She wrapped the spiral telephone cord nervously around her finger.

I could picture Linda's face as she considered the invitation, lips pursed, jaw set, still smarting from the humiliation of their last encounter. After a short silence, however, a tinny chirp down the line indicated assent.

My stomach gave a strange jolt. I was certain Debbie was planning to tell Linda about her meeting with David, but I would have to wait until the evening to hear what she had decided to do.

With a whole day to fill before Linda's arrival, I crept downstairs and headed out onto the parade. Christmas was now only a week away, and as I trotted along the cobbled streets I was jostled on all sides by harassed-looking shoppers laden with carrier bags. I hadn't even reached the end of the parade when a sudden hailstorm struck, and my body was pelted with icy pellets that stung, even through my thick fur.

I ran back to the café and rushed through the cat flap. Inside, the kittens had picked up on the excited air of festivity and were more skittish and boisterous than usual, chasing each other up and down the zigzag walkway, and making the customers shriek with laughter. But in my fretful state I couldn't face the ebullient atmosphere, so I kept my head down and slunk between the tables to the stairs. Finally finding some peace and quiet on the living-room sofa, I spent the day dozing and washing, watching the light levels change outside the window as the hours dragged by.

It had been dark for some time when Debbie finally came upstairs at the end of the day. She allowed herself a few minutes to recover, slumped on one of the dining chairs rubbing her knees, before busying herself in the kitchen. I paced the living-room floor agitatedly, both dreading and longing for Linda's arrival.

About twenty minutes later, the tinkle of the bell and the opening and shutting of a door downstairs made my heart lurch.

'Hi, Debs, it's me,' Linda called from below.

I smelt Linda before I saw her, my nose tingling at the cloying scent of her perfume, which preceded her up the stairs. My body tensed as Beau came bounding into view around the banisters, with his pink tongue hanging out. He darted past Linda's legs with a slightly deranged look, skidded into the living room and glee-fully began to smear his damp snout along the edge of the sofa cushions. Firing a withering look at him, I prowled out of the room, keen to keep within earshot of the sisters' conversation.

Debbie emerged from the kitchen with a look of determined good cheer. 'I'm just dishing up,' she said brightly, taking Linda's coat and hanging it on the rack.

'Great,' Linda replied, mirroring her sister's rictus smile.

When they carried their meals through to the dining table, I followed at a discreet distance, glancing sideways at Beau, who was proprietorially ensconced on the sofa cushion. His beady eyes tracked my progress across the rug, and I read some sort of victory in his look, but did my best to ignore him as I climbed into the shoebox. My attention was focused on the other side of the room, where the sisters had sat down on either side of the dining table and started to eat.

They didn't seem to know what to say to each other at first, and when they did at last speak, they made awkward small talk.

'The café's looking lovely. Very Christmassy,' Linda began politely.

'Thanks,' Debbie replied.

A pause, then, 'Where's Sophie this evening?'

'She went Christmas shopping with friends. They've probably gone for a burger.'

I was acutely aware of the clink of their cutlery, and the rattle of Linda's bracelets every time she lifted her glass.

'So, where've you been staying?' Debbie asked, with the slightly tense air of someone who knew she was straying onto dangerous territory.

'With friends,' Linda replied airily.

'Anyone I know?' Debbie persisted.

Linda kept a closed face, but I saw her jaw tightening as she answered, 'Just an old college friend.' She took a sip of wine, hesitated, then said, 'Although, with Christmas so close, I think I'm in danger of overstaying my welcome.' She kept her eyes firmly on her wine glass as she returned it to the table. 'I seem to be making a habit of that, at the moment,' she added wryly.

This comment seemed to be the cue Debbie had been waiting for. She lowered her fork and looked attentively across the table. 'Linda, I don't mean to pry, but . . . what's going on? Have you spoken to Ray?'

Linda pushed her food unenthusiastically around her plate. 'I've heard from his solicitor,' she replied, her voice brittle.

'Has it got to that stage already?'

Linda reached for her glass. 'Yup. Looks like I'll be spending Christmas as a homeless divorcee,' she said, taking a long gulp of wine.

Debbie hunched forward. 'Look, Linda. I met David a few days ago, to talk about Margery's legacy.'

Linda winced. 'Debs, let's not go over that again,' she pleaded. 'You were right – it's none of my business what you do with that money. I don't want to talk about it any more.'

Debbie smiled patiently. 'Linda, hear me out. I wanted to tell you that I've written to the solicitor to decline the legacy.'

If there was a flicker of disappointment in her sister's face, it was so fleeting as to be almost imperceptible. Linda assumed a look of benign impartiality. 'I'm sure you've made the right decision, Debs. You don't need to explain anything to me.' She set her cutlery down on her plate and took a deep, fortifying breath. 'I've been thinking about what you said on Saturday night and . . . you're right. I got carried away with my ideas for the café and the brand and . . . I went too far. I can see that now.'

Debbie had opened her mouth to speak, but Linda ignored her, fixing her gaze on the space above Debbie's shoulder.

'It really hurt when you said I was envious of your success, but perhaps you were right. I think I was a bit . . . surprised to see how you've managed to turn things around, and what a great job you've done with Molly's. I guess I thought that if I got involved in the business some of what you've achieved might rub off on me.' She met Debbie's eyes at last and her lips peeled back into a rueful smile. 'It sounds pathetic, really.'

'Oh, Linda. It doesn't sound pathetic at all,' Debbie said vehemently, leaning closer in. 'I didn't realize how serious things were for you, at first. I assumed you and Ray had just had a falling-out, and that you'd sort it out in time.'

At this, Linda's head dropped.

'Look, Linda,' Debbie said hastily. 'I didn't ask you here because I wanted an apology. I've got a proposition for you.'

Her sister raised her eyes in a questioning glance and, as I sat in the shoebox, my ears flickered attentively.

'When I said I've declined Margery's legacy, that was only part of the story,' Debbie explained. 'I agreed to do so on one condition: that I can use Margery's cottage in Oxford, for a year.'

Linda's face wore a look of blank incomprehension. 'But . . . I don't understand, Debs,' she stammered. 'Why would you want to move to Oxford? What about the café?'

I felt as though my heart had just dropped in my chest. The possibility that Debbie might move into Margery's cottage, leaving Linda to take over the flat, was not something that had ever crossed my mind. The very thought horrified me. The prospect of cohabiting with Linda and Beau for a year was almost as bad as the idea of moving in with David.

Linda's bewildered expression suggested that she shared my confusion, but Debbie reached across the table to place a hand on her sister's wrist. 'I'm not planning to live there myself, Linda.' She laughed. 'I was thinking of you!'

Linda's mouth fell open.

'It's only for a year, and the cottage will still belong to David,' Debbie explained quickly, 'but he's agreed to let me – us – be his tenants, for a peppercorn rent. It's been empty for a while now, and I think he's quite keen to have someone living there, to keep an eye on the place.' Linda's stunned expression had faded but, as she listened to Debbie, her shoulders began to droop. 'I thought it could give you a base of your own, while you're sorting out your situation with Ray,' Debbie went on, sensing that Linda needed reassuring. 'That is, if you want to, of course?'

'Debs, that's really kind, but . . . it doesn't feel right,' Linda said heavily. 'As you've pointed out to me before, Margery's intention was for Molly and the kittens to be taken care of. My using her cottage as a bolthole while I sort out my divorce isn't what she would have wanted.'

Debbie tilted her head and, with the patient look of someone explaining something to a small child, said, 'Linda, did you really think I was going to let you sleep on a friend's sofa over Christmas? Of course you've got to come back here. But we both know that you moving back into the flat isn't a long-term solution, either. We'd drive each other crazy, for one thing.'

Although her head was still bowed, Linda smiled.

'But it wouldn't be good for the cats, either,' Debbie continued. 'They're territorial animals and, living in a café, they need somewhere quiet they can escape to, somewhere calm and . . .' her eyes darted to Beau on the sofa, 'dog-free. So, the way I see it, finding you and Beau somewhere else to live for the next few months is as much in the cats' interest as it is in ours.'

Linda rubbed her forehead in consternation.

'It's all in the letter I sent the solicitor,' Debbie said, with an encouraging smile. 'I explained that I felt it would be in the spirit of what Margery wanted, and we would make sure that David isn't out of pocket. David's seen the letter and approved it.'

All of a sudden, Linda burst into tears, clamping her hand over her mouth to stifle her sobs. Debbie stood up and bent awkwardly over the table to hug her.

'Thank you,' Linda snivelled into her sister's shoulder.

'You're very welcome,' Debbie replied, rubbing her back. 'Oh, and if you don't mind the commute, I'd love you to carry on working in the café. Paid, of course – no more slave labour. You're a natural with the customers, and they've all been asking after you.'

Linda pulled away to look at Debbie. There were trickles of black on her cheeks where her mascara had run. 'I'd love to, thank you,' she replied, fresh tears springing into her eyes.

By the time Sophie returned home, Linda and Debbie had almost drained their second bottle of wine.

They were on the sofa, giggling at some shared memory of their schooldays, with a sullen-looking Beau relegated to the floor by their feet.

'Hi, Linda,' said Sophie, coming warily into the living room.

'C'm'ere, Soph,' cried Linda, seizing her niece around the neck in a one-armed hug.

Sophie raised her eyebrows at Debbie over Linda's shoulder, but her mother's eyes wore the same glassy, unfocused look as Linda's.

'Auntie Linda and I have come to a desh . . . a desish . . .' Debbie slurred. 'We've sorted a few things out. She'll be staying with us for Christmas, but—'

'Your mum,' Linda cut in, gripping Sophie's upper arms and looking up into her face earnestly, if a little blearily, 'is an angel!'

Sophie's eyes widened and her lip curled up into a sardonic smile. 'Okay, Auntie Linda,' she murmured politely, 'if you say so.'

26

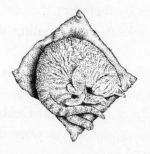

It was past midnight when Debbie and Linda finally agreed it was time to turn in for the night. Beau watched drowsily from the rug as Linda cleared away the wine glasses and Debbie prepared the sofa-bed.

Returning from the hall cupboard with an armful of pillows, Linda stumbled over a shoe and, flinging one arm sideways to regain her balance, dislodged a mound of jackets from the coat rack. Hearing her sister's yelp of alarm, Debbie abandoned her attempt to wrestle the duvet into its cover and staggered over to the door. She leant against the doorframe, giggling at Linda's clumsy efforts to reunite the coats with their pegs.

'Just leave them, we'll sort it out tomorrow,' Debbie hissed in a theatrical whisper.

Once Linda's bed had been messily assembled, I followed Debbie as she swayed upstairs. She peeled off her clothes, threw them across the bedroom in the general direction of the laundry basket and dropped, face-down, onto the bed. When I jumped up beside her, she mumbled something indistinct and ran her fingers through my fur, but her hand quickly fell still as she drifted off to sleep.

Through a gap in the curtains, the moon threw a strip of light across the quilt and I lay awake for some time staring at it, mulling over the evening's revelations. Now that I knew it was Linda who was being rehomed, and not me, I felt a little foolish. With the benefit of hindsight, I knew it was ludicrous to think that Debbie would consider giving me away; we had been through far too much together. I pressed closer to Debbie's side and lowered my chin onto her out-stretched fingers, purring with sleepy contentment.

When her alarm went off the next morning, Debbie sat bolt upright and looked around wildly, before batting the clock into silence. I chirruped at her, but she sank back on the pillows with a weak moan, shielding her eyes from the morning light with her arms. She had just drifted into a light doze when the relentless beeping started up again and, with a furious thrashing of limbs, she reappeared from beneath the duvet.

'I know!' she shouted, as if in mid-argument with some invisible adversary. 'I heard you the first time.'

She grabbed the clock roughly and switched it off, before heaving herself out of bed.

The kittens were pacing the hallway, waiting for breakfast with their tails expectantly aloft.

'Oh, all right, cats,' Debbie said, treading a careful path between them and the pile of coats still lying on the carpet. She was squeezing out a cat-food pouch with an expression of mild nausea when the living-room door opened.

'Morning,' Linda croaked groggily across the hall. The pristine baby-pink cashmere sweater she was wearing looked somewhat incongruous against her sallow skin smudged with make-up, and her scarecrow hair.

'Lovely top, Lind. One from Beau's carrier?' Debbie asked huskily, registering the telltale crease marks where the sweater had lain folded for the past few weeks.

Linda picked up the kettle and edged past Debbie to the sink. 'Perhaps,' she answered offhandedly, her cheeks flushing the same shade as her knitwear.

With the help of several strong coffees and a couple of paracetamol, the effects of the previous night's drinking seemed to subside, and Linda was back at work in the café as soon as she had fetched her belongings from her friend's house. The café was busy and Linda worked the room like a party hostess, asking customers about their plans for Christmas and chatting to them as if they were old friends. Her enthusiasm for Ming's Fortune Cookies was as ardent as ever, and soon the tables were littered with the telltale red cellophane wrappers and paper mottoes.

'You know what, Debs,' she said proudly, as she rooted around inside the Tupperware box of paper slips behind the counter, 'I'm going to have to print off a new batch of mottoes soon. We're nearly out.'

In an effort to prove she had abandoned her favouritism towards Ming, however, Linda made an impromptu addition to the Specials board – the '*Molly & Chandon* Champagne Tea' and persuaded several customers to order it on the basis that, 'If you can't treat yourself at Christmas, when can you?'

By closing time, both Linda and Debbie looked worn out. Blue shadows circled Linda's eyes as she wiped down the tables, and the sound of Debbie's yawns emanated from the kitchen at regular intervals. With her chores completed, Linda pulled up a stool to the serving counter, climbed wearily onto it and let her eyes settle on Ming, who was absorbed in a leisurely wash on her platform.

'Do you ever wonder what Ming's thinking?' she mused when Debbie came through from the kitchen.

'Can't say I've had the time to give it too much thought,' Debbie replied distractedly, searching for something on the shelf beneath the till. 'Why?'

'No reason,' Linda said lightly, stifling a yawn. 'It's just that, compared to the other cats, Ming always seems to be . . . in a world of her own. But then I don't really know much about cats, so it's probably nothing,' she added, self-deprecatingly.

Behind the counter, Debbie straightened up and looked over at Ming. 'Well, she hasn't fully integrated into the colony yet,' she said, but there was a note of concern in her voice.

Ming was cleaning her face with her eyes closed, licking the inside of her slender wrist, before using it to groom her whiskers punctiliously. She seemed oblivious, or indifferent, to their scrutiny. After a couple of moments of deliberation, Debbie peeled off her rubber gloves and stepped around the side of the counter. 'Ming?' she called tentatively.

Ming continued to wash, unperturbed. Making sure to keep out of Ming's eye-line, Debbie stepped nearer to the cat tree, held out her hand a few inches from the back of Ming's head and clicked her fingers. There was no reaction: Ming didn't startle and her ears didn't flicker.

'Oh my God,' Debbie said, turning to face Linda with a dismayed look. 'Linda, you're right. I think Ming might be deaf!'

I felt a dip in my stomach, of shock mixed with incipient guilt. I spooled through my memories, desperately trying to recall an occasion when I had seen Ming react to something – anything – that she had heard. None came to mind. I vividly recalled our first meeting, when she had snubbed my attempt to introduce myself and Eddie in the café. She had looked down at us from the armchair, and I had read imperious disdain into her expression and had taken her silence for rudeness. It had never crossed my mind that there might be another explanation: that she hadn't answered me because she hadn't heard me.

The following morning Debbie phoned the vet first thing, and shortly after lunch she hung up her apron and fetched the cat carrier from upstairs. Ming reacted with her usual placidity as Debbie lifted her into the carrier, her deep-blue eyes remaining entirely impassive as she gazed out through the wire door.

I watched them leave with a feeling of apprehension. Seeing Ming in the carrier brought back a strange stab of memory, of the time I had been to visit Margery. I had returned to find Ming on the window cushion, seemingly having made herself at home in my absence. I cringed inwardly as I recalled how the sight of Ming and the other cats looking relaxed in the café had driven me into a jealous rage; I had been so sure – so utterly convinced – that Ming had been talking to Jasper and the kittens while I was away. How ludicrous and mean-spirited my suspicions would prove to have been if it turned out that she was deaf.

As I awaited Debbie and Ming's return, my eye kept being drawn to the empty platform on the cat tree, and I found myself unable to settle. As the afternoon wore on, the chatter of customers began to grate on me, and the continuous chug and hiss of the coffee machine made my head ache. Craving fresh air, I slipped out outside and stood on the pavement, grateful for the chill breeze in my fur. The snowfall of the previous week had largely thawed, leaving only the occasional patch of grey slush on the pavements. A dustbin lorry turned the corner onto the parade and began its slow, growling progress up the street, so I ran along the pavement and darted into the recessed doorway of Jo's hardware store. Waiting for the lorry to pass, I peered through the door. With the shifting reflections of passers-by in the glass, I found it difficult to be sure, but I thought I saw a glimpse of a tabby cat striding down one of the shop's aisles.

The dustbin lorry pulled up outside the hardware shop and two men in luminous yellow jackets made their way towards the wheelie bins by the kerb. Keen to escape the lorry's ear-splitting hydraulics, I nudged at the shop's door. It swung open with very little resistance and, relieved, I slunk inside.

I had never been into Jo's shop before. I was struck

by its musty smell and the fact that, although it was similar in size to the café, the piles of stock that cluttered every surface made it feel smaller. I took a few tentative steps on the faded linoleum, past the serving counter on my right, where Jo was on the phone, complaining about an unpaid invoice. I could hear Bernard's snuffly snores as he slept by her feet. I padded slowly up the central aisle, past shelves lined with cardboard boxes full of screws and hooks. At the back of the shop, next to a wire rack full of tea towels and dusters, I sensed movement and spun round to find myself almost nose-to-nose with Purdy.

'What are you doing in here?' Purdy asked, her tone faintly accusatory.

'I thought I saw a cat through the window,' I said, somewhat pointlessly.

At that moment, the door swung open and a man leant in. 'Got any WD-40?' he said gruffly. Jo nodded and gestured towards the back of the shop. The man began to head in our direction, his face set in a stern grimace. Purdy and I instinctively darted away from him, dashing down the outer aisle and through the door, before it could swing shut.

In the parade, spots of rain had started to fall, adding to the urgency with which people strode past us. I stood facing Purdy on the cobbles outside Jo's shop.

'Do you come here a lot?' I asked.

'A fair bit. Why?'

For some reason I couldn't quite articulate, it stung to think of Purdy spending time in the hardware shop rather than at home. But there was something about her manner that made me want to proceed warily; she seemed to be avoiding my gaze, and her face wore a mask of impatient defiance.

'I know it's been difficult lately, with Ming, and Linda and Beau,' I prompted, feeling that she needed encouragement.

'It's got nothing to do with them,' Purdy replied evasively. 'This is just somewhere I can come to get away from . . . things.'

'Oh?' I said and, in the silence that fell between us, I felt the first tremors of misgiving in my stomach.

Her alert green eyes held mine for a moment and then she said, 'I just don't really like being in the café. I'm not sure I ever have.'

'I had no idea . . .' I replied, stalling for time while I digested her words.

Perhaps Purdy sensed my inner turmoil, because she began to explain. 'I don't like being on display, with strangers fussing over me all day. It's not really my thing. And sometimes there are just too many . . .' She trailed off, looking at the ground, uncertain whether to continue.

'Go on,' I urged.

'Too many . . . cats,' she said, glancing up at my face anxiously.

The rain was falling with increasing force and, all around us, people were shaking open umbrellas and quickening their pace.

'I'm sorry,' I said, feeling a sudden surge of remorse. 'I had no idea you were unhappy.'

'I'm not unhappy,' she corrected me, droplets of moisture glistening on her whiskers like crystals. 'I'm just . . . not as happy as I could be, I suppose.'

I knew our conversation would soon be curtailed by the weather, but I desperately wanted to say something to show that, although I was saddened by what Purdy had said, I was grateful for her honesty. But, instead, I heard myself say, 'Please, don't run away.'

The disappointed look in her eyes let me know that I had catastrophically misjudged my response. Purdy had found the courage to tell me how she felt, but rather than listen to her, I had panicked. Instead of reassuring her, I had put my own anxiety first, and sought reassurance from her.

'Of course I won't run away,' she replied breezily. Her tail had started to twitch and she glanced back over her shoulder, making no effort to hide her desire to be on her way.

I opened my mouth, wanting to undo the damage

caused by my clunky, ill-chosen comment, but it was too late. A car had passed too close to the kerb, splashing passers-by with murky water; and, in the ensuing commotion, Purdy turned and trotted away. Within seconds she had disappeared over a wall and I was left standing on the cobbles, with cold rain beating down on my back, and Christmas shoppers rushing past me.

27

I returned to the café and, ignoring the customers' good-natured overtures, headed straight for my window cushion. I turned my back on the room and stared out of the glass, castigating myself for the way I had handled the encounter. In my fretful state, Purdy's and Ming's suffering became conflated in my mind. I was convinced I was to blame for both, and that my self-absorption had blinded me to what they had been going through. If life in the café had been making Purdy unhappy, then surely, as her mother, I should have noticed? Similarly, as the colony's matriarch, I should have been less quick to judge Ming's odd behaviour. With both Purdy and Ming out of the café, however, I could do nothing except stare watchfully out over the damp street and wait for their return.

The rest of the day seemed to drag on inexorably,

and it was not until after closing time that Debbie finally brought Ming home.

'I'm back,' Debbie called, crouching down on the flagstones to unlock the cat carrier.

Ming crept out cautiously, glanced in both directions, sniffed the air uncertainly, then dashed towards the cat tree.

Linda came out of the kitchen with a querying look.

'We had to go to the animal hospital for tests,' Debbie explained as she made for the nearest chair and sat down.

'And?' Linda asked, pulling off her apron and hanging it on the peg.

'She's deaf,' Debbie replied sadly. 'Almost certainly since birth. A congenital defect, probably.'

I felt my breath catch in my chest.

'Poor Ming.' Linda sighed, pouting with concern.

Looking relieved to be back on her platform, Ming had started to wash, unaffected by the melancholy mood in the room.

'Do you think it's okay for her to stay in the café? I mean, is it cruel, if she can't hear anything?' Linda asked, looking sorrowfully at Ming.

'It's something to think about,' Debbie agreed. 'Perhaps she would be happier somewhere less . . . busy.'

Linda walked over to the cat tree and reached out

her hand to touch Ming's back. Startled, Ming turned towards her and, when Linda gently caressed her spine from her shoulders to her tail, blinked in pleasure.

'You know, if you think it would be for the best, I'd be happy to take Ming with me to Margery's cottage,' Linda said diffidently, as the room began to fill with Ming's rumbling purr. 'I should be the one to take responsibility for her, since it was me who brought her here in the first place.'

From her chair near the door, Debbie watched her sister closely. 'Thanks, Linda, I'll bear that in mind,' she said appreciatively.

Later, when Debbie and Linda had gone upstairs, I stared across the dimly lit café at Ming. She lay in a neat circle, the perfect arc of her body disrupted only by the single, angular protuberance of her left ear. I was struck anew by her effortless elegance, and the uncomfortable realization that Ming's beauty had been a major factor in my distrust of her. The adulation she had received in the café had stoked the flames of my envy, and I had never stopped to consider what coming to the café must have felt like for her. She had been an outsider, unexpectedly introduced to a colony of cats in an environment where privacy and solitude had not been an option. Any cat would have struggled in such circumstances, let alone one who couldn't hear. I felt a wave of pity rise up inside me. I had been determined from the outset to read disdain into Ming's reserved demeanour. Now I had to accept that, though there had been disdain, it had been on my side, not Ming's.

Sporadic twitches seized Ming's paws and whiskers as she dreamt, then she awoke with a sudden jerk. Her enormous eyes sprang open and she looked around in alarm, catching sight of me watching her from the window. Her dream had left her with a disorientated look, but I held her gaze for a few moments. Then, for the first time since meeting Ming, I blinked at her, slowly, in a sign of friendship. She tilted her head quizzically to one side before responding with a blink of her own, her azure eyes disappearing momentarily behind chocolate-brown eyelids.

I was overcome by a bittersweet elation. There was something so mundane, and yet so momentous, in that silent communication – the simple gesture of non-aggression that had passed between us. But my happiness was tinged with regret that it had taken me so long to attempt this most basic of feline signals, that I had wasted so much time looking for evidence to confirm my prejudices, rather than give Ming the benefit of the doubt.

Ming continued to look at me for a few moments, her cerulean gaze as steady and intense as ever and yet, this time, I saw it for what it was: curiosity about a baffling, soundless world, rather than an expression of her superiority. With a look of serene contentment, she lowered her head and licked the tip of her tail a few times, before tucking it neatly under her chin. Then she closed her eyes and swiftly fell back to sleep, to return to the world inside her head, perhaps the only world she would ever fully understand.

Sleep proved more elusive for me and when, after an hour of half-hearted washing and repositioning myself on my cushion, I did eventually doze off, I fell almost immediately into a dream. I was back on the rain-soaked street outside the hardware shop, watching Purdy disappear over the wall. I tried to call after her, but my voice was drowned out by growling lorries, and when I turned to run back to the café, I saw Ming cowering on the doorstep, staring at me dolefully through the rushing legs of pedestrians.

By the time the weak December sun rose over the rooftops, I had been awake for several hours, mulling over my situation and the way I had failed both Ming and Purdy. But I had come to a resolution: I was determined to make amends for my mistakes. Linda might have set her heart on taking Ming to the cottage, but I would do everything in my power to make Ming feel welcome, in the time she had left with us. As for Purdy, I would apologize for my reaction outside the hardware shop, and tell her that whatever she decided to do, I would support her.

Now I just had to wait for her to come home.

'But we thought you didn't like Ming,' Abby said, with a look of puzzlement. I had intercepted the kittens at the bottom of the stairs later that morning. They stood around me on the flagstones, listening attentively.

'We thought you didn't want us to talk to her,' Bella chipped in, trying to be helpful.

I looked from one inquisitive face to the next, acutely aware of the hypocrisy of asking the kittens to be friendlier to Ming when, in the past, I had sulked if they went anywhere near her.

'I never said I didn't like her,' I protested unconvincingly. If cats had eyebrows, Bella's would have shot up.

'But you were the one who . . . ' she began, but trailed off when she noticed my thrashing tail.

'That was before I knew she was deaf,' I replied sharply, aware that such a justification was feeble at best. 'I didn't realize that was why she was acting so . . . standoffish.'

I felt my cheeks burn beneath my fur as the kittens looked back at me with identical expressions of bemusement.

'I just thought she was shy,' Eddie remarked diffidently.

'Me too,' concurred Maisie.

Their guileless reaction compounded my guilt, confirming that I was the only one to have read superciliousness into Ming's silence. But I was grateful for their sweet-natured willingness to do as I asked, and for the fact that, if they did judge me for my hypocrisy, they kept it to themselves.

'Has anyone seen Purdy this morning?' I asked as they filtered out across the café floor.

'Not yet,' Eddie replied, and the others didn't disagree.

I left the kittens in the café and slipped through the cat flap. I felt a niggling suspicion that Purdy might have spent the night in Jo's shop. It was a cold, blustery day and the low clouds threatened rain. I had taken a few steps along the pavement when the hardware-shop door swung open and Jo came out with Bernard.

I halted mid-step, momentarily baffled by what I saw: rather than walking side-by-side with Bernard on his lead, Jo was carrying the dog like a baby, cradling his bulky hindquarters in her arms, while he rested his chin on her shoulder. Locked in their awkward embrace, they made an ungainly, slightly comical pair, but Jo's face was set in a look of tense concern. She hovered in the doorway, shifting Bernard's weight sideways as she locked the shop door behind her. Then, staggering slightly under his weight, she lurched towards the van, clumsily opened its rear doors and lowered Bernard carefully inside. I caught a fleeting glimpse of the dog's dejected expression, before Jo slammed the door shut and hurried round to the driver's seat. Within seconds, the van had accelerated away and disappeared around the corner.

I ran over to the shop door and peered through the glass, but it was dark and empty inside. Fighting off a growing unease, I made my way back round the side of the café to find Jasper sitting at the alleyway's entrance. After the events of the previous twenty-four hours, the wave of relief I felt at seeing him made my throat start to constrict. He seemed to sense my agitation, and our strides quickly fell into step as we walked together down the alleyway.

'So . . . ?' he prompted, as we pushed through the conifers into the churchyard. I took a deep breath; I had so much to tell him that I wasn't sure where to start.

'Well, you were right. Debbie wasn't planning to rehome me. Linda's going to be moving into Margery's cottage – that's all.' I braced myself for a response of the 'I told you so' variety, but Jasper merely blinked in tacit approval. Heartened by his reaction, I said, 'Also, Ming's deaf. That's why she never talked to any of us.'

At this, his eyes widened slightly. I waited for him to say something, but he maintained his diplomatic silence.

'Go on then,' I said, slowing to a halt among the headstones.

'Go on then, what?' Jasper replied.

'Say "I told you so",' I said, through clenched jaws.

'I never said I thought she was deaf,' he pointed out, generously.

'No, but you thought I had misjudged her, and you were right.'

Jasper looked away, apparently distracted by a pair of magpies cawing argumentatively in a nearby tree, but I suspected he was sparing me the embarrassment of having to look him in the eye while admitting that I was wrong.

'Just like you were right about Debbie not planning to rehome me,' I said sullenly.

'What's done is done,' he said, returning his gaze to the muddy turf in front of us. 'I'm sure Ming will forgive you.'

'I'm not sure she'll be around long enough to forgive me,' I replied churlishly. 'Linda wants to take her to the cottage when she moves out.'

At this, Jasper's ear flickered and his eyes narrowed a little. I wasn't sure whether his expression indicated surprise at Linda's offer, or disappointment that Ming might be leaving us.

'There's one more thing,' I said, glancing nervously at him. 'I'm worried about Purdy.' For a fleeting second I thought I saw a flicker of 'What now?' in his eyes.

'Why's that?' he said guardedly.

'She told me she doesn't like living in the café. I'm worried she might run away,' I explained. 'In fact,' I added, trying to fight my rising angst, 'she hasn't been home since yesterday.'

Jasper surveyed me calmly through his amber eyes. I knew what he must be thinking: no sooner had one of my anxieties been allayed, than another had rushed in to take its place. 'Purdy has an adventurous spirit. We've always known that,' he said steadily.

'I know,' I snapped, resenting his unruffled tone. 'But I think it's more than that.' I could feel my frustration suddenly rise up like bile in my throat. 'Do we just wait till one day she decides she'd rather live on the street than in the cafe? That is, if she hasn't already . . .'

I looked away. My eyes were tingling and I felt desperate as my conviction grew that it might already be too late to change Purdy's mind, and that, just as I had with Margery, I had wasted my last chance to say goodbye to her.

'She's half alley-cat, remember,' Jasper said, with a slight puffing-out of his chest.

'So?' I hissed, my tail twitching irritably.

'So,' Jasper replied with infuriating calmness, 'she's also a grown-up now. If she doesn't want to live in the café any more, there might be nothing we can do about it.'

28

I couldn't have felt less festive as I nosed back through the cat flap to be greeted by the sound of Christmas music and the smell of mince pies. I picked my way forlornly between the customers' coats and shopping bags, to take up my usual position in the window, and cast my eye around the café, on the off-chance that Purdy had returned during my absence.

It was the last working day before the holidays and the café was full. Debbie and Linda bustled between the tables with sprigs of tinsel pinned to their Molly's aprons. Some of the customers had brought gifts for the cats, little gift-wrapped parcels that Debbie placed in a pile beneath the tree. They smelt tantalizingly of catnip and cat treats, and as I surveyed the room I spotted Eddie prowling around them, sniffing greedily. Opposite me, Ming was meditating on her platform, with Maisie asleep in the domed bed beneath, and at the fireplace Abby and Bella were being entertained by a young girl who was dangling a toy fishing rod over the back of the armchair. But there was no sign of Purdy.

It was only since speaking to Jasper that I had acknowledged the possibility that, in spite of her promise, Purdy might already have run away. Out of the blue, a memory popped into my mind of the time Eddie had disappeared. I had asked Purdy if she knew where he was, and she had said, 'Maybe it was just the right time for him to go.' I had dismissed the idea as naive, certain that such a notion was out of character for Eddie. On that occasion, my instincts had been proved correct. But it hadn't occurred to me, until now, that there might have been more to Purdy's comment than I had realized. Had she, in fact, been trying to tell me that she felt it might soon be the right time for her to go?

Jasper was right, we had always known Purdy was more adventurous than her siblings, but I had never seriously considered what that would mean for Purdy as she entered adulthood. It hadn't crossed my mind that any of the kittens might crave a different kind of existence from the one they had been brought up in, or might have ambitions that a life spent dozing in the cat café could never satisfy. Perhaps, I realized with a dull pang of self-awareness, I had finally hit upon the nub of the problem: I had continued to think of Purdy and her siblings as kittens, long after they had left their kittenish ways behind, and had given little thought to their changing needs as they moved into adulthood. I had never questioned my assumption that what made me happy would also make them happy, and that their greatest need was to stay together, and to stay with me.

My eyes were drawn to Maisie, who had climbed out of her bed on the cat tree and was now sitting on top of the highest point of the dome, peering gingerly over the edge of Ming's platform above. When Ming looked across with her usual imperious gaze, Maisie responded by jumping up and cowering nervously at the edge of the platform. Maisie remained motionless with her head bowed, while Ming stepped closer and craned her neck downwards so that her nose was almost touching Maisie's fur. Ming took a few delicate sniffs, before delivering the briefest of licks across the top of Maisie's head. Maisie glanced up, their eyes met and Ming blinked at her benignly. Then, with a look of beneficent calm, she returned to the middle of the platform and resumed her meditative pose.

I felt myself succumbing to the overwhelming remorse that had been building since I had first learnt that Ming might be deaf. Witnessing Maisie's sweet-natured overture and Ming's affectionate response had brought a lump to my throat. There was no escaping the fact that my irrational dislike of Ming, and the kittens' desire not to upset me, had been the main obstacle to Ming's integration in the café. It was my resentment that had been the problem, not Ming's aloofness. I felt exhausted and knew I was descending into self-pity, but did not have the energy to fight it. Trying my hardest to block out the chatter and laughter around me, I turned my back to the café, lay down and went to sleep.

I was woken by a rhythmic swishing sound. I blinked and lifted my head; it was dark outside and I could see the café's bright interior reflected in the black glass. Behind me, Debbie was working her way across the empty café with a broom, sweeping crumbs into a dustpan, while Linda cashed up at the till. They were discussing the last-minute shopping that needed to be done for Christmas dinner.

'I'll go to the supermarket tomorrow, Debs,' Linda offered. 'I can pop in on my way back from Cotswold Organic.'

'Thanks, Lind,' Debbie replied gratefully, 'Going anywhere near the supermarket on Christmas Eve would just about finish me off.'

As Debbie swept the floor around the armchairs, she paused and pulled the broom-handle towards her chest. 'Linda, I hope you won't be disappointed,' she began, 'but I've decided to keep Ming in the café. She really does seem to be settling in here, and I don't think the upheaval of another move would be good for her.'

Linda followed Debbie's eye-line to the fireplace, where Ming was sitting on the flagstones, gazing beatifically at the glowing stove. Eddie was sprawled out on the tiles next to her, fast asleep with his jet-black belly exposed to the heat. 'You know what, Debs? I'm glad you said that,' she agreed. 'I was thinking the same thing myself.'

She pulled off her apron and went upstairs, and Debbie was about to lock up when there was a tap at the window.

'Hi, Jo,' Debbie said, opening the door to find Jo in the doorway, pale-faced and trembling. 'Is everything okay?'

'It's Bernard.' There was something strained in Jo's tone, and Debbie instinctively took a step closer.

'What's happened?' she asked, in a manner that suggested she already knew the answer.

'I had to take him to the vet this morning. He's . . . gone,' Jo replied in a shaky voice.

Debbie's face puckered with concern. 'Oh, poor Bernard. I'm so sorry,' she murmured, moving forward to envelop Jo in a hug. 'Come on, let me get you a cuppa,' she insisted, leading Jo across the room to the fireplace.

Jo lowered herself into an armchair while Debbie

stoked the embers in the stove, sending a burst of sparks flying into the grate. She left Jo staring with a dazed expression at the dancing flames while she went into the kitchen. Jo was startled out of her trance-like state by the swoosh of the cat flap, but her face broke into a smile – and my heart seemed to flip inside my chest – when Purdy stalked across the flagstones towards the stairs.

'Hello, Purdy,' Jo called fondly.

Upon hearing her voice, Purdy changed direction, veering towards Jo with her tail aloft. She cast a slightly shamefaced glance at me as she passed the window, but was soon pressed against Jo's legs, purring loudly as Jo rubbed the base of her tail.

'So, what happened?' Debbie asked, setting down two mugs of tea and taking the armchair opposite Jo's. Jo sat back and Purdy immediately jumped up and began to circle contentedly on her lap. The fire in the stove crackled and its orange glow lit their faces.

'When he woke up this morning, Bernard was struggling to stand. It was obvious that something serious had happened. I took him straight to the vet, who said it was probably a stroke and there was nothing she could do . . .' Jo took a deep, shuddering breath and dropped her head, allowing her curls to fall in front of her face.

'I'm so sorry, Jo,' Debbie said sincerely. 'He was such a lovely old boy. And so close to Christmas, too.'

Jo nodded and her shoulders started to shake. Debbie sipped her tea in tactful silence.

Eventually, Jo finished wiping her eyes with a tissue and reached for her mug of tea. 'He was with me for fifteen years. That's longer than my marriage lasted,' she said, with a watery-eyed smile, caressing Purdy's cheek with her free hand. They both sipped their tea, then Jo went on, 'Actually, Debs, there's something else I need to tell you.' She leant sideways and shakily placed her mug on the table. 'I've been meaning to tell you for a while,' she said, and there was something heavy about her tone.

'What is it, Jo? You're worrying me,' Debbie asked.

'Well, the thing is . . . I've given up the lease on the shop.'

Cradling her mug of tea, Debbie blinked confusedly. 'The shop? From when?'

'From next month,' answered Jo. Debbie's lips parted and her brow wrinkled but, before she could speak, Jo started talking again. 'The writing's been on the wall for a long time, Debs – the shop's been losing money for months. I'm cutting my losses before I get any further into debt. It's better to get out now, while I've still got my head above water.' She talked fast, as if she had rehearsed her words and wanted to get them out as quickly as possible.

Listening to Jo gave Debbie time to compose her face and, by the time Jo paused for breath, her friend's appalled expression had been replaced by a look of sympathetic understanding. 'I get it, Jo, I really do,' Debbie said quietly. 'I had no idea things were so bad. I mean, I knew business was slow . . .'

'You weren't to know, Debs,' Jo insisted vehemently. 'I've been telling myself business will pick up for over a year now, but after a point I realized I was just kidding myself and . . .' She trailed off helplessly.

They sat in reflective silence, the only sounds in the room the crackling fire and Purdy's sleepy purr. Debbie stared at her friend with fierce concentration. 'If you need a job to tide you over, I could find work for you here,' she said, her eyes shining hopefully.

'That's really kind of you,' Jo replied, 'but, well, I'll be letting the flat go, too. It's part of the lease.'

Debbie let out an uncontrolled yelp of dismay. 'But where will you go? You can't just give up your home and your business in one fell swoop.'

Jo took a long, fortifying breath. 'Don't worry, Debs, it's all sorted. I'm going to move back to the farm. Dad needs someone to take over running the place, and it'll give my finances a chance to recover.'

Debbie looked listlessly at her cooling cup of tea.

'Why didn't you tell me before? You must have been planning this for a while.' She sounded hurt.

'I'm sorry,' answered Jo with a guilty look. 'I didn't want to say anything until I was sure. I knew that you'd try and talk me out of it. Besides, you've had enough on your plate recently, without worrying about my livelihood as well.'

At this, Debbie cringed. 'I'm sorry, Jo. I know I've been banging on about my problems incessantly—'

But Jo lifted a hand to placate her, 'Debbie, please don't. This was just something I needed to work out for myself, that's all.'

Debbie looked suddenly drained, as if she had only just realized there was nothing she could say to change her friend's mind. 'I can see it makes sense. But it's strange to think of you . . .'

'Not being next door any more,' Jo completed Debbie's sentence for her.

Debbie's eyes suddenly brimmed with tears and she turned away.

'It's less than an hour's drive, Debs – I'll be back here all the time,' Jo said with a forced smile, although I could see her eyes were reddening, too.

'But it won't be the same, will it?' Debbie whimpered, wiping her nose hastily on the back of her hand.

Jo shook her head. 'I know. It won't.'

Their sniffing punctuated the unhappy silence and

then, from behind a scrunched-up tissue, Debbie said, 'You know, it's not too late to ask Linda to be your lodger.' She glanced at Jo and gave a tiny shrug.

Jo sniggered and the room suddenly felt lighter, as if a weight had lifted from them both, and they knew the worst was over.

'I'll be back in Stourton all the time, Debs, just you wait and see,' said Jo, blinking away her tears. 'We can still have our weekend takeaways. Besides,' she added, taking Purdy's face gently between both hands, 'I couldn't last long without coming back to see the cats. With Bernard gone, I've got to get my cuddles from somewhere, haven't I?'

That was when it struck me: an idea of such self-evident simplicity that I couldn't believe it hadn't occurred to me before. I sat up on the window cushion and fixed Debbie with a stare. She was looking at Jo intently over the rim of her mug and, in the dancing light from the fire, I thought I could make out the faintest trace of a smile around her lips.

I hoped and prayed she was thinking the same thing as me.

29

I rose before dawn on Christmas morning and slipped outside before anyone else was awake. The sky turned incrementally paler as I made a solitary circuit of the churchyard and, by the time I reached the square, the orange sun had peeped over the skyline to reveal a glittering frost on the rooftops. I sat beneath the elm tree and took a moment to enjoy the peacefulness of the scene, in anticipation of what I knew would be a hectic day. Sure enough, when I returned home, I climbed the stairs to find that the household had come to life during my absence.

A glance into the kitchen revealed the kittens, Jasper and Ming, breakfasting greedily from the food bowls, while in the living room Debbie, Linda and Sophie had gathered in their pyjamas to exchange gifts. I strode towards them with my tail aloft, pausing to look twice at Beau on the rug by Linda's feet. He was dressed in a lurid green elf costume, complete with jester's collar, faux buckle-belt around his belly and pointed hat. His face was a picture of abject mortification and, when he saw me looking at him, he lowered his chin miserably onto his paws, causing the tiny bell at the tip of his hat to tinkle.

Sophie was sitting on the floor by the sofa, happily engrossed in the instruction booklet for some new electronic device Linda had given her. Full of smiles, Linda stood up from the sofa and reached for a luxurious-looking gift box.

'Now, I know we said novelty gifts only, Debs,' she intoned grandly, 'but I saw this and . . . well, I just had to get it for you.'

Narrowing her eyes in a look of mild scepticism, Debbie took the box onto her lap and lifted the lid. She hooted with amusement as she unfolded a kitchen apron covered from top to bottom in a lurid montage of cats' faces, with the words *Crazy Cat Lady* printed across the front.

'Gosh, thanks, Linda,' she said. 'This makes me feel so much better about what I've got for you.' Her eyes twinkled and she handed over a rather more modestly wrapped gift to her sister.

Linda ripped open the wrapping paper to reveal a sweatshirt emblazoned with a photo of Ming wearing a Santa hat. *Have a Ming-ing Christmas!* the garment exclaimed in shiny gold lettering.

'I know how much you like Ming merchandise,' said Debbie mischievously.

Linda pulled the sweater over her head and gave a little twirl on the rug. 'I love it,' she gushed, striking a pose for Sophie, who had raised her phone to photograph her aunt. 'See, I told you Ming would wear the Santa hat!' she added with an air of vindication.

'She didn't,' Sophie said drily from behind her phone screen. 'It's Photoshopped.'

When everyone had showered and dressed, we all moved downstairs to the café. Debbie and Linda went straight into the kitchen to start work on lunch, but Sophie headed for the fireplace, where the pile of gifts from customers sat beneath the tree. 'Come on, cats,' she called, and the kittens trotted eagerly after her. Soon there was a frenzy of pouncing and shredding, as Sophie began to unwrap a seemingly endless succession of catnip mice and bags of treats.

'A laser-pointer – cool!' Sophie said, opening the last gift in the pile. She tore the pen-like toy from its cardboard packaging and aimed it across the room, making a dot of red light dance on the opposite wall, seemingly of its own accord. 'Maisie, look!' she urged, but Maisie and her siblings were more interested in the crinkling shreds of wrapping paper spread across the flagstones than in the dot of light on the far side of the room.

Ming, however, who until now had been observing the unwrapping process from her platform, appeared mesmerized. She jumped lightly down and prowled across the room, transfixed by the shimmering dot dancing across the wall. After a few stealthy wiggles of her hindquarters, she leapt upwards, her front legs outstretched and tail thrashing, trying to catch the wayward dot with her flexed claws.

'Nice moves, Ming!' Sophie giggled.

A few weeks earlier I would have delighted in seeing elegant, reserved Ming flinging herself around in such an ungainly fashion, but instead I felt touched that she had, finally, revealed her playful side. I took it as a sign of trust that she felt able, at last, to let down her guard with us.

As the morning wore on, a delicious aroma of roasting turkey began to drift out of the kitchen, drawing Eddie across the room to pace back and forth in front of the counter, sniffing the air hopefully. When John peered furtively through the window from the pavement, Sophie stood up to let him in, making sure to close the café door softly behind him. He placed a bag of gifts in an empty chair and immediately came over to sit beside my window cushion. 'There you go, Molly,' he whispered, adjusting my collar carefully with hands that smelt of soap.

John winked at me, then stood up and went over to the counter.

'Happy Christmas, ladies,' he shouted through the kitchen doorway. Debbie emerged from the steamy kitchen in her *Crazy Cat Lady* apron, wiping her forehead with the back of her arm. 'Nice apron,' John murmured, stretching over the counter to give her a kiss.

'Suits her, doesn't it?' Linda quipped, poking her head through the doorway from the kitchen. 'Shall we have a cup of tea?' she said cheerfully.

'Already, Linda? We haven't got the potatoes on yet,' Debbie replied, glancing anxiously at her watch.

'Yes, please,' Sophie piped up from the armchair in front of the stove.

'I'll make it. You two take a break for five minutes,' John said, pulling a stool over for Debbie.

Realizing she was outvoted, Debbie reluctantly sat down.

'I'll just get the Fortune Cookies,' Linda said brightly, as John made his way around the counter.

'Fortune Cookies?' Debbie repeated, looking puzzled. 'They're not exactly festive, Lind. If you're hungry, there are mince pies in the—' But Linda had already followed John into the kitchen, and Debbie found herself addressing the empty doorway. She tutted and rolled her eyes, drumming her fingers on the counter while John and Linda assembled the tea things in the kitchen.

After a couple of minutes, they emerged with a tray full of mugs and the Tupperware box of Fortune Cookies.

'I've got some new mottoes,' Linda explained, rummaging around inside the box. 'I'd like to know what you think.'

Debbie gave a defeated shrug and picked up a steaming mug, half-heartedly taking the cellophane-wrapped cookie Linda handed to her.

'I'll go first, shall I?' John said, unwrapping his cookie. '*Fortune favours the brave,*' he read.

Debbie nodded, albeit with a noticeable lack of enthusiasm.

'Okay, how about mine,' Linda said quickly. '*Some pursue happiness, others create it.*'

Debbie remained taciturn.

Sophie placed her mug on the counter and cleared her throat. '*Your heart knows the answer your head has been searching for.*'

'Um, I think—' Debbie began.

'You haven't read yours yet,' Linda remarked off-handedly, cutting her sister off mid-sentence.

Debbie sighed and unwrapped the twist of cellophane that she had absent-mindedly placed on the counter. '*If there is a day to act on the love in your soul, it is today.*' She looked around at their expectant faces and smiled vaguely, as if sensing that diplomacy was called for. 'They're good Linda. Although, if I'm honest, I think the last batch was funnier,' she demurred.

The backhanded compliment seemed to glide off Linda, and she gave a nonchalant shrug.

'Actually, Debs,' John said quietly, 'Linda didn't write the mottoes. I did.'

Debbie looked at him, nonplussed. 'I, don't, er . . .' she stammered in confusion.

'Molly's got your Christmas present,' John explained, taking her by the elbow and steering her across the room towards me.

Debbie looked utterly bewildered as she scanned the windowsill around my cushion. 'What do you mean, I don't see any—' Suddenly she gasped and one hand flew up to her mouth.

John knelt down in front of me and carefully untied the diamond ring he had attached to my collar with a ribbon. 'Good work, Molly,' he said, rubbing my head. Then, still kneeling, he turned towards Debbie and fixed her with a look that was at once hopeful and terrified. 'Molly's dying to know, Debs. Will you marry me?'

Across the room, Linda was biting her fist, and Sophie had taken out her mobile phone to film them.

Debbie uncovered her mouth and let her trembling

hand drop by her side. A suspenseful silence settled over the room.

'Yes, I will,' she whispered.

There was a shriek and a whoop from across the café and, beaming broadly, John stood up and slid the ring onto Debbie's left hand.

'I can't believe I just got engaged, wearing a *Crazy Cat Lady* apron!' Debbie wailed, smiling through her tears as John pulled her close and kissed her tenderly.

'At least John knows what he's letting himself in for,' Linda remarked, with an air of pragmatism.

'Don't worry, I know my place in the pecking order,' John said with a theatrical sigh, pulling Debbie towards him again and kissing her hair.

While Linda was in the kitchen fetching champagne there was a knock at the window, and I turned to see Jo waving feverishly through the glass.

'So, I take it congratulations are in order?' she asked excitedly when Sophie had let her in.

'Were you in on this, too?' Debbie replied in disbelief.

''Fraid so,' answered Jo, taking a glass of champagne from Linda. 'I've been waiting for Sophie's text all morning. I couldn't set off for Dad's until I'd come to celebrate with you!'

'I'm starting to feel like I've been set up!' Debbie said, looking alternately amused and aggrieved as she surveyed the grinning faces all around her.

'That's because you have been, Debs,' Linda replied matter-of-factly.

For twenty minutes they stood around, sipping champagne and laughing while Debbie repeatedly complained about being set up, bemoaned the fact that she looked ridiculous in her apron, and threatened Sophie with indefinite grounding if she so much as thought about posting online the footage of John's proposal. I watched them all from the windowsill, feeling a glow of pride for the part I had played.

Jo's glass was still half-full when she took Debbie's arm. 'I should be getting off,' she said softly.

Debbie turned away from the others and said in a low voice, 'Actually, Jo, there's something I want to ask you.'

They sat down at the little table nearest the window, just a few inches from my cushion. Debbie's eyes were shining, whether from emotion or the effects of the two glasses of champagne she had downed in quick succession, I wasn't sure.

She placed her fingertips on the table edge and said, 'Now I don't want you to feel obliged, but I was wondering . . .'

Jo looked at her keenly, but Debbie seemed to have suffered a loss of nerve. Her eyes danced worriedly across the tablecloth.

'I mean, I know it's a bit of a strange thing to ask,

what with this being a cat café and her being – well, a cat; and I know you've got a lot to think about at the moment, and that you're more of a dog person really.' Jo continued to stare at Debbie with an expression of patient bafflement. 'But I just thought, with you losing Bernard and giving up the shop, and moving to the farm, and I know you've always had a soft spot for her – oh!' A hiccup caught Debbie unawares. Looking faintly startled, she covered her mouth with the back of her hand and took a deep breath.

Jo smiled supportively. 'Debbie, I haven't got a clue what you're talking about,' she said at last.

'What I'm trying to say, Jo, is . . . how would you feel about, feel about . . . adopting Purdy?'

Confusion clouded Jo's face. 'Adopting Purdy? You mean, taking her to live with me?'

Debbie nodded. 'I just thought – after everything that's happened – it might be nice for both of you to live on the farm. Together.' She hiccupped again.

There was a pause as Jo absorbed Debbie's words, then: 'Debs, are you kidding? I'd *love* to take Purdy!' she said breathlessly. 'But are you sure you want to let her go? I mean, this is her home. Her whole family's here.' Jo glanced sideways, and I was touched by the concerned look she gave me.

'I'm *quite* sure,' Debbie answered emphatically. 'I think she's outgrown the café – it doesn't suit her any more. To be honest, she spends more time in your shop than she does here.' Her eyes started to well up and her face had flooded with colour. 'And I couldn't think of a b— a better life for her than on the farm with you,' she stammered, a tear sliding down her cheek.

Jo's eyes were suddenly brimful of tears, too. 'Well, if you think she'll be happy, Debs, I'd love to. You know I've always adored her. It'll be like taking part of Stourton with me,' she said with a watery-eyed smile.

'Exactly!' Debbie agreed. 'And of course it'll mean I have to visit you, to make sure you're looking after her properly.' She reached across the table to squeeze Jo's fingers.

Jo fished in her pocket for a packet of tissues and they each took one and dabbed their eyes. Then Jo glanced at her watch, gasped and stood up.

'And there was I, thinking you were going to ask me to be your bridesmaid!' she quipped, fastening her jacket.

Debbie's eyes lit up. 'Oh my *God!*' she shrieked, looking thunderstruck. 'I almost forgot! I'm getting married! Of *course* you'll be my bridesmaid, won't you?' Debbie shrieked. 'Along with Linda and Sophie of course,' she added, with a worried look across the room at the others.

'It would be an honour,' Jo replied, leaning in for a hug.

'I hope you both like taffeta,' Linda said drolly, before draining her champagne glass.

On her way out, Jo walked over to the cat hammock where Purdy lay fast asleep, her feet draped languorously over the edges. Jo rose up on tiptoes and stretched her hand out to rub Purdy's ears. 'Bye, Purdy. I'll see you again soon,' she whispered. Purdy lifted her head and blinked at Jo sleepily.

Even though she had her back to me, I blinked at Jo, too.

Linda had pushed several café tables together to form a row that stretched from the cat tree in the middle of the room to the window. She threw a deep-red cloth over the tabletops and, with painstaking attention to detail, arranged a magnificent display involving candles, garlands, snow-dusted pine cones and table confetti. With Ming's platform at one end and my cushion at the other, the layout had the unintended effect of looking as though Ming and I were joint heads of the table. I looked across the gilt candelabra at Ming, wondering what she thought of the lavish arrangement, but her eyes were closed. Looming sphinx-like and motionless above the red-and-gold tones of the table decor, she looked even more regal than usual. I had to admit, the grandeur suited her.

'Right, everyone, dinner is served,' Debbie shouted,

negotiating her way through the café with an enormous turkey on a platter. John and Sophie followed with the side dishes, and Eddie brought up the rear, trotting after them hungrily with his tail aloft. With admiring noises, they all took their seats. Napkins were unfurled, crackers snapped and glasses topped up, while John set to work carving the turkey. When everyone was about to eat, Debbie tapped on the side of her wine glass with her knife and said, 'I'd just like to raise a toast to Margery. Without her, I doubt we would all be here, celebrating Christmas together. To Margery.'

'To Margery,' the others repeated, clinking glasses gently, and a hush fell over the table. As they began to eat, I felt a wave of nostalgia spread through me. But the feeling was not only a longing for my past – for the time I had spent with Margery and the life we had shared – but also an appreciation of the present. It was beginning to dawn on me that this, our second Christmas in the cat café, would be our last as a whole family.

I let my eyes wander around the room in the knowledge that, one day, the scene before me would be no more than a fond memory. Jasper was sprawled out on the flagstones, the fire's orange flames lighting up his glossy black pelt; Maisie was nearby, playing with the last shreds of wrapping paper under the Christmas tree; behind them Abby and Bella were curled up together on one of the armchairs, washing each other contentedly with their eyes closed.

Eddie padded between the table legs, determinedly scouring the floor for dropped morsels of turkey. It was hard to believe that, only a few weeks earlier, I had been utterly convinced he had run away, and that I might never see him again. The irony of my situation did not escape me: whilst I had been racked with guilt about Eddie's disappearance, I had failed to notice that the kitten I was actually losing was Purdy.

I turned to the other side of the room and settled my gaze on Purdy, who was slumbering blissfully in the hammock. Her departure would break my heart, but I knew it was the right thing for her. The kittens' upbringing in the café had been unconventional and, in many ways, privileged, but for a self-sufficient cat like Purdy, it had become stifling. Living in a colony, and being on view to the public, did not suit her independent nature, and I knew that farm life would maker her far happier than café life. She would be free to roam as a solitary cat, and when she craved company, she would have Jo.

Although a part of me would always think of Purdy and her siblings as kittens, I had to accept that they had long outgrown their kittenhood. They were adults now, and their well-being could not be viewed collectively. My desire for them to be happy as individuals had to outweigh any sentimental notion of keeping my family together; and, as their mother, the best thing I could do was encourage each of them to follow the path that suited them best.

After all, I had followed my own path, a long time ago, when I had first lost Margery. I had found my way to Stourton, to Debbie and to Jasper. I was certain that my future would always lie with Debbie and the cat café, but the same might not be true for the kittens. Their future was an open book, a story waiting to be told, and it was my privilege to have come this far on their journey with them. Whatever happened, wherever they decided to go, I was confident that they had had the best start in life I could have given them; they had been safe, and loved, and happy.

Perhaps, when all was said and done, that had been my own legacy to them.

Acknowledgements

Much of this book was written either late at night or in the early hours of the morning, and it often felt like a solitary enterprise. Having finally emerged, blinking, into the daylight, I would like to acknowledge my debt of gratitude to some of the people who helped along the way.

Firstly I need to acknowledge the work done by the real cat cafés which inspired this book. In the interests of a good story I have put Molly, Ming and the other cats through ordeals that I am certain they would never face in reality. Cat-café staff take the utmost care of their cats' physical and emotional wellbeing, and I am quite sure they would be aghast at some – if not all – of the goings-on at Molly's.

I would like to thank my agent Kate Burke, and also Chloe Seager at Diane Banks Associates.

Thank you to everyone at Pan Macmillan. To my

diligent editor Victoria Hughes-Williams and the rest of the team: Natalie McCourt, Stuart Dwyer, Holly Sheldrake, Lloyd Jones, James Annal, Matthew Garrett and Jess Duffy. I appreciate all of your hard work behind the scenes.

To Debbie Nash, for being the ongoing inspiration for my (human) heroine, even though you are more of a dog person.

To my sister Emma, for your empathy, encouragement and support.

To my children, Suse and Louis, for your incredible patience throughout this process. Thank you Suse for being an eagle-eyed editor-in-training; your grammatical knowledge puts me to shame.

Lastly, and mostly, to Phil. Even with a broken leg, you kept the show on the road. Without you, this book wouldn't have happened.

MD, *2016*